W. SOLIMAN

UNFINISHED
BUSINESS

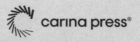
carina press®

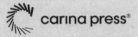

carina press®

ISBN-13: 978-0-373-00241-2

UNFINISHED BUSINESS

Recycling programs for this product may not exist in your area.

Copyright © 2011 by Wendy Soliman

www.CarinaPress.com

Printed in U.S.A.

"Sal, why haven't you said anything before now?" Kara asked.

"Well, because no one asked me. Not straight-out, anyway."

Kara looked at me and rolled her eyes. "Can't argue with that, I suppose."

"I tried to raise the subject with your family but was made aware, in no uncertain terms, that it was too painful for discussion." She paused. "I told Brett, though, years ago."

"I see." I didn't, though, not really, and needed to clarify a point or two. "Now, let's see if I've got this straight. Your best friend met some man, but she didn't tell you his name, or where she met him, or anything at all about him." I treated her to one of my infamous hard stares. "And you didn't think that might be a tad dangerous and try to talk her out of it?"

Sally's face flooded with colour but she stood her ground. "Have you ever tried to stop a tidal wave? When Jas made her mind up, there was nothing anyone could say to deter her."

"Must be a family failing." I flicked a sardonic look Kara's way.

"I prefer to think of it as a positive quality."

"Well, I think we've got it all straight now. Thanks for your time, Sally."

"Just one thing," Sally said. "Perhaps I didn't make myself clear. You said just now that Jas went off with a man. Well, it definitely wasn't a man she was going to London to meet. I wouldn't have let her do that, not without leaving me a contact number at the very least. No, Jas made it very clear that her appointment was with a woman."

**Also available from W. Soliman
and Carina Press**

RISKY BUSINESS
LETHAL BUSINESS

Dear Reader,

I was raised on the Isle of Wight, on the south coast of England, which just happens to be the headquarters of British yachting, famed for its regular visits from our royal family, and starting point for the world-famous Fastnet race.

I got plenty of chances to observe the glamorous yachting life at close quarters. I still can't believe the participants appeared to enjoy having regular drenchings in freezing salt water, took leaning precariously over the edge of boats tilted dangerously close to angry waves in their stride and didn't hop ashore praying for a quick and painless death. I decided at an early age that dry land had its advantages.

Many years later, helping my husband through a midlife crisis, I reluctantly agreed to take to the ocean waves, provided we were propelled by engines and not wind power. There were only so many sacrifices I was prepared to make. So started many years of a hate/hate relationship with the sea, during which I learned more about boats than I'd ever needed to know. The things I do for *lurve!* Still, never waste an experience, that's my mantra as a writer, and I spent many hours staring at great expanses of open ocean asking myself *what if?*

And so my Hunter Files series was born. The boat my hero, ex-policeman Charlie Hunter, lives on just happens to bear a striking resemblance to the one we owned. Many of the destinations he visits are also familiar to us.

Charlie gets a second chance at some of his old, unsolved cases, dragged back into a life he thought he'd left behind by a pretty girl with powers of persuasion that made it impossible to turn her down. In spite of my lukewarm enthusiasm for all things maritime, there's a certain camaraderie among the boating fraternity that holds an enduring appeal. I hope you enjoy reading about Charlie's cold cases. Do let me know what you think. I'd love to hear from you.

Enjoy!

Wendy

www.WendySoliman.com

Dedication

For Maggie,
longtime friend, confidante and drinking buddy.

UNFINISHED
BUSINESS

ONE

"EXCUSE ME, I'M looking for Charlie Hunter."

The spanner flew out of my hand and clattered into the bilge. "Shit!"

"Hello there, is Mr. Hunter on board? I was told to ask on this pontoon."

I swore again. The female voice responsible for breaking my concentration clearly wasn't going anywhere. Bare-chested and bloody-minded, I hoisted myself out of the engine room of my motor cruiser and slowly wiped the oil from my hands on the rag protruding from the pocket of my jeans. I took a moment to shake the hair out of my eyes and rotate my shoulders to smooth out the kinks before turning to the woman, ready to let rip. One look in her direction and the words stalled on my tongue.

The policeman in me took stock of the evidence. Midtwenties was my guess. Tall, slim, curly red hair tumbling down her back, big green eyes, a dusting of freckles across her nose, curves in all the right places, no wedding ring. The man in me couldn't help approving. She was just my type, or would be if I hadn't sworn off all women as being more trouble than they were worth. Still, there was nothing to say I couldn't indulge in a spot of window-shopping.

"I'm Hunter," I said tersely. "Something I can do for you?"

If the woman was discouraged by my churlish-
ness, she gave no sign. "My name's Kara Webb, Mr.
Hunter." She introduced herself as though it ought to
mean something to me.

"Congratulations."

"You don't remember me?"

"Can't say that I do." The name rang a vague bell
but I was willing to swear I'd never had the pleasure.
Kara Webb wasn't the sort of woman a man was likely
to forget.

"Is there somewhere we could go to talk? I could
buy you a coffee, or something." She nodded towards
the café on the landside of the approach to the marina.

"Can't see that we have anything to talk about."

"Please, I—oh!"

She broke off as Gil bounded out of the boat's salon,
a growl rumbling in his throat, long tail wagging like
crazy. Talk about mixed messages. I made a mental
note to have a chat with my dog a bit later on about
his duties. It would be useful if he could get into the
habit of warning me of imminent intruders *before* they
caused me to drop spanners in bilges.

"Gil!" Too late. He'd already leapt onto the pontoon and was jumping all over my lovely visitor. He's
a huge beast in an interesting variety of colours, and
although I wasn't about to admit that he's a big softie,
a lot of people were intimidated by his size. "Careful,
he's a bit edgy 'round strangers."

"So I see."

And then she smiled. I found myself silently re-
peating the words I'd said aloud when I'd dropped that
spanner. Miss Webb, when she smiled, could put the
sun itself to shame. It changed the whole tenor of her

face and dispelled the air of despondency I'd sensed when first checking her out. *Uh-uh, Charlie boy,* I told myself severely. *This looks like trouble. Don't let that bloody smile influence you into buying whatever it is she's come to sell.*

Kara reached out a hand to tickle the dog's ears. Gil, sensing a soft touch, had already rolled onto his back, ready to lap up any attention on offer.

"Gil," she said, "that's a strange name for such a handsome beast. Something to do with fishing?" She nodded towards the fishing rods attached to the roof of the cockpit.

"It's short for Guilty."

"Oh, I see." That usually stopped people in their tracks but Miss Webb didn't miss a beat. "Well, look, Mr. Hunter, I can see you're busy so I won't take up much of your time. If we could just—"

"As you said, I'm busy." Pointedly, I turned towards the engine room hatch.

"Mr. Hunter, please, don't you remember me? It's been fifteen years and I expect you've seen thousands of distressed families since then, but surely you remember my sister, Jasmine—"

"Jasmine Webb. Of course." Now the penny dropped. It had been one of my first cases after being made up to detective and I remembered it well. "But surely you're not the little sister—"

"The scrawny runt of the litter, you mean. The kid who got in everyone's way and kept asking awkward questions. Yes," she said with another brief smile, "that would be me. I was only twelve at the time and ignored by everyone. No one listened to what I had to say about

Jasmine's disappearance, except you, Mr. Hunter. I've never forgotten that."

"Yeah, okay." I was still trying to get over the fact that the awkward, gangling, tongue-tied kid I remembered had turned out like this. Just goes to show that you never can tell. "But your sister turned up alive and well."

"We heard from her, certainly, and you were satisfied that the call and subsequent letter we received from her weren't coerced, but we never saw her again."

"I don't see what you expect me to do about it. I don't mean to be rude but—"

"Please! What I have to say is important and it'll only take five minutes."

As soon as I saw the tears welling, I knew I was in trouble. I'm a pushover when women turned on the waterworks.

I sighed. "All right, come aboard."

She was already bending to take her trainers off. Obviously knew something about boats, then. It's the height of bad manners to step on anyone's craft wearing dark-soled shoes.

"How did you get into the marina, by the way?"

"Oh, that was easy. I simply waited for someone to leave, smiled at the guy and he held the gate open for me."

"Wonderful!" I rolled my eyes. The fancy electronic gate system was obviously about as effective as Gil's efforts to protect my new home. "Okay, one more question and then it's your turn. How did you find me?"

"I went to the police station and asked for you by name. It was a long shot after all this time but I thought you might still work there. It didn't occur to me that you would have retired. You seem a little young, if you don't mind me saying so."

"They wouldn't have told you where to find me at the nick," I said, ignoring the implied compliment.

"No." A hint of mischief lit her eyes as she followed me into the salon. "They were most unreasonable and wouldn't tell me a thing. And so, oh—"

"It's being refitted." Her gaze travelled 'round the spacious cabin, which was devoid of all furniture except Gil's bed and a folding canvas chair. The light oak walls were complete, but the cabinets were still halfway through construction, and wires hung from the ceiling. "We'll be more comfortable in the cockpit. And it's instant coffee or nothing. I wasn't expecting visitors."

I expected her to ask if I had any tea, probably something fancy like camomile—she looked like the type to drink that sort of muck—but to her credit she said instant coffee would be fine.

I removed a carton of milk from the fridge, sniffed it and poured the contents down my new sink. "Hope you don't take milk."

"No, just as it comes."

We stepped into the cockpit and she sat on the cushioned bench. It would be a seriously bad idea to get too cosy with her, so I took the teak lounger on the other side of the table, putting a physical barrier between us. She elevated her brows, obviously not used to men making excuses to keep their distance from her, even if my one-man dog felt no such compunction. He ignored me, made a beeline for Kara and gazed up at her adoringly through liquid brown eyes, tongue lolling stupidly from the side of his mouth. His tail thumped against the deck as she smiled and stretched forward to tickle his ears.

I added loyalty to the list of subjects I needed to discuss with my dog.

"You were going to tell me how you tracked me down."

"Oh yes. Well, after I failed to get anything out of the miserable desk sergeant at the station, I took myself off to the Royal Oak—"

I groaned. The hostelry of choice for Brighton's finest. It told me all I needed to know, and more. One look at those big sorrowful eyes of hers and half my ex-colleagues would sell their souls in order to get on her good side, always supposing they still had souls to sell, which was questionable.

"Who spilled the beans?"

"Someone called Jimmy Taylor."

"That figures."

"Look, I'm sorry to come barging in on you like this. I can see you value your privacy but this is important to me." She looked directly at me, fastened those magnetic eyes on my face, and I knew I was in danger of going the same way as Jimmy Taylor *et al.*

"Yeah, okay. You're here now and have my attention, so you might as well tell me what's on your mind."

"What do you remember about my sister?"

I threw my head back and closed my eyes, dredging up the details from the recesses of my brain. "Jasmine Eleanor Webb, just seventeen, in her first year at sixth-form college. Red hair, green eyes, good-looking, same height as you are now, which would be about five foot seven. Good student, popular and hardworking, no known boyfriends, no known problems, reported missing by her father when she failed to return home after college. Assumed abducted because nothing was missing from her room to suggest she'd left home of her own free will." I opened my eyes again and looked directly at her. "Assumed abducted by everyone except you, that is."

"You have a good memory," she said. I shrugged off the compliment. "I *knew* she hadn't been abducted but no one would listen to me. It was like I didn't exist."

"Because her teddy bear was missing? The one she'd had since she was a kid."

"Yes, and her diaries, as well. Why would she take the things that really mattered to her to college on that particular day? It wasn't something she usually did."

"It seemed odd that your father insisted she had no reason to run away and nothing was worrying her." I felt myself being sucked into Kara's problems in spite of my determination to remain detached from them. "All teenagers have worries that seem insurmountable."

"My father's always right." Kara's voice dripped sarcasm. "If he'd decided Jas didn't have any problems then that's the way it was going to stay."

"But two days later she phoned from London and followed up with a letter. We knew she was alive, the investigation was wound down, and she became just another runaway."

"Yes, and we never saw her again."

"I don't mean to be rude, Kara, but why are you dragging this up again after all this time? And more to the point, why have you taken so much trouble to find me?"

"Because I still don't know where she is or why she

left. I've never stopped thinking about it and I can't get on with my life until I have some answers."

"Yes, but even so—"

"And," she added sombrely, "because my brother was killed in an accident last month."

"Ah, I'm sorry." That would account for the despondency then. Her family seemed to be dogged by bad luck. "I remember your brother. Brian?"

"Brett."

"Yes, Brett. What happened?"

"A boating accident. He was helping to deliver a boat from France to Weymouth." That figured. Her father was a marine engineer and keen sailor, and all the kids had the sea in their blood. "They got the yacht there, went ashore and let off some steam. The other two went back to the boat but Brett stayed in the bar for one more." She wrinkled her brow. "That's the part I don't really understand because he wasn't a great drinker. Still, they'd had a force six with them all the way so I imagine he needed to unwind." She shrugged. "That's all we know for sure. He was pretty drunk and it looks as though he slipped into the water on his way back to the boat. The other two were out cold and didn't notice Brett hadn't come back. They raised the alarm the next morning, a search was made and his body was washed up with the afternoon tide."

"I'm sorry," I said again. "I assume there was an inquest."

"Yes, and it was declared an accidental death. He had a high alcohol content in his stomach and water in his lungs that implied...well, that implied—"

"That implied he'd been alive when he hit the sea,"

I finished for her, giving her time to recover her composure.

"Yes, and there were no marks on him to indicate that it was anything other than an accident."

"So what do you want me—"

"I was going through Brett's things the other day and found this." She rummaged in her bag and handed me a photograph. "That's Brett," she said.

"Okay, but who's the woman with him?"

"Jasmine."

I shot her a look. "But you said none of you had seen her since she disappeared."

"I didn't think we had."

"It doesn't look like Jasmine as she was described to me." She was a looker all right but Jasmine had been described as a redhead and this woman was blond. Still, women are always messing with the colour of their hair so I supposed it didn't mean much. "How can you be sure it's Jasmine?"

"Apart from the fact that she looks just like me? Turn the photograph over, Detective Inspector."

Feeling dense for the second time in as many minutes, I followed her advice. The names *Brett and Jasmine*, *Weymouth* and a date a few months prior was printed on the back. In spite of my best efforts to remain disinterested, I felt the familiar tingling in my spine that I used to get in the job when an interesting or unusual case came along. I didn't like coincidences and here were several all at once. A long-lost sister found alive and well and living in Weymouth but Brett hadn't bothered to inform the rest of his family. Brett then jumps at the chance to deliver a yacht to Weymouth, presumably because he hoped to see his sister once he got rid of the rest of the crew. Then the young man turns up dead in circumstances that could be accidental but might well not be.

"Okay, but I still don't see—"

"My sister's defection, as my father still refers to it, tore our family apart, Mr. Hunter."

"Call me Charlie."

"Okay, Charlie. Dad was a bit of a tyrant, a control freak if you like, before it happened but afterwards… well, let's just say I bore the brunt of his caution. I wasn't allowed out. Wasn't allowed boyfriends unless he gave them the third degree first. Makeup was out of the question, as was the sort of clothing all my friends wore." She spread her hands. "I'm sure you get the picture."

"Yeah, that must have been tough for you but I suppose you can see his point of view."

She shook her head. "I'm not looking for the sympathy vote. That's not why I'm telling you all this."

"Then why?"

"To try and make you understand how I feel about my sister. Jasmine and I were never close, there were five years between us, and five years is more like an eternity when you're that age. But I looked up to her and wanted to be like her. And then she just upped and ran away for reasons I've never been able to fathom." She fondled Gil's ears almost aggressively. "Brett found her but didn't tell us, and now I need to try and figure out why."

"It's probably better left alone. Look what happened to your brother."

"I can't leave it. Especially not since Brett. That's why I went to the trouble of tracking you down. I was hoping you might still be a serving policeman with access to the necessary resources to find Jasmine. Still, you know how these things are done, and I want to hire you to help me find my sister."

"I'm not for hire."

"Please! It won't take long and then I'll leave you in peace."

"Have you tried putting a notice in the local rag, asking for information?"

"If she's intent upon staying hidden I doubt she's using her real name." She narrowed her eyes. "I thought you were a detective."

"I retired."

A man walking along the pontoon called to me. "I've got the impeller for the generator, Charlie. I'll fit it this afternoon and should be able to finish tweaking the engine on Monday, then you'll be able to give her a nice long sea trial and put her through her paces. I know that's what you've been dying to do."

"Thanks, Ben." Thanks for nothing, I added beneath my breath when Kara's face lit up.

"There you are then. Weymouth is far enough away to put the boat—" she stood and leaned over the transom, reading the name upside-down "—the *No Comment* through her paces. Unusual name," she added with a lilting smile that immediately put me on my guard.

"Kara, just so we're clear. I am *not* going to take you to Weymouth."

She pouted, suddenly looking very young and vulnerable, but I pretended not to notice. "So you won't help me then?"

"*Can't* would be a more accurate answer. It's a wild-goose chase after all this time. Do you know how many people go missing every single day?"

"Yes, actually, I did some research."

"Well, there you are then." I couldn't quite meet her eye. "It's a wild-goose chase."

"Not necessarily. A lot of those people are eventually located and we have somewhere to start."

"People gone for a long time are only found if they want to be, and your sister clearly doesn't. Otherwise, why would Brett not have told you that he'd seen her?"

She scowled. "I know. That's what's been bothering me."

The fact that she'd given up trying to coerce me softened my stance. "Tell you what, I'll have a word with my old partner and see if he remembers anything about the case that I don't, but that's the best I can do."

"Well, that's something, I suppose." She didn't sound especially grateful and I was already regretting my impulsive offer. "Will you do it now?"

"Nope. What I'm gonna do now is take my son fishing."

I've never been a great one for smiling. Personally I think it's a grossly overrated gesture and seldom means what it says. But the one thing guaranteed to make my face break out in a great big goofy grin is the sight of my son barrelling towards me, all enthusiasm and gangly limbs, and the prospect of having him all to myself for two whole days. Kara's eyes were trained upon me as my smile broadened. I returned Harry's wave but didn't look at her. Presumably even she wasn't insensitive enough to hang around now.

"Okay, then." She gathered up her bag and gave Gil's

ears one final scratch. "I'll leave you to the mackerel. Call me as soon as you can."

I didn't respond. Instead I caught my son up and twirled him above my head as he hurled himself on board.

"By the way, it's a magnet you need," Kara said as she bent to put her shoes on.

"Come again?"

"A magnet, Charlie. It's the best way to get tools out of the bilges. Surely you know that."

NADIA LAY IN her husband's arms, post-coital contentment for once failing to soothe her. Afternoon sunshine filtered through curtains that weren't fully closed, hurting her eyes.

Igor's hands ran the length of her body, soft yet possessive. They came to rest on her waist and pulled her closer until she was spooned against him.

"What is it, my darling?"

She thought she'd hidden her tears, but he caught one on his finger as it trickled down her cheek.

He leaned over her, his brow furrowed. "Why are you so sad? Did I not give you pleasure?"

She met his gaze. "You always give me pleasure, Igor, you know that. You're my life."

"Then what? Are you thinking about your brother still?"

"I can't seem to help it." She made the confession in a tiny voice, afraid he might be angry with her. "I feel responsible for what happened."

"Because he was in Weymouth? How could that be your fault?"

"I—I don't know."

Nadia usually told Igor absolutely everything but didn't dare admit that Brett had known where she was. Igor would be angry with her for not telling him, and she couldn't handle that right now. He almost never lost his temper with her but when he did…well, she shuddered at the mere prospect. Being married to a man who looked upon violence as one of life's givens sometimes worked against her. Brett's death had been a freak accident, no more than that, and she should stop dwelling upon it. The past couldn't be undone, and Igor was right when he said they should concentrate on what lay ahead. But somehow she couldn't get it out of her head that Brett had delivered a boat to Weymouth simply to try and see her again, even though she'd told him it would be impossible for them to meet.

"You shouldn't have seen the report in the paper about his death. I gave most specific instructions." Igor's voice had taken on a hard edge. The one he often employed when speaking to his underlings but never used with her. "Whoever left it hanging about will answer to me for his carelessness."

"They weren't to know."

"Then what do I pay them for?" His voice lightened again as his fingers slowly traced the outline of one of her breasts. "You get more beautiful every day." He bent his head and slowly, expertly, kissed her. She felt some of the tension leaving her as he gently agitated her passions. "If another man were to lay so much as a finger on you, I'd kill him with my bare hands. And then I'd kill you." He smiled but there was a chill behind his words and Nadia knew he was in deadly earnest. "That's how much I love you." His hands left her body and he levered himself from the bed with a heavy sigh. "I have some things I must do but you stay here and rest, my love. Take your pill, and when you wake everything will seem better."

"But the children. I must get them from school."

"Anton will do that."

Nadia didn't have the strength to argue. She, who'd once been so full of vitality, was permanently tired nowadays. Resigned to never seeing her family again, she was surprised how much it still hurt when she thought of her baby brother, dead because of her. And so she tried not to think about it. Igor would look after her, just like he always did. She washed down the pill he handed her with a swig of water and waited for blessed oblivion to claim her.

TWO

Kara waved over her shoulder as she made her way up the pontoon with a deal more elegance than Emily was achieving as she advanced in the opposite direction. I shook my head in reluctant admiration. A bloody magnet. Why hadn't I thought of that?

"Who was that?"

Emily seemed to have forgotten she'd forfeited the right to ask. She was about to clamber aboard but clocked my expression and changed her mind. Emily was at pains to remain on good terms with me, and decorating my new teak decks with stiletto heel marks would hardly further her cause.

"No one." I tousled my son's mop of unruly brown curls, a mirror image of my own crowning glory. "Hi there, champ. All ready to get at those fish?"

"Yeah, Dad! Can we go now?"

"In a minute, I just want to have a word with your mum first."

Emily wouldn't leave until she'd told me at least a dozen times exactly how to look after Harry. As though his teeth would fall out if he didn't clean them at least twice a day. I put the boy down and he fell to rolling around the deck with Gil.

"Hurry up then, Dad, the fish won't wait."

Chuckling, I stepped onto the pontoon. "Too right they won't."

"Don't leave him aboard alone! He might fall in."

"He won't fall in," I said with exaggerated patience.

"You don't know that. You should never—"

"Isn't there somewhere you need to be?"

"Why can't you live in a house like a normal person?" Even by Emily's standards her sigh was overdramatic. "When you left the police, I really did think you'd be able to develop a proper relationship with your son. Make up for all the years you missed. But what do you do? Grow your hair and adopt an alternative lifestyle like an ageing hippy, that's what."

"It was you, I recall, who accused me of letting Harry down when I was in the job. A job you didn't have a good word to say for because it always came first. Well, in the six months since I got out, I don't recall having to break a single arrangement with my son." I fixed frosty eyes on the former love of my life. "You can't have it both ways, Em."

"But this boat thing. I just don't understand."

"No." I shook my head, already weary with a conversation that was going nowhere. "I don't suppose you do. I'll drop Harry back by six tomorrow evening."

"No, no, I'll come and get him. I won't have a moment's peace if I think of him riding on *that* contraption."

I made allowances for the fact that she worried obsessively about our son and didn't take her to task for her disparaging remarks about my beloved Harley.

"Cor cool, Dad, you got it!" Harry emerged from the salon, clutching a shiny new child's crash helmet, eyes round with excitement. He squashed it onto his head and grinned at us from beneath the visor.

"Do you want to tell him he can't use it?" I asked Emily pointedly.

If looks could kill… Her eyes swivelled between Harry and me but for once she had the sense to keep her thoughts to herself and made do with slowly shaking her head.

"I thought not. Don't worry, I'll return him tomorrow with the requisite number of limbs still in place, although I can't guarantee how clean they'll be."

"Bye, Mum," Harry shouted cheerfully.

Harry and I lost no time in assembling our gear and setting off in pursuit of the mackerel. We caught several off the breakwater, took them back to the boat and grilled them on the small barbecue in the cockpit. I showed my son how to fillet the fish, avoiding all the bony bits. He bit his lip in concentration, meticulously following my lead, causing me to suppress a wry smile. I doubted whether he'd eat mackerel if his mother was foolish enough to put it in front of him. But catching them himself seemed to elevate the humble fish to burgerlike status.

After we'd eaten we caught a bus to Rottingdean. We were in luck. The bus driver, at whose discretion Gil can or can't travel, didn't seem to object to his presence and he got his run on the downs. By the time we got back to the boat, Harry's eyes were already drooping from an overdose of fresh air. I rubbed the worst of the grime off his limbs and put him to bed. His teeth would just have to take their chances. He'd survived the day without watching television, playing video games or consuming junk food and didn't seem to have missed any of it. Instead he'd had a cracking time simply behaving like a kid.

"Phil says fishing's dangerous," Harry mumbled sleepily.

"Does he now." I wasn't too sure how to handle that one. Phil was Emily's new husband, an accountant, adequately suited in my opinion to his dull profession. But Phil was steady and reliable, the complete antithesis to the unpredictability that went hand-in-hand with my profession. Emily finally had all the stability she could possibly want but I sometimes wondered if it was a case of beware what you wish for. Why else did she drop Harry off every other weekend, tarted up to the nines, and make excuses to linger? Poor Emily, didn't she realize our relationship had been over long before she finally threw me out, and that I'd only clung on for as long as I had for Harry's sake? "Fishing's only dangerous if you're irresponsible, and we're never that, are we?"

"No, 'course we're not. Can we go out on the Harley tomorrow, Dad?"

"How about taking it to Stamford Bridge?" Now was the time to spring my big surprise.

"What!" Harry sat bolt upright, wide awake again, his eyes sparkling. "Chelsea are playing Spurs in a preseason friendly. You've got us tickets?"

I nodded solemnly. I'd been pleased but not surprised to learn that Phil didn't like soccer, which cast me as the exclusive guardian of my son's passion for the game. It was a responsibility I took exceedingly seriously.

"Wicked!"

"Yeah, well, get some sleep. Kickoff's at twelve so we'll have to be on the road early."

"Okay. And can we go to McDonald's on the way home?"

I rolled my eyes. So much for the abandonment of junk food. I ruffled Harry's hair, turned out the light in the little bunk cabin I'd created especially for him, and closed the door behind me, leaving Gil snoring across Harry's feet and taking up most of the bed. Gil was technically Harry's dog. He'd found him wandering in a park and had been distraught when his mother said they couldn't keep him because Phil was allergic to dogs. So yours truly took pity on Harry, and the mutt, who was turning out to be good company, even if he was somewhat lacking in the requisite guard dog qualities.

I wandered back into the salon. I'd be glad when the refit was complete and I could finally put the boat through its paces. I inherited the ten-year-old fifty-footer from my uncle. She was designed to his unique specification, and mostly built by him too. There isn't another *No Comment* anywhere on the planet, and many seafarers might suggest that's not such a bad thing. She's not pretty to look at, nor is she a fancy gin palace. As a sturdy single-engined trawler yacht, built to take the unpredictable seas around the south coast at a stately cruising speed of eight knots, we suit one another just fine. There's nothing wrong with eight knots if you're not in a hurry to get anywhere.

My first thought when I inherited the boat was to sell it on. It had been neglected both mechanically and internally for the last few years and would be a full-time project to restore. I'd never be able to find the time. But, aware that I'd reached a crossroads in my life, something made me hesitate about putting it on the market. The more I thought about it, the more appealing the prospect of freedom from bureaucracy became. So, at the age of forty, after twenty-two years in the job and thoroughly disillusioned by the direction the police force was moving in, I took my pension, the small amount of money left to me after the marital home was sold, the little bit of cash my uncle also left me and turned in my papers. I then sold everything else except the Harley and set about living the dream.

The *No Comment* has a wheelhouse in lieu of a fly bridge, accessed via a few steps up from the salon. I headed in that direction and gazed with satisfaction upon my newly installed navigational equipment. No expense spared here. A state-of-the art plotter, radar, GPS, the works. The wheelhouse has a comfortable helm position and seating areas behind it on either side of the central steps. I'd ripped one of these out and replaced it with a desk and floor-to-ceiling shelves for my books. Some navigational, a lot of biographies and some fiction, none of it devoted to crime.

I fired up my laptop, attached the lead from my digital camera and downloaded the pictures I'd taken of Harry that day, chuckling as they came to life on the screen. This was the first time Harry had landed a fish all on his own, and his gap-toothed grin as he held up the modest results spoke volumes. I printed the pictures out and put them beside Harry's bunk so they'd be the first thing he saw when he woke up in the morning. A defining moment in the career of Harry Hunter, intrepid fisherman, preserved for posterity.

I poured myself a beer and returned to my laptop. Dragging my mind away from my son's achievements, I rummaged in the drawer where I'd thrown the card Kara had given me. Time to find out a bit more about my visitor before I did anything about her request. The card was for a business called It Takes Two and gave a website address. I typed in the URL and was confronted with what looked like a dating agency, with a difference.

Kara's name was given as one director and a Sam Bryce as the other. Samuel or Samantha? There were no pictures of either director so I had no way of knowing. I read the promotional stuff on the home page and discovered It Takes Two didn't attempt to pair lonely hearts but instead offered organized activities for single people. Walking, dancing, trips to the theatre, stuff like that. As I read on I learned Kara's singles were enjoying meaningful eye contact over a line-dancing session that very evening.

Clever. The dating thing had been done to death, but Kara and the genderless Sam had hit upon a niche in the market, getting like-minded people together in a social environment and letting nature take its course— or not—rather than trying to match them up through their star signs, or a mutual desire to save the planet, or whatever the fuck it was that supposedly made strangers instantly compatible.

By the time I'd finished studying the site I knew little more about Kara than I had at the start. The address on the card was in Hove but I had no way of knowing if that was just her business premises or if she lived there too. Time to make Jimmy Taylor pay for thinking with his prick and blabbing his mouth off. I rang the nick and was in luck. Jimmy was on duty and in the squad room. One of my ex-colleagues yelled for him and his voice was soon on the other end the phone.

"Hey, mate, how's it hanging? That little cutie found

you all right the other day, did she? Lucky bastard! Don't know how you do it."

"Charm, mate, charm. I wouldn't expect you to understand. Anyway, that's what I was calling you about. As a penance for telling her where to find me, you've been selected to do me a favour."

"Uh-uh, I don't like the sound of that."

"This one's within even your limited powers of detection."

"Cheeky bastard!" Jimmy sighed. "Okay, give, what do you want?"

"Very gracious."

"The man rings me for a favour and expects *me* to be grateful."

"Okay, I owe you a pint."

"Too right, you do. Now, give."

"Well, I just want all you can get for me on Kara Webb. Age about twenty-seven. I need to know where she lives. I've got an address you could start with but I don't know if it's her business premises." I reeled off the one from the card.

"Kara, hey, isn't that the redhead from the other day? Hello, hello, don't tell me she's broken through heartless Hunter's cynical barricades?"

"You lack the ability to think outside the box, Jimmy, that's your trouble. Get back to me as soon as you can."

I cut the connection and dialled another number from memory. My old partner, Joe Newman, now in his early sixties, had mentored me in my early days as a detective and taught me almost everything I knew about being a good copper. He's one of the most principled people I've ever met and still enjoys my unadulterated respect. He's retired now and lives in a bungalow close to Brighton racecourse. He answered the call on the second ring, his booming voice echoing down the line as forcefully as ever.

"Hey, Charlie boy!" He sounded delighted to hear from me, which made me feel guilty. He was lonely and I didn't see as much of him as I should. "What's up?"

"Well, I reckon the bass ought to be running a few miles out about now, and since my engine's in need of a tryout, I thought we could combine the two things on Tuesday."

"You're on. I'll bring beer."

"Now you're talking." I paused for a moment and then got down to the real reason for my call. "Oh, and Joe, go back through those meticulous records of yours between now and then and tell me all you can remember about a missing person, Jasmine Webb. It was about fifteen years ago, just after I joined the squad."

"It rings a vague bell but why on earth are you asking me about that all this time later?"

"Well, her sister came to see me—"

"Ha!" Joe's barking laugh resonated in my ear. "I might have known there'd be a woman involved."

"No, nothing like you're thinking. You've got a dirty mind. She just needs closure and I said I'd see if there was anything you could remember that might help her."

"Gotcha."

JOE ARRIVED AT the marina weighed down by fishing tackle, a heavy-looking cool box, and his daughter, Sarah. I sighed, exasperated. Joe was being his usual less-than-subtle self, and Sarah had yet to learn to take no for an answer. A few years younger than me, she

was an attractive divorcée with a daughter the same age as Harry, which she seemed to think joined her and me at the hip.

I'd foolishly given way to loneliness a few months back and had a brief fling with her. I thought she understood the score and was as wary of the relationship thing as me, but that had proved not to be the case and she'd been a thorn in my side ever since. It didn't help that Joe encouraged her and took every opportunity to throw us together. Ah well, at least Sarah knows one end of a fishing rod from the other so there was nothing I could do other than to make the best of it.

"Hi." Sarah waved. "Hope you don't mind me tagging along."

"Hi, yourself." I kissed Sarah's cheek and avoided the more personal form of greeting she appeared to have in mind by stepping onto the pontoon and relieving Joe of his burden.

I disconnected the shore power, brought the cable on board and started the engine. The tension left me when it sprang smoothly into life. Joe let the lines go and I edged the boat away from the pontoon, elated to at last have the chance to put to sea, albeit on an unusually calm day, which wouldn't be particularly testing.

Once we were clear of the marina, I set the autopilot and left Joe on watch several times as I visited the engine room. Two-hundred-and-fifty horses sang to me as I lifted the hatch, no spewing of oil, water leaks or unnatural clanking to spoil the melody. It was a cramped area for a man of six foot two, but I didn't notice the discomfort as I bestowed one of my rare smiles upon the hunk of metal that had become as familiar to me

over the past few months as the curves on a particularly voluptuous woman's body.

Sarah busied herself in the newly fitted galley. I didn't have a clue what she was doing and had no intention of asking, but if she attempted to reorganize my stuff I'd go ballistic. Joe's eyes were glued to the Fish Finder screen above the helm position, which showed the seabed immediately below us and gave warning of any marine life unwise enough to be lurking within range of the fishing rods waiting in the *No Comment's* cockpit.

"Looks like you were right about the bass." Joe pointed to the screen after we'd been at sea for about an hour.

I checked the screen for myself and nodded. "So what are we waiting for? Let's go and make their acquaintance."

I cut our speed to idle and we adjourned to the cockpit. Sarah materialised with a platter of sandwiches and hot coffee.

"Can't fish on empty stomachs."

She brushed her breast against my arm as she moved past me to place the plate on the table.

I pretended not to notice and concentrated on setting up the rods.

I didn't want to broach the subject of Kara with Sarah in earshot. Predatory females have a tendency to put two and two together and come up with seventeen, which would only make for more trouble I didn't need. So it wasn't until we got back to the marina and Sarah scuttled off to collect her daughter from school that I could finally ask Joe if he'd remembered anything.

"Well, it's funny." He popped the ring pull on a can

of beer and took a long draught. "But once you mentioned it, I remembered the case without looking it up."

"I did too but then it was one of my first as a detective." I took a swig of my own beer. "What made it stand out for you?"

"Something about the father got my hackles up on that one. He was all over us, threatening us with God alone knew what if we didn't drop everything and find his daughter. He did the funny handshake bit, said he played golf with the ACC and had his ear, that sort of stuff."

"I suppose he was a bit aggressive, but aren't all parents like that when a kid goes missing? Christ, if anything were to happen to Harry, I don't think I'd—"

"Yeah, but this guy was bombastic and arrogant beyond belief, whereas the wife barely said a word. Didn't even look as though she'd shed a tear. And that didn't seem natural either."

"People cope with grief in different ways, Joe, you know that."

"Sure they do, but then the kid phoned home and suddenly the father was just as anxious for us to back off." Joe shrugged. "You know how it is, after the first flush of relief that the kid's safe, they usually want us to deploy half the Met to track them down."

"That's right. Webb did a complete about-face."

"Yeah, he said she was safe and that was all that mattered. She'd told him on the phone she was struggling with college work and needed some space, which he intended to give her."

"So he did. He didn't know where she was or who she was staying with but was adamant she'd be all right." Didn't sound like the reaction of the control freak Kara had described to me. "He said she'd be back home in a week or two and we didn't need to do anything else."

"I didn't buy that and nor did you," Joe said. "You wanted to carry on delving into it but the brass pulled us off."

"Yeah, I was a bit suspicious because no one at her college thought she was struggling."

"No, but we didn't get the chance to ask many questions before the plug was pulled, remember? You still wanted to go back and sniff around a bit more."

"Well, there's keenness for you."

I remained in the cockpit for a long time after Joe left, drinking beer, listening to Hank Jones on the stereo and staring up at the sky. I mulled over the whole business of Jasmine Webb's disappearance and her parent's peculiar reaction to it. Presumably they'd got over that but now had the death of their son to cope with. Coincidence? Somehow I didn't think so. Why, I couldn't say but none of it made sense and I'd bet the *No Comment* there was something very wrong with the whole shebang.

SOMETHING TICKLING HER eyelids woke Nadia from a sleep invaded by images of Brett. She tried to brush it away, but it persevered. Cautiously she opened her eyes, unable at first to remember where she was, and stifled a scream. A face, Brett's face as it had been when he was no more than seven or eight years old, stared directly into hers. Relief flooded through her. He wasn't dead. She must have imagined it all. The pills Igor gave her sometimes messed with her head. She waited for the fuzziness to dissipate. As it did so she wondered why Brett looked so young.

"Brett, what—"

"Mummy, wake up, Mummy."

Her relief fizzled out when she realized it wasn't Brett, but Sergei, her seven-year-old son. Nadia loved him unconditionally but couldn't quite suppress her disappointment when the brutal truth struck home. The fact that her son was a mirror image of her brother at the same age had once given her comfort. It now only added to her torment every time she looked at him. She hid her reaction by hugging the child close.

"Why are you always sleeping in the daytime, Mummy?" he asked accusingly.

"I'm not always sleeping, darling." She sat up cautiously, aware the room would spin if she moved too quickly. "Where's your sister?"

"Here, Mummy."

Saskia was seated at Nadia's dressing table, still in her nightdress, red hair—the same colour Nadia's had once been—a tangled mass around her shoulders. The priceless diamond choker Nadia had worn last night to wow Igor's guests was wrapped 'round the four-year-old's neck. She was in the process of applying her mother's scarlet gloss to her lips, missing her target and smearing most of it over her face.

"Why aren't you both at school?"

"It's Saturday, Mummy," Sergei said impatiently. "And you said we could go sailing today."

"So I did." The thought of spending the day on the water with her children ought to have cheered her, but she doubted she'd be able to summon up sufficient energy to go through with it. Since Brett had died—since she had caused his death—she didn't seem to have enough energy for anything. "What time is it?"

"Almost nine o'clock."

Nadia nodded. Igor would have been up for hours. He was one of those people who didn't seem to need much sleep and was always busy, keeping on top of his business affairs. Cautiously she eased her legs out of bed. A tap at the door and the children's nanny entered.

"There you are," she said in heavily accented English. "I'm sorry, madam, if they disturbed you."

"They didn't, Olga. Why should they? Have they had breakfast?"

"Not yet."

"Then see to it, please." Nadia couldn't face any breakfast herself. "Then we'll go sailing."

Olga frowned. "Mr. Kalashov didn't say anything about going sailing."

"Did he not?"

Nadia disliked the Russian woman her husband employed to care for the children. Since her first day, she'd insisted upon speaking in Russian almost all the time even though she knew Nadia's knowledge of the language had been sketchy at the time. It was as though she was trying to make her an outsider in her own family. She'd ignored Nadia's early attempts to win her friendship and refused to address her as anything other than "madam." She was a distant relation of Igor's. Nadia had never been able to work out exactly where she fit into the extensive Kalashov family tree and couldn't rid herself of the feeling that Olga spent as much time watching her as she did caring for the children.

That was ridiculous, of course. She was being paranoid. Igor loved her without reservation. Why else had he gone to such lengths to persuade her to marry him? It was just that, as he often explained to her, he had many enemies who might try to get to him through her, or anyone else close to him. That was one of the reasons why she'd agreed to change her identity and never see her family again.

"Well, Olga, I'll tell Mr. Kalashov of our plans myself."

"You can't. He's out for the day."

"Well then, it hardly matters. Is Anton here today?"

"Yes."

"Good, he can come with us."

Nadia wasn't permitted to leave home without one of Igor's men to protect her. To protect her from what exactly she'd long ago given up trying to figure out. Sometimes ignorance was a good thing. Anton was her favourite amongst her husband's employees. The children liked him too. Nadia suspected he was a little in love with her. Not that he'd dare to do anything about it, and Nadia certainly didn't encourage him. She loved her husband and, besides, she had no wish to cause problems for Anton by forming too close a friendship with him. All the same, it would be a relief to have someone with her whom she felt she could trust and with whom she could be herself—or as close to the person she'd become over the past fifteen years as it was now possible for her to be.

Viktor, her husband's right-hand man, sometimes watched over her but seemed to think the duty was beneath him. Something about his attitude gave her the creeps. His flat eyes never betrayed any emotion, reminding her of a dead fish. She was glad she wouldn't have him with her today.

"As you wish," Olga said coldly. "Come along, children."

She left the room, talking in rapid Russian as she closed the door behind them. Nadia sighed, crossed the room on unsteady legs and headed for the shower.

THREE

"JOE DOESN'T REMEMBER anything about your sister's case that's likely to help." I leaned back and lifted the bottle of lager Kara had just bought me to my lips. "So you've had a wasted journey, I'm afraid."

"What exactly did he say?" Kara fastened her eyes intently upon me. "Did he remember Jas?"

"Yeah, it stood out for him because your father was keen for us to find Jasmine and equally keen for us to stop looking once he knew she was alive. And that much we knew already."

"Yes, I suppose we did." She lapsed into silence. I made the most of it, knowing it wouldn't last. "You know," she said speculatively, "I've never understood why he didn't do something himself to look for her when you lot pulled out. You know, hire someone to track her down, start a poster campaign, offer a reward for information. That sort of thing. There was loads of stuff we could have done, but when I suggested it he was adamantly opposed. He said she'd be home when she was ready."

"Hardly the sort of reaction you'd expect from a controlling father with a young daughter adrift in the big city."

"No, I can see that now."

We were at a table outside a pub on the upper storey of the parade of shops and restaurants attached to the marina. Gil was spread-eagled on the floor with a bowl of water, the type that comes in a fancy bottle and costs as much as a beer. Kara insisted on purchasing it for him in spite of my assurances that the tap variety possessed all the necessary components to titivate Gil's doggy palate.

I'd phoned her that morning and told her I hadn't been able to find out much, hoping it would make her appreciate the futility of her task. But I wasn't holding my breath. Which was why I hadn't been surprised when she'd pushed for a face-to-face meeting. I reluctantly agreed but knew it was a mistake when she made it clear she wasn't going to let the matter rest and fully intended to enlist my help.

And the bugger of it was that my interest was piqued, my mind already buzzing with other ways to pursue the enquiry. Did she but know it, she wouldn't have to push too hard to keep me involved.

"So, that's it, I'm afraid. I can't do anything else."

"Now, you know you don't mean that." Her dazzling smile told me she wasn't buying it. "You want to know what happened to Jas almost as much as I do. Don't feel bad. You can't help yourself. You're a detective through and through and can't throw off your sleuthing instincts just because you're no longer a copper."

"You wanna put money on that?"

"Come on, Charlie, you can't fool me. You *know* there's something not quite right about the whole business, and it will eat away at you until you get some answers."

"Even if that's true, I don't have the authority to poke my nose in it anymore."

"All the better, surely? You don't have to abide by

all the silly new regulations that used to frustrate you
so much and—"

"What makes you say that?"

"Lucky guess."

I harrumphed. "You watch too much television."

"Everyone knows the police service is bogged down
with bureaucracy nowadays. When did you last see a
bobby walking the beat?" She had me there. "Anyway, just think, if you helped me there wouldn't be
any paperwork at all. That has to be worth something,
surely?"

"Kara, just so we understand each other. I'm *not*
going to help you look for your sister."

"Oh, all right then." She pulled an injured face and
took another sip of her wine. "If that's the way you
feel, I'll manage without your help. Just tell me what
you'd do next if you were me, and I'll try to make sure
I don't have a fatal accident like Brett did."

"Emotional blackmail won't work with me, sweetheart. I don't have a conscience."

"Sure, you do. Everyone does." She leaned towards
me and rested her fingers on my arm. Possibly unintentionally, but I couldn't be sure—the movement afforded me a good view of her full breasts encased in a
lacy white bra. She followed the direction of my gaze,
realized what she'd done and hastily sat up again. Definitely not intentional then. "Come on, Charlie, give. I
really need your help."

"Okay." I sighed, dragging my mind away from her
impressive assets, a subject I'd infinitely prefer to focus
on. Close proximity to Ms. Webb was seriously testing
my resolve not to get involved with another woman, to
say nothing of remaining aloof from her investigation.

"I suppose I'd talk to all the people who were closest to her, if you can still find them, that is." I frowned. "There was a best friend, wasn't there?"

"Yes, Sally Austin. They went through school together and then moved on to college. They were inseparable."

"We spoke to her at the time, but she couldn't shed any light. There was a teacher at the college, too, but I can't recall his name."

"Ramsay."

"That's it."

"She was doing A levels in English, history and economics, but English was her first love and Ramsay had high hopes of her getting an A grade."

"Yeah, we spoke to him too but never got to follow that up." I sat back and concentrated on my lager, satisfied I'd given her a dead end to chase. After fifteen years, both Sally and Ramsay must have moved on. "So, I guess that's it."

"Come on then." She drained her glass and stood up.

"Come on where?"

"Sally lives in Hassocks. She's married with three kids and doesn't work, so if we hurry we should be able to catch her before she does the school run."

I groaned. "Just a minute, I don't remember saying I'd go with you."

"No." She offered me another of her killer smiles. "But you will."

"Oh, all right." I revised my opinion about the flash of her breasts being unintentional. If my mind hadn't been diverted, I'd never have been outmanoeuvred so easily. This girl knew just how to get what she wanted from a man, although I doubt she usually had to try this hard. "If I agree to see this Sally with you, will you leave me in peace afterwards?"

"Of course." Her expression was suspiciously innocent. "Provided she doesn't tell us anything that leads us somewhere else, of course. Oh, and after we've seen Ramsay, naturally."

I rolled my eyes. "Why do I get the impression you know where to find him too?"

"Because I do. He's still slaving away at the Sixth Form College. He taught me when I did my A levels."

"Come on then," I said, resigned. "I assume you have a car and won't mind Gil slobbering all over the backseat."

I picked up Gil's Frisbee but made the mistake of letting him see it. He threw back his head and let out a series of earsplitting howls that caused everyone in the place to stare at him with varying degrees of disapproval. Gil was addicted to his Frisbee, and excitement got the better of him whenever he laid eyes on it. I was embarrassed but Kara just laughed and ruffled his ears.

"Don't encourage him." I hid the Frisbee inside my jacket.

"Well, I think he's sweet."

We headed for the car park. "I'm not even going to ask you how you know where Sally lives," I said. "I'm not sure I want to know."

"Oh, there's nothing sinister about it. She married Brett's best mate. Brett was best man at their wedding and I was a guest."

I took a moment to process that. "You know her well then?"

"Not really. We exchange Christmas cards, stuff like that, that's all."

We reached the car park and I knew which vehicle was hers even before she unlocked a yellow VW Beetle with the remote. Jimmy had come through with that information. And quite a bit more besides. Gil squeezed into the back and then sat centrally, leaning his head between the two of us, distributing his favours evenly.

"If Sally has been all but part of the family for so many years," I said as we drove down the ramp, "how come you haven't discussed Jasmine with her before now?"

"Don't forget I was only twelve when she went AWOL, and no one spoke to me about it at all. I didn't see Sally for another five years and by then Jasmine's disappearance, by parental decree, wasn't a subject for after-dinner conversation." She shrugged. "I suppose it became a habit to keep quiet about it."

"But that shouldn't have prevented Sally from saying something, surely? Your father couldn't control her."

"No, but if Jasmine's name is ever mentioned in front of him he goes all quiet and, believe me, my father should have patented the recipe for stony silences. No one does them better. He's a master at making people feel uncomfortable if they talk about something he doesn't want to hear. Asylum seekers, gays, the government's soft take on crime—believe me, you don't want to get him started on any of those."

I grunted, knowing the type.

"But Jasmine's disappearance…sorry, *my elder daughter's selfish defection*, has yet to be toppled from the coveted number-one position in his all-time greatest bugbears' list."

"You've barely mentioned your mother in all this. What's her take on it?"

Kara kept her eyes focused on the road ahead, considering the question before she responded. "It's hard to say really. She never talks about it either but she hasn't been the same since Jas left."

"In what way?"

She frowned. "It's difficult to be specific. She didn't have a breakdown or anything obvious like that. Quite the opposite. She refused to see a doctor and declined the offer of counselling. But something inside her changed. I suppose the best way to describe it would be to say that she lost her sparkle." She flashed me a quick sideways glance. "Does that make any sense?"

"Sure. It stands to reason she must feel bitter and disappointed. What mother wouldn't in the circumstances? Deep down she probably blames herself."

"Perhaps."

"And now she's lost her only son, as well."

"Yes, and I can't help feeling for her. Brett and I both worked unorthodox hours so we tended to go and see Mum during the day when we knew *he* wouldn't be about. But Brett was much better at making time to visit than me. Perhaps that was because he was Mum's favourite child." Kara sighed. "A preference she didn't bother to hide. And now she's only got me."

"Did her relationship with your father get stronger as a result of their joint loss?"

"No, just the opposite," she said. I raised a brow, mildly surprised. "She's always been cowed by my father, just like the rest of us, only we grew up and moved away. She didn't have that option."

"She could have divorced him."

"Huh, you wouldn't say that if you knew my father." She pulled a face. "Appearance is everything to him, which is why I've always thought he couldn't forgive Jas. But still, a daughter doing a runner isn't in the same league as his wife seeking a divorce, which implies direct criticism of him as a husband."

"You've got to be joking." I paused, impressed by the economical way she changed down a gear and overtook a slow-moving van. "Divorce carries no stigma nowadays."

"You're making the mistake of applying rational thinking to the situation. Dad would feel humiliated by the very suggestion of divorce and find a way to stop Mum going through with it."

"You think she stayed out of fear rather than love then?"

"I'm not sure but, as I said, after Jas went she changed. After a couple of weeks she moved out of the marital bed and into Jas's room."

"Did she now." It was the first thing she'd said that truly surprised me.

"She said she couldn't stand Dad's snoring, that it kept her awake, but I never really believed that." She flicked the left-hand indicator as she reached a T-junction and pulled out before an ancient Volvo hogging the crown of the road got close enough to hold her up. "She still sleeps in Jas's room to this day."

"When did you and Brett leave?"

"As soon as we could." Kara lifted her shoulders, her eyes still fixed on the road ahead. "And we never went back. I suppose she could leave if she's not happy but, then again, she's never worked and he holds all the purse strings. I don't think she's ever written a cheque. She certainly doesn't have her own bank account. She has a Visa card but I don't expect it has much of a limit on it. Certainly not enough to start another life."

"But she'd be entitled to half the joint property."

"Sure, but if she went to a solicitor, Dad would find a way to paint her as the guilty party and drag matters out for years."

"He sounds like a real charmer."

"He can be when it suits his purpose. Right, here we are." She indicated again and pulled up outside a neat semi with a front garden full of children's toys. "That's Sally's car." She nodded towards the people-mover parked on the drive.

Sally answered the door wearing jogging bottoms, a stained T-shirt and a tired expression, a toddler balanced on her hip. When she saw Kara, her eyes softened with sympathy and she somehow managed to hug her without squashing the child.

"How are you holding up, Kara?"

"I'm okay, Sal, thanks. Sorry to call unannounced but I need a quick word. This is Charlie," she added, almost as an afterthought. "Can we come in for a moment?"

"As long as you pretend not to see the mess."

"Mess? What mess?"

"Attagirl! Can I get you both something?" Sally asked as she led the way into a cluttered kitchen and put the child in a playpen.

"Tea, Sal, if it's no trouble." Kara took a seat at the table. "Do you have green?"

I covered a half smile with my hand. She wasn't really the instant-coffee type at all.

"Nothing for me, thanks," I said when Sally looked in my direction.

Kara played briefly with the child in the playpen, made the obligatory enquiries about the other two and listened with commendable patience to the long-winded responses. Then she got down to business. "Charlie is helping me to try and track Jasmine down."

"Okay." Sally assimilated this news calmly. "But why, after all this time?"

"She deserves to know about Brett."

"Yes, I suppose, but if she's taken no interest in any of you for all these years…well, I'm sorry, Kara, but do you think she'll care?"

"I honestly don't know, but this is for me as much as her. I need to understand what happened. Charlie was the detective who looked into her original disappearance, if you recall."

"Knew I'd seen you somewhere before, Charlie. I never forget a handsome face."

For some reason that escapes me, women find me attractive. I have a reasonable physique, I suppose, but when I look in the mirror I honestly can't see what all the fuss is about.

"Handsome?" I quirked a brow and treated her to one of my infrequent smiles, just to soften her up.

"Ah, no, if you're fishing for more compliments you've had all you're going to get out of me. Vanity is a terrible trait in a man."

"I'll bear that in mind." I stretched my legs in front of me, crossed them at the ankles and cut to the chase before vanity got the better of me. "I remember when Jasmine went missing you told me she had no problems you knew about and that she was doing well at college. Was that true?"

"Well, not precisely. There *was* something on her

mind, I'm sure of it. She'd been short-tempered and withdrawn for weeks but she refused to tell me what was wrong."

"Now that does surprise me." Kara sat forward and rested her arms on her knees, tea forgotten. "You two told each other absolutely everything."

"Yes, but not this time. The more I probed, the more adamant she became that nothing was up. But I knew she wasn't being honest and got the impression something had happened at home. Something to do with your father that she couldn't bear to talk about. She couldn't stand the sound of his name anymore and started referring to him as Alan, as though that somehow distanced him from her."

"But you're sure you don't have any idea what was bugging her?" I asked.

"None whatsoever."

"What about you, Kara?"

"No, sorry, but then I'm the last person she would have confided in."

"Did she have any boyfriends?"

"Half the upper-sixth were wetting themselves to take her out."

"Anyone special?"

"Yes, Billy Simpson. A good-looking guy, we all fancied him, but he only had eyes for Jas."

"And did she? Go out with Simpson, I mean?"

"Once or twice, just in a crowd, I think. Kara's probably told you how hard it was for any female in her family to have a normal teenage life. No guys like being raked over the coals when they call to take a girl out on a casual date." Sally shook her head. "Mr. Webb was Dickensian about that sort of thing, which is why Jas didn't put the boys through it, I always thought. It was just too embarrassing."

"Okay," I said. "What about college? Was she doing okay there?"

"She had been, but that last term her grades had really slipped."

"The downturn coinciding with her mystery problems, presumably."

"Yes. I know Ramsay was concerned and had her in his office for several long heart-to-hearts but, again, she wasn't very forthcoming about their discussions."

"That's okay," Kara said. "We're going to see him next and I expect he'll tell us."

Are we? That was news to me. I treated Kara to a scowl, which she blithely ignored.

"It sounds as though she'd become rather secretive in those weeks before she disappeared," I remarked. "Couldn't have been anything to do with Ramsay, could it? I remember him being quite young and got the impression a lot of the girls had a thing for him."

"Yes." Sally grinned. "He wasn't that much older than us and we did all rather fancy our chances. But as far as I know he steered clear of the lot of us. Must have known what would be in store for him if he tried it on and got reported. Even though we were all above the age of consent, something like that on his record would hardly enhance his career prospects."

"Yes," Kara added, giggling. "He was still considered to be a bit of a heartthrob in my day."

"I do remember there was a rumour, though," Sally said.

"About Ramsay?"

"Yes, he joined the college the year before Jas and I

went there. Before that I think he'd been in a big London comprehensive for a couple of years."

Kara frowned. "Wonder why he left after only two years."

"Probably preferred the idea of sixth-formers. Kids who actually *wanted* to learn." Sally drained the last of the tea from her mug. "Anyway, when Jas and I got to the college, there were rumours amongst the upper-sixth about a girl called…hell, can't remember her name offhand but it'll come to me in a minute. Anyway, she'd been a great favourite of Ramsay's but didn't return to college after her first year—"

"Like Jas, you mean?" Kara said keenly.

"Well, I don't think the circumstances were quite the same. The rumour was that Ramsay had been giving Suzanne Longhurst, that was her name, more than extra coaching and a complaint had been made against him. We thought it was just the other girls being catty because she'd been the Chosen One. Anyway, her family moved away from the area, the rumours died and, as far as I know, Ramsay kept his nose clean after that."

"Well, that's interesting," I said, "but I dare say the girl's family moved away for reasons that had nothing to do with the college."

"But it must mean something, Charlie," Kara said. "It's our first lead."

"As to Jasmine's actual disappearance, Sally, when I spoke to you at the time you said you didn't know where she'd gone and that her vanishing was a complete surprise to you." I focused my eyes on her face and didn't blink. It was a basic police tactic that was supposed to fool the person you were interviewing into believing you knew more than you actually did. "That wasn't completely true either, was it?"

Sally didn't hesitate for long. "No, it wasn't."

"What!" Kara leapt from her seat. "Why didn't you say something at the time?"

"Later, Kara," I said. She glowered at me but resumed her seat. I wanted to hear what Sally had to say before she had the chance to think better of it. "Go on, Sally."

"Well, she was very excited about something. She reckoned she'd got it all figured out at last and that she'd soon be out of this dump, as she referred to it, forever."

"And you never said!" Kara was getting all agitated again.

"Sorry, but I was sworn to secrecy. She only told me because she didn't want to disappear and have me thinking something had happened to her."

"She didn't care what we thought then."

"I think she did, but I also think she was too preoccupied to worry about anything other than getting away. Anyway, I said I'd keep quiet for a day or two, provided she got in touch with your parents and let them know she was safe. Whatever her beef with your father, and God alone knew she had enough reasons to resent him, they didn't deserve to spend however long she planned to stay away not knowing if she was dead or alive. Besides, I knew she'd be reported missing, obviously, and that the police would get involved and I didn't fancy lying to them indefinitely."

"It's okay," I said. "Everyone does it. We kind of expect it."

"Yes, but even so."

"Where did she go?"

"London, but I don't know who with, she wouldn't say. All I knew was she'd met someone who was going to make her rich and happy. She said she'd never have to be dominated by anyone ever again."

"Those were her exact words?"

"More or less."

"Sal, why haven't you said anything before now?" Kara asked.

"Well, because no one asked me. Not straight-out, anyway."

Kara looked at me and rolled her eyes. "Can't argue with that, I suppose."

"I tried to raise the subject with your family but was made aware, in no uncertain terms, that it was too painful for discussion." She paused. "I told Brett though, years ago."

"I see." I didn't, though, not really, and needed to clarify a point or two. "Now, let's see if I've got this straight. Your best friend met some man but she didn't tell you his name, or where she met him, or anything at all about him." I treated her to one of my infamous hard stares. "And you didn't think that might be a tad dangerous and try to talk her out of it?"

Sally's face flooded with colour but she stood her ground. "Have you ever tried to stop a tidal wave? When Jas made her mind up, there was nothing anyone could say to deter her."

"Must be a family failing." I flicked a sardonic look Kara's way.

"I prefer to think of it as a positive quality."

"Well, I think we've got it all straight now. Thanks for your time, Sally."

"Just one thing," Sally said. "Perhaps I didn't make

myself clear. You said just now that Jas went off with a man. Well, it definitely wasn't a man she was going to London to meet. I wouldn't have let her do that, not without leaving me a contact number at the very least. No, Jas made it very clear that her appointment was with a woman."

WITH THE WIND in her face and a brisk breeze pushing the boat smoothly through the water, Nadia felt almost normal for the first time since Brett's death, heralding a fresh bout of guilt. How could she dismiss her brother from her thoughts so readily? But it was such a perfect day for sailing, the wind exactly right, and somehow she couldn't remain sad. Her children were like monkeys, running all over her forty-foot ketch in response to her instructions. Saskia was already a competent sailor, just as Nadia herself had been at the same age. Anton sat in the cockpit, alert but unobtrusive. He said little and each time they tacked he moved without needing to be told. She tilted her face until she was looking up at the sky, enjoying the familiar sensation of the wind burning her cheeks, thinking this was a far better way to assuage her grief than filling herself with Igor's pills. She didn't understand why she hadn't tried it before and, inside her head, she dedicated this perfect day on the water to Brett.

Only reluctantly did Nadia turn towards home when the children tired and started to bicker. The bridge that would let them back into the marina lifted on the hour. If they hurried they would just make the four o'clock. By the time she slid the *Nadia* into her berth, Saskia was curled up asleep in Anton's lap. Her eyes clashed with the serious young Russian's and they smiled at one another. Nadia then returned her attention to berthing the boat, instructing Sergei to leap ashore and slip the lines over the bollards when she was close enough to the pontoon for him to do so safely.

Anton drove them home, pressing the remote inside the car to open the electronic gates to their massive detached house. As soon as they stopped by the front door it opened and Igor, all smiles, was waiting to greet them. Saskia, awake again, ran from the car and hurtled herself straight into his arms.

"Papa, we went sailing and I did two tacks all by myself."

"No, pumpkin, surely not?" Igor opened his eyes wide in faux astonishment. "Someone must have helped you."

"Nooo, Papa, it was all me!"

Nadia smiled as she struggled to follow the conversation. Igor always spoke to the children in Russian but if she concentrated she could understand most of what was said nowadays.

"Off you go now, both of you." He patted his son's head. "Olga is waiting for you." He extended his hand to Nadia. "I didn't know you intended to take the boat out today, darling." He slipped an arm 'round her waist and walked her into the house. "Was that wise? You're not strong enough."

"But, darling, I had a wonderful time."

"I can tell that from your animated face." He smiled and kissed the end of her wind-burnt nose. Nadia noticed Anton watching them, an unreadable expression on his face. "Come, my love." Igor led her towards the stairs. "We should rest now."

Nadia knew what that meant and her pulse quickened at the prospect. For the first time in over a month she felt a brief flare of sexual desire. Igor was a passionate man and not many days passed without his making love to her at least once, almost always in the afternoon. His lovemaking was strenuous and inventive, and in fifteen years she hadn't once tired of it. Until the death of her brother deprived her of all her finer feelings.

They reached their room and Igor removed her clothes frustratingly slowly, plastering her body with sensual kisses as he tantalised and teased, sensing the return of her interest perhaps and punishing her by making her wait.

"You have returned to me, my darling," he said afterwards, his now flaccid penis still buried deep inside her. "I rejoice. But you have done too much today. Rest awhile and I'll get your pill."

"No, Igor. Today has done me good and I think I can sleep without it."

"No, my love, it's too soon. And don't forget we have guests tonight. I need you to sparkle and win them over with your charm. Monika will be here soon."

Nadia hid her dismay with difficulty. Monika was Igor's daughter from his first marriage. Just a few years younger than Nadia, she resented her father's new wife—a fact she was at pains to hide from him but which she made crystal clear to Nadia at every opportunity.

"I need your help, my darling. So you must take the pill, for my sake."

And so, of course, she did.

FOUR

A WOMAN? I hadn't seen that one coming. Still, it didn't necessarily mean what Kara clearly thought it did. She walked out of Sally's house as though in a trance, hands shaking as she fumbled for her car keys. No big surprise there. She'd spent fifteen years wondering what had become of her sister. Young as Jasmine had been at the time of her disappearance, her actions demonstrated a selfish determination to put herself first that I found hard to forgive. To Kara, discovering that her sister planned it all in advance and had gone off without a second thought for those she left behind must feel like a brand-new betrayal.

Kara finally succeeded in extracting the keys from the bottom of her bag and promptly dropped them on the ground. I reached out a hand to steady her, picked them up and ushered her into the passenger seat.

"I'll drive. You need time to get your head together."

Without argument she meekly slid into the car. She didn't say anything and stared fixedly ahead, absently fondling Gil's ears as he leaned across from his back-seat perch and licked her face. I've never been one to underestimate the value of silence and left her to her thoughts. She'd speak when she realized she had questions she needed to ask. I estimated that would take about five minutes.

"Is the answer as obvious as it seems?"

I glanced at the dashboard clock. Four and a half minutes. "Not necessarily. There could be dozens of reasons why she'd go off with a woman without telling any of you."

"Like what?"

"Well, she might have thought she was being recruited for a modelling agency or something like that. She certainly had the looks and the figure."

"I suppose so, but why didn't she say?"

"Would your father have let her?"

"God, no!"

"Well, there you are then."

"Yes, but she could have told me. I'd never have let on to Dad."

"She might have thought you were too young to understand or that you couldn't be trusted to keep her secret once the pressure was on."

"Perhaps, but I still think—"

"Or she might have thought she was going to be interviewed for some glamorous job somewhere and the woman might have been offering her accommodation." I paused, glancing at Kara's profile as I waited for the lights to change. "But, even if what you're thinking is true, would it matter?"

"Not really, it's just not something I've ever considered. Not once in all the hours I've spent speculating about the reasons for her disappearance."

"Well, if it's true, and it's a very big *if* we're talking about here, it would explain why she's never been home again. She wouldn't want to deny who she really is and you did mention that homophobia is high on your father's pet-hate list."

"True, but I just don't buy it, Charlie." She shook her

head. "Not that I have anything against gays, not like my father. Each to their own, as far as I'm concerned. But the Jas I remember took a healthy interest in the opposite sex and didn't display any of the tendencies."

"Knew what to look for, did you, at the age of twelve?"

"No, I suppose not."

"Are you all right now?"

"Yes, I'm fine, but I'm glad you were with me back there."

"No sweat."

"Charlie, what Sally told us about that other girl, surely that means something?"

"Not necessarily."

"Oh, come on! Two girls in succeeding years, both favourites of Ramsay's and both disappearing in questionable circumstances."

"Don't jump to conclusions, Kara. We don't know that Suzanne actually disappeared. Sally said her family moved away."

"Yes, that's what she *said* but I doubt if she really knows." The dull sheen of disappointment in Kara's eyes had been replaced by a gleam of determination I was starting to recognize. I wasn't sure if I was pleased she'd recovered so quickly or wary about her renewed determination to continue with this wild-goose chase.

"If the girl had disappeared, there would have been a police search, lots of publicity and appeals for information locally. You'd have been bound to hear about it."

"Yes, you're right." She briefly lapsed into silence. When she spoke again she appeared to be having trouble containing her excitement. "But, Charlie, if a complaint was made against Ramsay, wouldn't there be something on record somewhere? Perhaps one of your old colleagues would be able to find out what it was?"

"Nope, I'm afraid not. It would have been a disciplinary matter at the college. The girl would have been over the age of consent so no law would have been broken."

"Oh damn! I was so sure we were on to something."

"This place hasn't changed much," I said, pulling into the college car park.

Ramsay was taking his last class of the day but Kara was recognised by the college secretary and we were allowed to wait in reception even though we didn't have an appointment. A steady stream of students of both sexes wandered past us in tight clusters. From the snippets of conversation I overheard, a party at someone's house on Saturday night and the thorny question of exactly who had or hadn't managed to snag an invitation appeared to be the only subject under discussion. I was tempted to smile, remembering just how important such things had once been to me. Times change but people obviously didn't.

"Kara." Ramsay approached us a short time later with a broad smile for his ex-pupil. "What a pleasant surprise."

The man didn't seem to have aged much. He was tall and lean, wearing an open-necked shirt with the sleeves rolled back, no jacket and well-tailored trousers. He looked suave yet approachable. More like an athlete than a teacher. His hair was thick and slicked back with that wet-look goopy stuff but kept falling forward across one side of his brow. Call me a cynic but I couldn't help wondering if it was a deliberate ploy to encourage his female students to fantasise about pushing it back into place.

His clear blue eyes were focused on Kara with evident appreciation. But that was no reason for me to regard him with suspicion. His reaction to her was no different than I'd expect from any red-blooded male, myself included. But still, there was something about him that put me on red alert. My copper's nose told me there was more to this guy than just a pretty face. In my experience, when someone seems too good to be true they almost certainly are.

"Sorry to call unannounced, Mr. Ramsay," Kara said, shaking his proffered hand.

"Oh, Colin, please, you're not a student anymore."

"Colin, then. This is Charlie Hunter."

I took my turn to shake the man's hand. His grip was firm and there was no anxiety in his expression. He was clearly curious to know what brought us knocking at his door but too polite to ask outright. I took a backseat as Kara and Ramsay caught up. How was college? What are you doing now? Why don't you come to our reunions? The usual insincere crap. Still, it gave me the opportunity to watch Ramsey in action, to get a feel for the man. He didn't seem to be anything other than genuinely interested in Kara's activities since leaving college, and nothing in his body language suggested he found it a strain chatting to Jasmine's sister.

"Charlie was the detective who investigated my sister's disappearance," Kara said, finally getting down to business.

And there it was. A lightning-swift cloud passed through those suspiciously bright blue eyes—coloured contact lenses, I was willing to bet. It was fleeting and if I hadn't been watching him closely, I'd have missed it.

"You still haven't heard from Jasmine, then?" Ramsay recovered with commendable speed.

"No, but you see, my brother was killed in an accident—"

"I'm so sorry, Kara. I didn't know, otherwise I would have—" He broke off and covered one of her hands with his so I never did learn what he would have done. "That must have been a terrible blow."

"Yes, thank you, it was, but we're coping. The thing is, though, I think Jasmine ought to know and so I've started looking for her."

"And you think I can help?" He shrugged. "I don't see how. It was all so long ago. Still, anything I can do, I'll be only too glad. I expect you have some questions."

"I remember interviewing you at the time," I said, breaking up Ramsay's cosy little tête-à-tête with Kara by reminding him of my presence. "You said she was an exceptional student."

"She was. I had high hopes of getting her to Oxbridge."

"Yes, but you didn't tell me her grades had started to slip."

"They hadn't slipped exactly—"

"Well, either they had or they hadn't," I said in my most reasonable voice.

If Ramsay realized I was deliberately trying to provoke him, he gave no sign and answered me in the same courteous tone he'd employed throughout the exchange. "She was preoccupied and had turned in a couple of essays that weren't up to her usual standard, that's all." He shrugged. "It happens. Kids, especially ones of that age, suddenly realize there's a life outside the schoolroom and their attention slips. Jasmine was a good-looking girl." He paused and offered Kara an oily smile. "It runs in the family, obviously, and I dare say she had the lads chasing her 'round the block. It was bound to distract her."

"So what did you talk about in your one-to-one sessions?"

"Oh, the usual. Was there anything wrong? Did she think she was giving her work the attention it deserved? Was there anything she wanted to tell me? That sort of thing."

"And was there? Anything she wanted to tell you, I mean."

"No, she said everything was fine. She admitted not having given as much attention to her work as she should have done, but she didn't say why. She said she'd get back on track because she didn't want to fail."

"And you didn't talk about anything else?"

He wrinkled his brow. "Not that I can recall."

"And I don't suppose, during your little chats, she happened to let anything slip about where she was planning to go."

"Sorry, Mr. Hunter, I'd like to help but it was a long time ago and hundreds of students have passed through my hands during the intervening years." He lifted his shoulders, still addressing his comments to me, but his eyes were resting upon Kara's face, and he treated her to a commendably sincere smile of regret. "I really can't remember anything else about Jasmine."

"Yes, but if you could just cast your mind back—"

"Thanks for your time," I said, cutting Kara off and

standing up so she had no choice but to do the same. "We'll get out of your hair now."

"If I remember anything, is there anywhere I can reach you?"

The question was addressed to Kara but before she could hand over her own card, which I thought was probably Ramsay's true objective, I gave him one of my own. I shook the teacher's hand, waited patiently whilst Kara made more protracted farewells and led her back down the long corridor that so reminded me of my own schooldays. I expected, any minute, to be chastised for not walking in single file.

"Why did you stop me like that?" Kara demanded. "I wanted to ask if he saw Jasmine with any particular boy."

"And you think he'd know that when her best friend didn't?"

"It's possible."

"No, Kara, you're clutching at straws. There wasn't anything else he could tell us."

"You think he told the truth then?"

I didn't but knew better than to encourage Kara by saying so. "If there's anything he didn't tell us, I don't think it's connected to Jasmine's disappearance."

"I don't see how you can be so sure if you didn't let me ask any more questions."

"You wanted me to tag along so you must have thought I knew the right questions to ask."

Her expression indicated that she remained less than impressed by my irrefutable logic.

"If he knew anything and didn't say so at the time, he could hardly do so now without creating problems for himself. Teachers still have responsibility for their students, even in this blame-free culture we've created for ourselves. It wouldn't do much for his future career prospects if he admitted to holding back information about a missing minor."

"I suppose not." She turned to look at me. "So, Charlie, what do we do next?"

"Nothing. I said I'd see those two with you and I did. There's nowhere else to go with this. Your sister doesn't want to be found and you should leave it at that."

"But if we just went to Weymouth—"

"And do what exactly?" I eyed her impassively. "Stand on a corner and hope she obligingly strolls past? Weymouth's a big place and we don't have a clue where to start looking."

"Yachts. Whatever she's doing, it'll be connected with the sea. She was the best sailor of us all and loved everything to do with the sport, which must be how Brett found her."

"Give it up, Kara." I leaned back to open the rear door for Gil as we pulled into the marina. Then I gave Kara a quick peck on the cheek and jumped out before she came up with more reasons to delay me. "There's nothing more you can do."

I WAS TOO busy over the next few days to spare any thoughts for Kara. The salon cabinets were finished and the U-shaped seating in muted shades of grey and blue was fitted. The colours were designed to withstand the nefarious activities of small boys and large dogs, so the upholsterers would have it. The matching blinds had just been installed, and the fitters despatched with a healthy tip, so when someone knocked on the hull I assumed one of the guys had forgotten something.

Instead, to Gil's delight, Kara was standing on the pontoon, a suspiciously innocent smile on her face. There was a bottle of wine under her arm and she was carrying a bag bulging with takeaway cartons. It was the first time I'd seen her wearing a skirt but the wait had been worth it. Her legs were endless, and slim, and—*hell, Hunter, don't go there.*

"Kara," I said guardedly, "to what do I owe the pleasure?"

"I come bearing gifts as a thank-you for trying to help me. Can I come aboard?"

No, you bloody can't. Not looking like that. It will definitely not be in your best interests to come within range. Well, that was what I should have said.

"Okay," I found myself saying instead. "Just so long as you've given up all thoughts of persuading me to take you to Weymouth."

She smiled sweetly. "As if I'd do anything so underhanded."

"As if!"

I reached forward and took the bag from her. She kicked off her high heels and I took her hand to help her aboard. In that skirt it wasn't ever going to be an elegant manoeuvre, even with my help, but perhaps that was her intention. The fabric rode well up her thigh as she stretched a leg over the gunwale, and that was when I knew that I was definitely in trouble.

Big trouble.

This girl wasn't about to abandon her search for her sister. Knowing how determined she could be, how could I ever have supposed that she would? But worse, she obviously thought I could be persuaded to help her, and there didn't seem to be much she wouldn't be prepared to do in order to cajole me. Just for a moment I considered finding out how far she'd be prepared to go.

But only for a moment. If I became more intimately acquainted with her, there was no way my conscience would allow me to turn my back on her afterwards. That was the downside of having standards.

"Oh!" She stepped into the salon and looked around her. "It's lovely, Charlie. When was it finished?"

"About five minutes ago."

"So we can celebrate then."

I shrugged. "Why not?"

I opened the bottle of Shiraz she'd brought with her and left it on the counter to breathe. As I unloaded the cartons of Chinese food she'd provided for our supper, she prowled 'round the boat, taking an interest in everything.

"I didn't know what you liked so I got a little of most things."

"So I see."

I joined her in the wheelhouse, where I found her examining my books.

"Is that your son?" She pointed to the framed picture fixed to the wall above my desk.

"Yes, that's Harry."

"How old is he?"

"Eight."

"And your wife, what does she do?"

"Ex-wife. She's married to an accountant now."

"It must be hard for you not being with Harry all the time. I saw how much he means to you the other day."

"It's tough, but Emily will tell you I never saw him much when we were together because of the job—"

"Is that why you separated?"

"Yeah, it's a cliché but true for all that. Policemen, good policemen, are married to the job and it causes havoc with relationships. Em is high maintenance in terms of attention-seeking, and my ability to supply always fell short of her demands."

"But when you left, couldn't you and your wife have patched things up?"

"It was too late by then." I shrugged, surprised not to find myself resenting her intrusive questions. "I suppose the sparkle had gone out of it years before. The usual stuff, you know, marrying too young, expectations too high. It's better like this. I get what the experts call quality time with Harry and have a civilized relationship with his mother and her new husband. Everyone wins."

"I suppose so. I know something about dysfunctional families myself."

"Anyway," I said, having no wish to get onto the subject of her family. "Let's refill these glasses and attack that mountain of food."

"Sounds good."

"Tell me something about yourself," I invited, between mouthfuls of sweet and sour.

"What don't you already know?"

"What makes you think I know anything?"

"Because you agreed to help me and wouldn't have done that without checking me out first."

I actually chuckled at that one. "Okay, you tell me about yourself and I'll let you know if it agrees with what I found out."

"Fair enough." She took a sip of wine and recited her life story as though reading from a script. She acted like it was a question she'd been asked by millions of men millions of times before and wanted to get it over with before she died of boredom. "I did A levels you know where, did a degree in psychology at UCL and then went to work for one of the big multinationals." She pulled a face. "Why do those companies always assume female graduates are only good for human resources?"

"What are human resources?" I asked, deadpan.

Kara smiled. "Stop playing dumb."

"How come you didn't take a gap year? Isn't that the done thing nowadays?"

"What, and have *him* pay for it and still control me?" She shuddered. "Not on your life! I wanted out. I lived on campus and, when I left uni, I got my own flat straightaway."

"But you didn't take to corporate life?"

"Nope, too many pointless meetings for my taste. And as for office politics and having to watch your back all the time, well…"

I nodded, understanding precisely where she was coming from. "Okay, I get the picture. Not everyone thrives in that sort of environment. It's usually the ones with brains and the will to use them who don't slot in and refrain from asking awkward questions."

"You must have had similar problems in the modern police force."

I took a swig of wine and deliberately didn't answer. I'd worked out her tactics now and wasn't about to be caught out for a second time. She wanted to get all cosy and intimate, and I'd played into her hands by asking her about herself. Talking about personal things would make it that much harder to turn her down when she finally got 'round to the real reason for her visit. The silence between us lengthened and Kara finally broke it, just as I'd known she would. People usually find silence unsettling. Especially when they want something.

"On the day my life changed I was really peed off about something ridiculous that had happened at work. I can't even remember what it was now, but I went to a wine bar to let off steam and bumped into Sam Bryce."

"Who's Sam?"

"An old friend. We were at uni together and had meant to keep in touch, what with both of us hailing from Brighton, but somehow that didn't happen. Anyway, we linked up again and were complaining about the futility of our respective careers, as you do. That led on to him having a good moan about his inability to meet women." Ah, so it was Samuel. "It Takes Two was launched over a bottle of house plonk in a bar off the Lanes."

"Is it successful?"

"We're getting there. You'd be surprised how many people are too busy with their lives to meet a significant other, or too frightened to go to a regular dating agency. They're not all saddos like you might imagine, just busy people who don't know how to connect with the opposite sex. Also men like Sam, who are brilliant but a bit lacking in self-confidence, have problems with today's more assertive women. You know, the ones who give the impression they might eat you alive if you say something to upset them."

"He's got a point," I said, thinking of Sarah.

"Well, they don't have to worry about that with us. All we do is bring groups of lonely people together, for a fee of course, over some shared interest and let them get on with it. Friendship is very often all people want anyway, and with us they can get precisely that, no strings attached."

"Sounds interesting."

"Want me to sign you up?"

"I'll pass on that, thanks."

"Yes, somehow I can't see you having trouble attracting female companionship."

"Do you live in Hove?"

"Now, Charlie, you know I don't, so stop asking trick questions." She wagged a spare rib under my nose. "That's Sam's abode and we've registered the business from there, although as it's all done online we can work from anywhere we like."

"That's good."

"I have a flat in Sussex Square, as I'm sure you're aware."

"Very salubrious address."

"So is the rent."

We placed the empty cartons in the trash compactor and I offered her brandy.

"No, thanks. I have to drive and I'd hate to have to explain to any of your ex-colleagues that you're responsible for me being over the limit."

"Coffee then?"

"Only if it's instant."

I chuckled. "Right answer."

"So, Charlie, before we part forever," she said casually, as we settled onto my new seating unit with our drinks, "can we sum up, for my own peace of mind, what we learned about Jas?"

Her words immediately put me on my guard. We'd got to the real reason for her visit at last, and when I disappointed her she'd probably get all upset, throw a wobbly, call me all sorts of names and storm out of my life forever. Now I remembered why I didn't want to get involved in another relationship.

"I wondered when you'd get 'round to asking."

"Now, don't be like that. After all, I bought you dinner and livened up your evening with an abundance of witty banter, didn't I?"

"Just get on with it," I said grouchily, "if you must."

"Okay, I'll go first then. Jasmine was doing fine until a few months before she disappeared. Then she discovered something, almost certainly at home, that upset her but she wouldn't even tell her best friend what it was. Her English teacher probably fancied her and treated her as a favourite but we don't know if it went any further than that. When her grades suffered, he had long one-to-ones with her but his explanation for what they spoke about doesn't account for the amount of time they were closeted together. Then she disappeared, not with a man but a woman." She shrugged as she counted off the points on her fingers. "That's it, unless there's something you picked up that I missed. The only new fact we've learned is that she went away with a woman but it still doesn't make any sense. Why did she do it?"

"Instead of why, have you stopped to ask yourself how?"

"What do you mean?" Kara sat up straight, put her cup down and stared directly at me. "Is there something you're not telling me?"

"No, you know everything I do. But just bear in mind it was a woman, not someone her own age she went off with. We think she lived in London because that's where Jasmine's phone call and letter came from, and it's also where she told Sally she was going." I paused to sip my brandy, wondering if I was doing the right thing in setting Kara's mind on this particular detour. But she'd never let me stop now I'd started, so I ploughed on. "If her movements were so closely guarded by your father, where did she get to meet this mystery adult and have lengthy discussions about a career change?"

"Sailing," Kara said, her face brightening. "It must have been. We raced all the time at weekends and met all sorts of different people at the various clubs. Dad would have intervened if she'd spoken to any of the men for too long but he wouldn't have minded about a woman."

"Well, there you are then," I said, stretching my arms above my head. "All you have to do is revisit all the sailing clubs you went to fifteen years ago and ask all the women you meet in them if they remember Jasmine."

"Not funny, Charlie!"

"Sorry. Do you still sail?"

"Yes, I have my own thirty-two-footer that I can manage single-handed. I keep it at Hamble."

I knew this already, of course, thanks to the diligent research carried out by Jimmy. I also knew, courtesy of the same source, that Suzanne Longhurst had not been reported missing sixteen years ago, and her family had moved away from the area for reasons that had no apparent bearing on Colin Ramsay.

"Why Hamble?"

"Well, there isn't anywhere much to sail to from Brighton, and Hamble is more convenient for Cowes. That's where Brett lived, and I often used to go over for weekends and stay with him. We'd either sail my tub together or he'd get us on something a bit faster as crew."

"That must have been something to look forward to."

"It was."

A tear ran down her cheek. Powerless to help myself, I arrested its progress with my forefinger, gently smoothing it away, and traced the outline of her lips with that same finger.

"Hey, sweetheart, don't be sad." I snaked an arm 'round her and pulled her head towards my shoulder. I was probably playing right into her hands but what the hell. "It'll be all right."

"Charlie, I wanted to ask you if you would—"

My mobile, charging in the wheelhouse, shattered the mood by chirping into life. Just touching Kara had got me all stirred up, and if the phone hadn't saved the day, nothing on this earth could have prevented me from kissing her, which was presumably her intention, even though I thought her tears were genuine. And then I'd have felt honour-bound to carry on helping her.

Saved by the bell, Hunter.

"Excuse me." I stood to answer the phone, careful to keep my back to her. She didn't need to see the physical evidence, proof positive that her plan had come within a hair's breadth of succeeding. "Yes, Em," I said, recognising my ex-wife's number on the display, "what is it?" As I listened to her near hysterical voice, my heart went cold. "What! When? Calm down and tell me exactly what happened." I glanced over my shoulder. Kara was standing directly behind me, frowning. "All right, I'll be there as soon as I can…No, no, don't call the police, let me see it first. Have you got it there?… Fax it over now and don't worry, it's probably nothing."

"What is it?" Kara asked. "What's happened? You've gone ghostly pale. Has something happened to your son?"

"You could say that. Someone planted a threat in his backpack." My jaw felt painfully taut as I fought to contain my fear. When I got my hands on the nameless bastard who'd been cowardly enough to use my son to get to me, he'd regret the day he was born. "Emily found it just now when she was packing his lunch box for tomorrow."

"My God, why? What did it say?"

"We're just about to find out."

I wrenched the paper from the fax machine as soon as it came through. Kara peered 'round my side and gasped when she read the chilling words typed in bold print across the page.

Tell your dad to leave Jasmine Webb alone. She doesn't wish to be found.

NADIA WOULD HAVE been late for dinner if Igor hadn't woken her with a gentle kiss. The pills he gave her sapped her energy and made her fuzzy-headed. Even now, several hours later, she still hadn't completely shaken off the effect. She really must stop taking them. She didn't need them anymore and, besides, she'd hate to become addicted. All the ridiculous things she'd said, the accusations she'd made when Brett died, now seemed to be exactly that. Ridiculous. It was easy to see, now that she was thinking more rationally, that her reaction had been an instinctive means of dealing with the grief and guilt by transferring blame to someone else.

She smiled across the table at Igor, who blew her a

kiss. His eyes were all for her so he probably didn't notice Monika's scowl. Nadia did but she ignored it, rev-
elling in the adoration she could detect in the eyes of
her intelligent, handsome, powerful and oh-so-charm-
ing husband. How could she ever have imagined Igor
had anything to do with Brett's death? He idolised her
and would never knowingly do anything to cause her
pain. He hadn't chastised her when she said those terrible things, seeming to understand that she needed
to blame someone, anyone, other than herself. Well,
she was over that now and would apologise later, as-
sure him she hadn't meant what she'd said and make
it clear to him that she no longer needed to take his
tranquillisers.

Nadia answered a question put to her by the Span-
iard sitting on her left. Her response was light and witty
and she could detect approval in Igor's eye as their male
guests looked towards her with identical expressions
of admiration. Good, she'd pleased him.

She tuned out the conversation when it turned to
business and found her mind drifting back to the day
when Brett had accosted her outside the Jubilee Retail
Park. It was so long since anyone had addressed her as
Jasmine that she hadn't responded. What did make her
turn her head was the tenor of the voice. A tingle of recognition trickled down her spine as she slowly looked
into her brother's face. Her breath came in short, nervous gasps, the years fell away, and she hardly dared to
believe what she was seeing with her own eyes.

Fortunately Anton had been with her that day. He
asked no questions when she flung her arms 'round a
complete stranger, tears streaming down her face, and
said she was going to have coffee with him. He even

let Brett take a picture of the two of them together. Nadia shouldn't have permitted it but couldn't bring herself to disappoint her brother over something that must have seemed so trivial to him. She knew without having to ask him that Anton wouldn't mention the meeting to Igor.

She told Brett as gently as she could that it wouldn't be possible—or safe—for them to meet again. But nothing could stop her from asking about Kara and her mother. She had a folder full of pictures of both her siblings supplied regularly by Igor. But now she knew something about their lives, as well. Neither of them referred to their father, and as they parted Nadia asked Brett not to mention to Kara or their mother that they'd met.

She left him with fresh tears in her eyes, having convinced him it would be impossible for them ever to meet again.

But three weeks later Brett again accosted her. This time Viktor was with her. He placed himself between her and Brett, and they didn't even get to speak. She knew Viktor would take pleasure in telling Igor she'd been approached by a bloke claiming to be her brother.

She waited for her husband to ask her about it but he never did. Instead, the next time Brett came to Weymouth he finished up dead.

But it was just a coincidence.

It had to be.

FIVE

"CHARLIE, MY GOD!" Kara clutched my arm. "Is Harry all right?"

"Yes, I guess so. He hasn't seen the note."

"But who could have written it and got close enough to put it in his bag?"

"That," I said with barely suppressed rage, "is something I have yet to establish."

"This is all my fault." Kara looked distraught. "What the hell have I got you involved in?"

"It's not your fault. All you wanted to do was to find your sister." I reached for my biking jacket and then changed my mind. "Can you drive me to Shoreham? It'll be quicker than getting the bike out."

"Of course. Is that where your ex lives?"

"Yes." I gathered up my wallet and mobile. "Stay, Gil!" The dog's tail, wagging in anticipation of his usual evening run, flapped to a halt.

"He can come if you—"

"No, I want him to guard the boat."

Kara frowned. "You don't think that anyone would—"

"Until I get to the bottom of all this, I don't know what to think." I locked the boat and helped Kara onto the pontoon, a whole raft of possibilities flitting through my mind. "But one thing's for sure, if they know where Harry goes to school, then they sure as hell know where I live."

"Yes, I suppose."

Kara drove in silence and with the swift efficiency I was beginning to expect from her. She concentrated on the road, seeming to appreciate that I needed the space to think without any distraction from her. The roads were quiet for once and we reached Shoreham pretty quickly. Kara pulled up outside the house I directed her to and turned off the car's lights.

"I'll wait for you here." She touched my hand. "Good luck."

Phil had obviously been looking out for me and opened the door before I could knock. He wasn't spitting expletives at the upset caused to his wife but I figured he must resent the disruption to his orderly life.

"Hello, Charlie, come on in."

His tone, calm and friendly, took me by surprise. "How's Em?"

"Pretty upset, but perhaps you can say something to calm her down."

I didn't share his confidence. In Em's eyes I would now be enemy number one. "I'll see what I can do," I said, heading for the lounge.

"I'm sure there must be a rational explanation for all this." Phil followed me into the room. "Charlie's here, darling."

Emily, red-rimmed eyes staring from an ashen face, leapt up from the sofa. "What's going on, Charlie?" Her high-pitched voice stopped just short of being hysterical. "What have you got yourself mixed up in that involves Harry?"

"Nothing and it doesn't." I spoke with a calm assurance I didn't feel as I guided her back to her seat. "I'll get it sorted, Em, and Harry won't be dragged into it again. On that you have my solemn promise."

"Would you like a drink, Charlie?" Phil asked. "I think we could all do with one."

"No, I'm all right, thanks, Phil, but I expect Em could use one."

"Is that still your answer to everything?" she cried accusingly. "A few shots of whisky and all the world's problems magically disappear."

"It was my suggestion, darling." Phil sat beside his wife and handed her a glass of brandy. He encouraged her to lift it to her lips and take a sip. "Now, why don't we stay calm and let Charlie tell us what's going on? We both know he'd never deliberately put Harry at risk."

"Thanks, Phil." I was grateful for his lack of emotion, which seemed to temper the worst of Emily's histrionics. "Harry's all right, I assume."

"Yes, but he could easily have found that note. It's only good luck that he didn't."

"It wouldn't have meant anything to him, even if he had. Anyway, I think I know who's responsible for the prank."

"Someone connected to this Jasmine Webb, presumably," Emily said sarcastically. "Even I worked that one out. Who is this woman, Charlie, and why are you looking for her?"

"She's a runaway, or was, fifteen years ago. Her brother died recently and the rest of her family wants to let her know. They came to me because I was involved when she first went missing and I said I'd ask a few questions."

"You expect me to believe something so innocuous

resulted in a direct threat to our son's safety?" Emily
was getting all worked up again. "Don't treat me like
an idiot, Charlie. There has to be more to it than that."

"It's the truth. I wouldn't try to pull the wool over
your eyes when it comes to Harry's well-being, you
know that."

"Not intentionally, but I know you when you get your
teeth into a case. You become totally obsessed. Even
after all these years, you still haven't let your mother's
murder go. Perhaps that's why you and I couldn't—"

"Leave it, Em."

My tone was glacial. My mother's murder was something I *never* talked about, not even with Emily, who'd
helped me get though the aftermath. I supposed that
made her one of the few people entitled to an opinion
on the earth-shattering, pointless crime that deprived
me of the mother I adored, changing the entire direction
of my life. It didn't help matters that Emily was right.
My disinclination to talk to her about it hadn't exactly
helped to cement our rocky relationship.

"You're not being fair, darling." Phil's calm voice
filled the brittle silence. He covered one of his wife's
hands with his own and smiled. "Charlie's told us that
he'll sort it out."

"Yes. That's what he *says* but you don't know that
he can deliver and neither does he. You have no idea
what it was like—"

"I'd done all I could about Jasmine and was going to
let it drop," I said, in no mood to listen to one of Emily's
tirades about my myriad shortcomings as a husband.

"Well, that's all right then," she said ungraciously.
"That's what they've asked you to do and it means
Harry will be safe."

"There, darling, I knew there'd be a simple—"

"Just a minute." She eyed me suspiciously. "What do you mean, you *were* going to let it drop? Surely you don't intend to carry on looking for this woman? Not now, after what could have happened to Harry."

"I can't have people threatening my child." Ice trickled through my veins. I exist on a pretty short fuse at the best of times and was almost frightened by my determination to inflict physical damage on the people using Harry. No longer being an officer of the law, I was fast discovering, had its advantages. "What sort of father would that make me?"

"Our child, Charlie, our child, in case you've forgotten. You're not the only one involved."

"I'm only thinking of Harry."

"Then do what's best for him, report this to the police and let them sort it out."

"And what would the police do?"

She hesitated. "You'd know better than me."

"Right. What they'd do is question Harry and everyone connected with him at school to see who could have got access to his bag. Do you really want to upset him like that?"

"They have people specially trained to talk to children. With all their resources, they'd probably catch whoever's behind this much quicker than you can."

"Let me deal with it. I'm not bound by their restrictions anymore."

"That makes sense, darling," Phil said.

"These thugs seem to think I know a lot more about Jasmine's disappearance than I actually do," I said, thinking aloud. "And unless I find out why, then the threat to Harry won't go away."

"Oh God!" Emily buried her face in her hands. "I don't believe I'm hearing this. Whatever possessed me to marry a policeman?"

"Em, you, Phil and Harry are going off to your parents' place in Spain when term finishes in a couple of weeks, aren't you?"

"Yes."

"Well then, why don't you take Harry out of school and go tomorrow? I know it's a bit earlier than planned, but your mum and dad would love it and so would Harry." I turned to Phil with an apologetic shrug. "I guess it would be a bit inconvenient for you, Phil, but it would mean they'd both be safe and you can still join them in a fortnight." My expression probably reflected the grim determination I felt, because neither of them tried to interrupt me. "And by the time you get back to England, I'll have this sorted."

"I think that's the most sensible thing that's been said this evening." Phil surprised me again by siding with me.

"But I don't want to go without you," Emily said to her husband, her voice a pitiful wail.

"I'll only be a couple of weeks behind you, love, and I'd rather be alone for a few days than be worrying about you both all the time I'm at work." He smiled at his wife. She didn't look overjoyed at the change to her plans but her objections dried up and she retreated behind a sullen silence. Phil obviously had a handle on Emily's need for attention and knew how to keep her sweet. "I'll see if I can change their flights," he said to me, getting to his feet.

When he left us alone, Emily stared at me through hostile eyes and refused to speak. I felt guilty for inadvertently having caused her so much grief and was relieved when Phil returned brandishing online boarding passes.

"I've got them on a flight out of Gatwick early tomorrow morning," he said.

I turned to him with gratitude, having been obliged over the past ten minutes to revise my opinion of the man. There was none of the superiority I would have expected at the turn events had taken. Just the calm, no-nonsense attitude of a meticulous man who loved his wife and stepson and would do what was necessary to keep them safe. I shook his hand and offered to pay for the flights. Phil waved the suggestion aside.

"Can I see him for a moment?"

"He's asleep," Emily snapped. "No thanks to you."

"I won't wake him."

"Oh, all right, I suppose it can't hurt."

I ran up the stairs and into my son's room. Harry was sprawled on his back, arms and legs flung at impossible angles, the light from the landing illuminating soft features slack with sleep. The room was a shrine to his Chelsea football heroes, posters covering the walls, books and magazines about the beautiful game cluttering the little desk in the corner. His prized possession of a programme signed by some of the players was propped up beside the bed. I was amused to notice that his new crash helmet was there too. I gazed down at the boy who was my life and felt my heart inflate with a love that was almost too painful to bear. My determination to keep him safe swelled with it. Careful not to wake him, I gently brushed the hair from his brow.

"You be careful, champ," I said in an undertone,

"and I'll get the bastards who dared to threaten you before you even know it."

Back in the car I briefly told Kara of the arrangements I'd made for Emily and Harry.

"I'm so sorry, Charlie. If I'd known what I was getting you into, I never would have asked you to help."

"It's okay, we'll sort it."

"We?" About to start the car, she paused and blinked at me in evident astonishment. "You surely don't want to know anything more about it now?"

"You don't have me pegged as a quitter, do you?"

She pulled away from the curb. "Well, no, but I realize what Harry means to you and I guess you can do without the hassle."

"I didn't want to know anything more about it *before* this happened and I really wouldn't have let you persuade me." I glanced sideways at her. "No matter what you had planned to try and get me to change my mind."

"It looks as though you'll never find out." She grinned. "Pity that. Anyway, what do you intend to do now?"

"By threatening my son, those scumbags have achieved the one thing they were trying to avoid." My anger escalated. "I'll let you know what I discover," I said when we arrived back at the marina.

"No need because I'm coming with you."

"Afraid not. This could be dangerous."

"Yes, I suppose you're right. It's now more your fight than it is mine, and I don't want to get in your way." She glanced at me. "Where will you start?"

I was too preoccupied to be suspicious about her easy capitulation. "How do these people know I've been asking questions?"

"From someone we've spoken to, presumably."

"Smart girl. And who have we spoken to?"

"Only Sally and Ramsay."

"Right, and I'd stake my bank balance on Sally not being involved."

"You think Colin Ramsay told the people behind Jasmine's disappearance that we'd been asking questions?"

"Don't see who else it could have been. Unless you've spoken to someone I know nothing about."

"No, no I haven't. I haven't even discussed it with Mum or Dad. I know how they'd react to the mention of Jas's name, especially now when they're still so devastated about Brett."

"Well, there you are then."

"So what will you do?"

"I shall pay a little visit to our friend Ramsay before the start of college tomorrow." I got out of the car. "Thanks for the lift."

"At least let me come with you for that. He'll see me but may not be available for you."

"Oh, he'll see me, make no mistake about that." My tone was imbued with steely determination. "I don't need you there, Kara. This is between him and me now, and you'd only be in the way."

"Take care, Charlie."

She blew me a kiss and drove off without a backwards glance.

I found the boat still intact, with nothing to suggest that uninvited guests had come calling during my absence. Gil greeted me with enthusiasm and finally got his run, which afforded me the opportunity to have a good think. Returning to the *No Comment*, I rang the squad room but it was too much to hope that Jimmy would be on duty again. With no time to waste, I passed my request for any information they had on Colin Ramsay to another of my ex-colleagues. I didn't have to wait long for the return call, which confirmed Ramsay had no record and no complaints recorded against him, throwing the theory that had been incubating in my mind back into touch.

I set out early the next morning on the Harley to intercept Ramsay as he arrived at college, counting on the element of surprise to act in my favour. I had nothing more than gut instinct to support my conviction that Ramsay was involved in the disappearance of Jasmine Webb, and nothing but the anger still churning inside me to make the smarmy bastard admit it. It would have to be enough.

Ramsay drove an unremarkable midrange car and slotted it into a space in the corner of the staff car park, which was already almost full. In black leather and still wearing my helmet with the tinted visor covering my eyes, I must have appeared pretty intimidating. Well, I hoped so anyway. I blocked Ramsay's path and took the teacher completely by surprise.

"What the—"

I pulled off the helmet, shook the hair out of my eyes and grabbed Ramsay by the elbow. "We need to talk."

"Mr. Hunter, you half scared me to death."

I scowled. "Think yourself lucky that I'm in a lenient mood."

"Look, I really don't know what you want from me but I haven't got time for this now. I'm already late for my first class."

"And I need some answers." I steered him against

the wall with a vicious twist of the elbow I was still crushing.

"But I can't help you. I've already told you everything I know."

"Cut the crap, Ramsay, I'm in no mood to play games."

"You can't treat me like this. There are rules. I'll report you to your superintendent."

"Good try, but I'm not a serving policeman anymore."

"But Kara said—"

"Kara said I looked into her sister's disappearance fifteen years ago."

"So, if you're no longer a policeman, what are you now?"

"The person who's going to make your life a living hell if you don't start telling the truth." I spoke quietly, an unmistakable note of menace underlying my words. "Who did you talk to after Kara and I came to see you?"

"No one, I…"

His words trailed off and I knew what must be going through his mind. Should he try to talk his way out of this, call for help or simply tell the truth? When I detected signs of real fear in his eyes, I knew he wouldn't hold out for long. Not with me in such an uncompromising mood, governed by no one's rules except my own and in no frame of mind to play fair.

"Is everything all right, Colin?" One of his female colleagues who'd just parked her car was regarding me with suspicion.

"Oh yes, no problem, thanks, Celia. Just having a chat with an old friend."

Yep, definitely a coward. He could have got his colleague to call security but he must know if he did that he'd only be delaying the inevitable.

"Whoever you spoke to is such a fucking coward that he's threatening my eight-year-old son," I hissed as Ramsay's colleague walked slowly away, frequently turning to look back at us over her shoulder. "As you can imagine, that's pissed me off big-time. Now start talking and don't even think about lying."

Ramsay shook his head just once. I increased the pressure I was putting on his elbow and the shake turned into a nod. "All right, I'll tell you what I know, which isn't much. Let's go inside. But just for the record, I didn't tell anyone you'd been to see me, and that's the truth."

Against all the odds, I believed him.

Ramsay headed for the same room as before and closed the door in the face of a student waiting to see him. "All I've ever wanted to be is a good teacher," he said, slumping into the chair behind his desk and rubbing his elbow. "To impart knowledge and try and instil some appreciation for literature into the young minds I'm entrusted to shape."

"Very noble of you."

"Well, what can I tell you? I was young and idealistic and soon learned that it's not that straightforward. If the kids don't want to learn, there's not much a teacher can do about it. It's not like it was in my day anymore."

"This is all very touching but what's it got to do with Jasmine Webb?"

"I'm getting to that." He stood and paced the room, making it difficult for me to read his expression. "Like I said, when I first qualified I was full of enthusiasm, a bit like you when you joined the police, I should think.

Anyway, no fancy private schools for me. Oh no! I wanted to teach in a big comprehensive and see if I could make a difference for some of the less privileged kids in society." He made a scoffing sound at the back of his throat. "I figured that in order to get through to them, I needed to connect on their own level. Dress like them, speak their language, stuff like that."

"Can't see clued-up kids falling for that one." I felt myself being drawn into Ramsay's account in spite of myself, satisfied that so far he'd told the truth.

"That's what the old hands told me but, of course, I thought I knew better and didn't realize at first that the girls misinterpreted the way I was behaving. I didn't know either that I'd made a rod for my own back until it was almost too late."

"Complaints were made against you?"

"Not at the time, but one fifteen-year-old did start a rumour that I'd come on to her." He met my gaze head-on. "It was complete nonsense, nothing was made official, but I knew my card had been marked."

"So, let me guess, when a vacancy came up here you decided to apply?"

"I was persuaded that it might be in my best interests. I was told that if I went for it, nothing would be said about the allegations."

"I see."

"Yes, well, the ideology was already wearing off and sixth-form college suddenly didn't seem like quite such a bad idea."

"So what happened?"

"The girl from the comp who'd made the allegations, she was a bit unstable, got into trouble and was sent for counselling. Some navel-gazer persuaded her to purge her demons by making her allegations official." He paused and looked me directly in the eye again. "There was no foundation in the complaint. I didn't touch the wretched girl but it could have ruined my career, regardless of whether or not I was found guilty."

"But the case never made it to court?"

"No." He stopped pacing and threw himself back in his chair. "No, it never did."

I sensed that we were getting to the crux of the matter at last. "Why was that?"

"Well, out of the blue someone I'd never seen before approached me in a pub some of us use regularly. He knew all about the allegations, which shook me because not many people did. He said they could be made to disappear if I did one small thing for him in return."

"Name?"

"Never knew it. All he gave me was a phone number and a warning not to tell anyone else about our conversation." Ramsay levelled his eyes on my face. So far at any rate he hadn't lied to me. "He scared the shit out of me, I'm not ashamed to admit it, and I wasn't about to cross him."

"What did he want you to do?"

"He was on the lookout for a girl of Jasmine's age, someone good-looking who knew something about boats. Someone intelligent. I guess they thought girls at a college on the coast would be more likely to fit that bill."

I ground my teeth, suspecting I knew where this was going and attempting to keep my temper in check. "Go on."

"The girl had to be dissatisfied with school and on the lookout for another way to make easy money."

"And you gave them Jasmine?" I couldn't believe what I was hearing. "Without even knowing what it was they wanted her to do. You're supposed to protect the young, not feed them to the bloody lions."

"It wasn't like that." He flapped his hands. "You don't understand. I knew she wasn't being recruited for prostitution and was told if she wasn't interested in their proposition she'd be allowed to walk away." He looked away and concentrated his gaze on the surface of his littered desk. For the first time he wasn't looking directly at me, which could only mean he was about to start lying. "It seemed to be the solution to both our problems, Jasmine's and mine."

"You told me you didn't know she had any problems."

"Well, obviously, her work was slipping so I'd had those long chats with her—"

"Only chats?"

"All right." He still wouldn't look at me. "We had a bit of a thing for a while, I admit that. But I wasn't her first, and it was her who pursued me. She was a bit wild, not interested in lads of her own age. And Christ, she was attractive." He pushed his hair away from his face, swiping his forearm across his brow as though removing sweat. "I'm only human."

I glowered at him. "That's a matter of opinion."

"It's true," he said with quiet dignity. "And it was more than just a thing, from my perspective anyway. But sadly, not from hers."

"What do you mean?"

"Isn't it obvious? I fell for her. Hard." He ran his hand through his hair for a second time and kept his eyes focused on the surface of his desk. I thought I could detect genuine pain in his body language as he recalled the doomed relationship. "I wanted us to be together when she finished college. I could have helped her through university." Ramsay finally lifted his eyes, met my gaze and held it. "I wanted to marry her."

"But she didn't feel the same way?"

He flushed. "She laughed in my face. Said she had no intention of tying herself down to anyone and wasn't interested in university."

I hitched a brow. "Then what was she interested in?"

"I never found out. All I knew was that she was planning on going off to London. I don't know why, she wouldn't say, but she was adamant that she couldn't stay here any longer."

"What had changed?"

"I honestly don't know. She clammed up whenever I asked her but she was determined to give up her education, and so I offered to set her up in a flat. She turned that proposition down too."

"So you got your revenge, salved your wounded pride, by recommending her to someone whose intentions had to be questionable?"

"No, I knew she wasn't in danger. I still loved her, in spite of the fact that she seemed to be toying with me, and I wouldn't have put her at risk."

"That's not how it looks from where I'm standing."

"No, I don't imagine it does." He sighed. "And I'm not proud of what I did. I suppose I just hoped that if she got what she wanted through my recommendation, if I gave her the space she obviously needed, she'd come back to me when she was ready." He looked embarrassed. "Pathetic, isn't it, but, like I said, I fell for her hard. Anyway, it didn't work because I never heard from her again."

"But, if you loved her, I still don't see how you can be sure you weren't putting her in danger."

"Isn't it obvious?"

"Not to me."

"How do you think the allegations the girl made so conveniently disappeared after I gave them Jasmine?"

"Hang on, let me get this straight. Are you saying the people who wanted a girl like Jasmine were linked directly to the police?"

MONIKA ESCORTED THE three Spaniards to one of Igor's cars and climbed into it with them. Viktor was behind the wheel. Nadia felt Igor's arm slide 'round her waist as they waved to their departing guests. She turned her face into his shoulder and closed her eyes. The evening had been a huge strain and she felt tired again. She hoped Igor wouldn't want to make love and would let her go straight to sleep.

She'd always pretended she didn't know what her husband did for a living, how he made so much money but, of course, she did. It was impossible not to. He'd never given her chapter and verse, and she knew better than to ask, but over the years she'd got a pretty good handle on things. Her Russian was better than anyone realized. They spoke in front of her about things they thought she wouldn't understand, and she absorbed information that brought home to her the dangers Igor faced every waking minute of his life. He didn't seem unduly troubled and thrived on the stress, but she was continually anxious about his safety.

But things would soon improve. Igor was mostly legitimate nowadays and planned to invest a lot of money in a building project somewhere on a Spanish costa. Lots of his countrymen were jumping on that particular bandwagon, which was partly why he'd entertained these men tonight. They were local politicians from the area that interested Igor. No doubt they wouldn't be averse to taking bribes in return for pushing his building applications through.

She was delighted he was gradually shedding his old ways but change didn't happen overnight. Monika, her glamorous stepdaughter, ran her father's escort agency based in the West End of London, staffed mostly by East European girls smuggled in via Igor's organisation. He kept another house in Weymouth, and Nadia supposed that was where Monika was headed now. No doubt attractive feminine companionship awaited the Spaniards, which would all but seal their commitment to her husband.

"You did well tonight, my love." Igor guided her to the stairs. "Perhaps we'll live permanently in Spain when the building's complete, and you can have a free hand in designing our house." His voice was reflective, as though he'd only just thought about making the move, but Igor never did anything without considering all the angles first. "Would you like that?"

Nadia didn't respond immediately. She wasn't sure how she felt about leaving England behind forever, and it must have shown on her face.

"What is it, darling? You don't look overjoyed at the prospect." He opened the door to their room and ushered her inside. "I thought the idea of a fresh start would please you."

"It does, Igor, but I thought we'd agreed to send the children to school in England."

"There are good schools in Spain, as well. We'll find the very best for them." He pulled her into his arms. "There's nothing more for you here. The memories are too painful."

"No, Igor, I'm better now, really I am. Going out on the water today did me a world of good. I'm sorry, I shouldn't have said all those terrible things to you. I didn't mean them."

"I know you didn't." He grazed her forehead with his lips. "But I'm glad you realize it too. It shows you're making progress. Now, come to bed. You look exhausted."

"I don't need pills anymore." She shook her head at the one he was holding out to her.

"Take it, darling. It's too soon for you to stop them."

"Well, at least let me take less of them. I'm sure I can sleep tonight without one."

"No, my love." He smiled but a trace of intransigence entered his voice as he slipped the tiny pill into her hand, closing her fingers around it. "The last time you tried to sleep without one you woke up in the middle of the night screaming. I don't want you to feel like that ever again."

"But, Igor—"

"No arguments, darling. Trust me to know what's best for you."

She did trust him. Of course she did. So she took the pill.

SIX

A POLICEMAN?

I walked back to the Harley, shaking my head, half wishing now that I'd listened to Emily and left this thing alone. If I'd taken the coward's way out, I wouldn't be wrestling with the unpalatable possibility that one of my former colleagues was batting for the opposition. The prospect filled me with sadness as much as anger, and before I even got back to the bike I was halfway towards convincing myself there had to be another explanation. If one of my mates—someone I'd trusted to cover my back in tight situations—was bent, surely I would have known? How could I have worked with someone for all those years and not even suspected?

The answer was that I couldn't have, so I must be overlooking something vital. Either that or Ramsay had lied to me.

A fulminating anger coursed through me as I considered the teacher's cavalier actions, taken to save his own skin, fifteen years ago. Christ, wasn't it supposed to be women who got all vindictive when they were scorned? The way Ramsay tried to justify what he did by painting himself as the innocent party made me want to go back and break his knees. I made do with thumping the saddle of the Harley instead and forced myself to face facts.

If Ramsay had told me the truth, then I was the one responsible for the threat to my son. By appealing to my ex-colleagues for help, I'd inadvertently warned the dirty copper of my interest in Jasmine Webb. The insider had every reason to suppose the case would remain buried forever but had presumably flagged the computer file, just in case. My sudden interest in it must have come as a bolt out of the blue.

I rode the bike back to the marina feeling sick, the taste of betrayal bitter on my tongue. I weaved recklessly in and out of traffic, ready to commit murder. There was *nothing* worse than a bent copper, and when I discovered his identify, which I now fully intended to do, I wouldn't be held responsible for my actions.

Kara. Bloody hell! I almost swerved into a slow-moving van as a thought struck me. I'd blithely sent her home last night, thinking she was safe because the threats were being directed at me through Harry. But the insider would know all about her too. I needed to warn her, and considered pulling off the road to give her a call, eventually deciding it could wait another ten minutes until I got back to the boat.

I was still at the other end of the pontoon when I realized no call would be necessary. I knew who the figure sitting on a bollard outside the *No Comment* had to be, even before I saw all that red hair pulled back in one of those things that looks like a bulldog clip. She was leaning against a bulging holdall and working on her laptop as though she didn't have a care in the world. As soon as she saw me she snapped her computer shut and jumped to her feet.

"How did it go? I thought I'd come over and find out what Ramsay had to say."

"Looks like you thought you might be in for a long wait." I nodded towards her holdall, trying to keep the amusement out of my expression. Did she but know it, she was playing straight into my hands.

"Ah yes, well, about that… Charlie, I *know* you plan to go to Weymouth and I really think I ought to come with you."

I shrugged. "You know more than I do then."

"Listen, it's quite a way to go in a slow boat, and you'll need someone to crew for you and help you keep watch. I could tie a bowline before I learned to lace my shoes, I can cook—"

"Okay."

"Look, don't say no until you've heard me out." She was focusing on her feet, presumably searching for a more persuasive argument, and it took a moment for my capitulation to register with her. "Hang on, what did you just say?"

"I said okay, you can come." I wasn't about to tell her she could be in danger and the best way for me to look out for her was to keep her close. I lifted her heavy bag with one hand and almost dropped it in the water. "Christ, what the hell have you got in there?"

"Oh, just one or two essentials." She smiled angelically. "You know how it is."

I didn't, but I figured I'd soon find out.

Unhampered by the restraints of a tight skirt this time she leapt agilely on board without my assistance. I unlocked the boat and Gil did his usual thing of jumping all over Kara, knowing better than to try the same routine with me. I tossed Kara's bag onto the bed in the spare cabin and rejoined her in the salon. She looked completely at home making coffee in the galley.

Succinctly I outlined all I'd learn from Ramsay. Well, most of it.

"I'm so sorry, Charlie," she said. "It must come as quite a blow to realize one of your colleagues was involved."

"Not your fault."

"Any idea who it might be?"

"Not yet, but it must be someone who's still there, otherwise they wouldn't know I'd been asking questions. Unfortunately it also means it's probably someone I've known and trusted for a long time."

"Does that narrow it down?"

"A bit." I rubbed my chin as I gloomily pondered the question. "Problem is, it needn't be someone in the squad. It could be a uniform or even a civilian worker. It's hard to know where to look first."

"If whoever enticed Jas away had contacts in the police fifteen years ago, presumably he still does, so it may not necessarily be someone you know."

"Thanks for trying to make me feel better, sweetheart." I squeezed her shoulder, touched by her concern and glad, suddenly, of her company. "Thing is, even if he has a new generation of poodles reporting to him, in my day it must have been someone I knew." I thumped my fist against the galley surface. "I've been a bloody fool, charging in like that, asking questions willy-nilly and endangering Harry."

"Maybe it wasn't your questions that did it?" She poured hot water into two mugs. "Perhaps it was me going to that pub and asking after you that alerted the insider?"

"That's a possibility." But it didn't make me feel a whole lot better.

My mobile rang. I checked the display and took the call.

"Are they airborne yet?" I asked, not bothering with any preliminaries.

"Yes, they took off right on time."

"Thanks, Phil, I appreciate you letting me know.

"Well," I said, pocketing my phone, "at least Harry's safely on his way to Spain."

"Good, that must be a relief."

"You have no idea." I let out a long breath, took the mug of coffee she was holding out to me and sipped it. "Ouch, that's hot!"

"Don't be such a baby, Charlie. Coffee's supposed to be hot."

"Not that hot."

"Anyway," she said, "I think we should stop worrying about who, how and why for the moment and think about what we're going to do when we get to Weymouth. How are we going to find Jas, assuming she's there, of course? Presumably you have some sort of plan."

"Yes, but there's something we ought to do here first."

"Oh yes, and what would that be?"

"Have a chat with your mother."

"But why?" Alarm flashed through her eyes. "She doesn't know anything."

"Possibly not, but you did say she changed towards your father once Jasmine disappeared."

"That's hardly to be wondered at."

"Then let's see if she's willing to tell us why. Just like Sally, there's probably stuff she knew at the time but didn't say. Perhaps she'll reveal things that might help, if she knows you want to find your sister." I glanced at her. "I assume she doesn't know you've decided to look for her."

"No, I haven't told her. Now isn't a good time for her. She's got a lot to deal with and I don't want to upset her more than she already is."

"What do you mean?"

Kara tutted with impatience. "Her only son and favourite child just died, remember."

"And her remaining daughter has questions that need answers." I met her gaze and held it, challenging her. "Do you want to find your sister or not?"

She only hesitated for a second or two longer. "Yes, okay, let's do it."

"Okay, good. Will she be at home this morning?"

"I expect so but I'll check."

Kara extracted her mobile from the pocket of her jeans and called home. She had a brief chat to her mother and broke the connection.

"She's there." She grabbed her bag and car keys. "Let's go."

I was getting used to Kara's habit of doing everything at breakneck speed. She headed for the door without even checking to see if I was following her. I gave Gil a rawhide bone as compensation for being left behind, locked up and followed her.

"How do you want to play this?" she asked as she drove us towards Lewes.

"Depends how she reacts to our questions. You should start by telling the truth. You contacted me hoping I'd help you find Jasmine so you can tell her about Brett. I'd be interested to see how she takes it."

"Badly, is my guess."

"Look, if you don't want to do this, you only have to say."

I didn't add that nothing on this earth could stop me from delving deeper, not now that Harry had been threatened. One of my ex-colleagues had most likely been instrumental in posing that threat, and the key to discovering his identity was the whereabouts of Jasmine Webb.

"No, I want to know what happened to her more than ever. It's just the thought of Mum being disappointed in me."

"Why should she be?" When Kara didn't respond I pushed the issue. "Come on, Kara, talk to me. Why should your mother be disappointed because you want to know what happened to your sister? Just because your parents don't talk about it, that doesn't mean you've got to keep stum, as well." My eyes raked her body with the suggestion of a smile. "You're a big girl now."

She rolled her own eyes but wisely didn't comment. Instead she lifted her shoulders and the indicator simultaneously. "No, you're right, of course. It's just that old habits die hard and talking about Jasmine to either of my parents seems like heresy. Okay, here we are." She pulled into the driveway of the detached house I vaguely recalled and opened her door before she'd even turned the engine off. "Come on, let's get this over with before I change my mind."

She climbed out, squared her shoulders and led the way 'round the side of the house. We entered through the kitchen door and Kara called out, "It's only me, Mum."

The sight of the woman who shuffled into the room a

minute or so later took me completely by surprise. I remembered an attractive woman, elegant and composed. She'd taken the disappearance of her elder daughter in her stride and held the family together when it was in danger of self-destructing. All right, so it was fifteen years on, but the person confronting me now bore no resemblance whatsoever to the image I retained of Kara's mother. Mrs. Webb had put on at least two stone since I'd last seen her. Given that she was several inches shorter than her daughter, it was weight that didn't sit comfortably on her petite frame. Her once flaming red hair was now dull and heavily streaked with grey. There was no style to it and it badly needed cutting. Her complexion had that dried-up sallow appearance I associated with heavy smokers. She wore a shapeless dress that did nothing to improve her appearance, and her bare feet were pushed into slippers with the backs trodden down. They slapped against the tiled floor each time she took a step. Her face was completely expressionless. She glanced at Kara with apparent disinterest and didn't address a word to her.

I reminded myself she'd just had to deal with the death of her only son and mentally cut her some slack. I knew all about death and could empathize. Perhaps because of my firsthand dealings with the Grim Reaper, breaking the news of death to the loved ones of the deceased had always been the part of the job that got to me the most. I was glad when Family Liaison Officers were drafted in to take the brunt of the pressure off us in that respect. I was also mightily relieved I hadn't had to tell this woman about her son. I didn't suppose she was getting much support from her husband and couldn't see them helping each other through their grief. But the deterioration in her appearance hadn't happened overnight. She must have given up on life and started letting herself go long before Brett's accident.

"Mum, this is Charlie Hunter."

Mrs. Webb offered me a limp handshake but didn't say anything, nor did the mention of my name light a spark in her lifeless eyes. That surprised me. It also put me on my guard. In my experience, parents of missing children never forgot the names of the investigating officers, regardless of the passage of time. I waited for her to ask why I'd come calling with Kara in the middle of a weekday morning.

Nothing.

This was one zoned-out female, difficult to like, harder still to make excuses for.

"Let's have some coffee." Kara's artificially bright voice filled a silence that was in danger of becoming embarrassing. She bustled about the kitchen, filling the kettle and pulling mugs from a cupboard. "How have you been, Mum?"

"How do you think?"

Kara winced at her mother's acerbic tone and I felt a moment's anger on her behalf. Mrs. Webb wasn't the only one hurting here. She should be taking comfort from the feisty daughter who remained to her. A little maternal empathy wouldn't go amiss.

Once we were seated 'round the kitchen table with our coffee, the conversation stilted and one-sided, I decided to take the lead. Kara, usually so forthright and sure of herself, seemed to regress in her mother's presence, becoming awkward and tongue-tied.

"I don't know if you remember me, Mrs. Webb, but

I was one of the detectives who came here when Jasmine disappeared."

Her head snapped up. At last there was some animation in her slack features as her gaze darted from Kara to me and then back to her daughter. "Why did you bring him here?"

"Mum, I just wanted to—"

"What do you think you're playing at, dragging that business up again?"

Kara flinched at her mother's accusatory tone and I couldn't altogether blame her. Mrs. Webb's reaction to the mention of Jasmine's name was way too extreme. After all this time, she ought to be able to handle it without flying off the handle at her one remaining child. Even if her elder daughter was no longer spoken of in this house, her mother wouldn't be human if she didn't still think about her. And wonder.

I tried to make allowances, but just observing the way she was glaring at Kara with an expression that bordered on dislike was enough to make my hackles rise. Along with my growing suspicions. Did she know more about Jasmine's disappearance than she was letting on? Was that why she hadn't shown any grief at the time? Or was she just a naturally cold fish? Questions in need of answers jostled for position in my brain. I cut to the chase, hoping to shock a genuine reaction out of the woman.

"Kara asked me to come here today because she thinks Jasmine should know about Brett," I said.

Mrs. Webb let out an ugly laugh. "Why? What good do you suppose that will do?"

She fumbled in a drawer, extracted a packet of cigarettes and lit up. After inhaling, she blew a long stream of smoke in my direction but kept her eyes focused on a spot on the wall above Kara's head. Her fingers were stained with nicotine and her hands were shaking. I thought I could detect an element of fear behind her aggressive expression. And that got me wondering some more.

"Mum, please try to understand." Kara touched her mother's hand. "Brett's gone and now we have—"

"You don't need to remind me that Brett's gone. It's not something I'm likely to forget in a hurry."

"I know you're hurting, but—"

Mrs. Webb shook Kara's hand away as though she couldn't bear the thought of being comforted. For the first time since we'd entered the house I noticed an emotion other than anger on the woman's face. Her guard had slipped and the abject grief she felt at the loss of her son was written all over it. There was none of the stoic acceptance she'd shown when Jasmine went missing. Just stark, unadulterated misery.

Feeling like the intruder I was, I looked away, concentrating my attention on the large rear garden, which was in full bloom and meticulously maintained. Not Mrs. Webb's work, I was willing to bet. Probably her husband paying someone else to keep up appearances.

"Everyone's gone, and all I'm left with is—"

Mrs. Webb's words trailed off. Whatever she'd been about to say, she'd clearly thought better of it. Kara was staring at her as intently as I was but her mother refused to look at either of us. Instead she drew on her cigarette so deeply she was afflicted by a spasm of coughing.

I stood, found a glass in the cupboard Kara had taken the mugs from and filled it with tap water. It didn't exactly come as a big surprise when I handed it to the woman and received no thanks. Shrugging, I waited for her to bring her coughing under control before I spoke again.

"You're left with a lovely daughter who's a credit to you," I said, finding it hard to keep the anger out of my voice. "And another daughter who's made a life for herself somewhere else. Kara thinks it's time to find out where she is and I'd have thought you'd agree."

"You're hardly in a position to know what I think."

She'd got me there. "True, but all the same, I—"

"Anyway, you don't know Jas has made a life elsewhere. You don't even know if she's still alive. None of us do."

"We know she was alive, Mum. We had that letter and phone call."

Mrs. Webb dismissed her daughter's words with a careless wave of her hand. "That was fifteen years ago. Anything could have happened to her since then."

"Surely we would have heard."

"Not necessarily. She could be abroad. She could be anywhere. She's never bothered to get in touch, so why would she care about Brett?"

The words were spoken with a finality, presumably intended to discourage argument. But I was in an argumentative mood. Besides, I couldn't help wondering why she was so keen to close the door on her elder daughter. Was she so devoid of maternal feeling that she no longer cared? I shifted my position and stretched my legs out. No, there was more to it than that. Mrs. Webb was frightened about something, and I reckoned her emotionless display was a mask she'd perfected to disguise that fear. Time to apply some pressure.

"Oh, she's still in this country. Well, she was a few months ago anyway."

Mrs. Webb didn't show any surprise. "How do you know?"

"I know because Brett saw her a few months ago."

This time my bombshell produced the desired effect.

"What!" Mrs. Webb's eyes swivelled and rested upon her daughter, her first uncontrived reaction since our arrival. "What lies have you been spreading to drag him into this?"

"It's true, Mum, I found—"

"If Brett had seen Jas, he would have told me."

"*If* he didn't," I said, "presumably he had a good reason."

"I don't believe you!" Mrs. Webb folded her arms and stared at the opposite wall.

Exasperated, I nodded at Kara. Looking miserable, she rummaged in her bag and produced the picture of Jasmine and Brett together. Wordlessly she slid it across the table.

Mrs. Webb grabbed it with both hands and held it out in front of her at arms' length, as though she was short-sighted but avoided wearing glasses. Unlike me, she didn't need to be told to turn the photo over. She groaned when she saw Brett's neat handwriting on the back and dropped the picture as though it hurt her to touch it. Hands shaking more violently than ever, she lit another cigarette from the butt of the first.

"It's a trick." An uneasy silence ensued. I kicked Kara's ankle under the table when she opened her mouth as though to fill the void. I wanted her mother to digest all we'd told her and show some interest but half a cigarette was reduced to ash before she did so. "Brett didn't say. Jas didn't—"

"Jas?" said Kara and I together.

"How often does she ring you, Mrs. Webb?"

"Mum?" Kara's eyes were luminous with shock. "What does this mean?"

When Mrs. Webb showed no immediate signs of responding, I spoke for her. "It means your mother knows where Jasmine went to. She's always known, which is why she didn't seem particularly upset when she first went missing."

"No, I—"

"And I suspect she talks to her on a regular basis, even if she doesn't actually see her, which is why she was so surprised to learn your brother met her again. She thought one or the other of them would have told her."

"You think you know it all," said Mrs. Webb, a noxious smile of her face. "But you're wrong. I have no idea where Jasmine is."

"Perhaps not but I still maintain you knew in advance she intended doing a runner." I ran a hand through my hair and locked eyes with Kara's mother. "I think she went with your blessing and still keeps in touch with you."

"Oh God!" Kara propped her elbows on the table and dropped her head into her splayed hands. "I don't think I can take much more of this."

I squeezed her shoulder. Now wasn't the time to tell her I'd told her so. But, if nothing else, presumably her distress would elicit some sort of response from her mother.

It did, but not the one I'd been expecting.

"Don't listen to him," she said. "He's way off the mark." She turned eyes full of scornful reproach upon me. "But then he's a policeman, so what else can you expect. Just as well I *did* know Jas intended to leave. His lot were worse than useless."

I met her hostile gaze with detachment and disciplined myself not to respond. Out of respect for Kara's feelings, I'd only get heavy with the woman when I was able to see her alone.

"Charlie?" Kara's voice sounded tiny and ridiculously full of hope.

"I don't think I'm wrong."

"Mum says you are."

"Well, she would, wouldn't she." I paused and sipped cautiously at my coffee but it tasted fine and was exactly the right temperature. Kara was a fast learner. "For starters, my partner and I both remarked at the time that your mother wasn't particularly distressed when your sister went missing. Any natural mother would be prostrate at the thought of what might be happening to her child." I frowned as I conjured up images of the woman's unnatural self-possession fifteen years previously. "But you, Mrs. Webb, were almost as poised then as you are now."

"I don't wear my heart on my sleeve but that doesn't mean you have any idea what I feel inside. Can you even begin to imagine what it's like?"

Oh boy, could I. But I said nothing.

She looked at me with an expression of unmitigated dislike. "No, you're a man so I don't suppose you can. We all bear these things differently, Mr. Hunter. Don't slot me into one of your neat little pigeonholes and think you know it all."

At last, a genuine reaction from her. "I was new to CID at the time," I said, "so I didn't make as much of it as I should have. But I've been involved in dozens of similar situations since then, and even the most slap-dash mother falls apart when a child goes AWOL. But I don't recall even having to call a doctor to give you a sedative."

She sneered at me. "And that's your evidence for supposing I know where Jas is?"

"That and the fact that you gave yourself away just now." She snorted smoke down her nose and said nothing. "We both heard you. And you're frightened about something. You don't want to talk about Jasmine."

"Do you have children, Mr. Hunter?"

"One. A boy."

"If he disappeared and you managed to somehow put it all behind you, would you want strangers traipsing into your house and raking it all over?"

"Kara's your daughter," I said icily, "not a stranger."

"You know what I mean."

"Actually I don't, but it'll be easy enough to get to the bottom of this. Perhaps we'll discuss it with your husband, see what he knows. What time is he due home?"

"No!"

I shrugged. "It's your call."

"Charlie, I don't think—"

I cut off Kara's protest by gently kicking her ankle again.

"Oh, all right." Mrs. Webb drew herself up to her full height, her eyes burning with resentment as they rested upon me. "I knew Jas was going to leave and I didn't try to stop her. There, is that what you want to hear?"

MONIKA AND IGOR were closeted together for most of the next morning, and Nadia was left to her own devices. Her head was as fuggy as ever and she had trouble keeping her eyes open. Igor remarked on it over lunch and, when the meal was finished, he insisted that she rest. He accompanied her and made gentle but hurried love to her, which was unusual for him. He devoted his full attention to everything he did, and she'd never known him to rush her in bed before. She failed to climax and he didn't seem to notice. He was clearly preoccupied about something. Instead of causing him more problems, she supposed she ought to be supporting him but was too droopy-eyed to let the guilt bother her.

"Rest now, my love. I have people waiting for me next door." He nodded towards the connecting door to his study, his thick mane of iron-grey hair falling across faded blue eyes, which gentled as they caressed her face. "Take a pill and have a long sleep. You'll feel much better when you wake up."

The last thing Nadia wanted to do was to take one of his wretched pills. They were starting to make her feel nauseated, and she worried that she was becoming addicted to them. But there was something about Igor's attitude today that prevented her from protesting, and obediently she took the pill from his outstretched hand. He watched her swallow it, nodded in satisfaction, kissed her and disappeared through the connecting door.

He had barely left her when Nadia's stomach gave

several violent lurches. She just made it to the en-suite bathroom before falling to the floor and being violently ill. She rested her head against the cool porcelain when she finished retching, wondering what could be wrong with her. Perhaps she was pregnant again. She loved her children but the thought of bearing another didn't fill her with joy.

Igor, on the other hand, would be delighted. He had three grown children from his first marriage and often lamented that he and Nadia hadn't been blessed with more of their own. She sighed. That was one aspect of his character she would never understand. She knew family was very important to him—half the people who worked for him seemed to be related to him in some way—but she failed to appreciate why he felt he had a duty to overpopulate the world.

When she was sure her legs would support her, Nadia got up from the floor and headed back to the bedroom. She paused when she heard raised voices emanating from Igor's study—his, Viktor's and Monika's. Wondering what they could be arguing about, since few people dared to argue with Igor, she pressed her ear to the door. They were talking in Russian, of course, but perhaps she'd pick up a few key words.

Her interest was piqued when she heard her own name but she struggled to understand in what context it was being bandied about. She wondered why they were talking so loudly, especially if they were discussing her. They knew she was next door asleep and would be bound to hear them. Although, of course, as far as they were concerned she'd taken a pill, which always knocked her out for the count. Was that why Igor had insisted she take one? No, that was ridiculous! Nadia felt disloyal for merely thinking such a thing. Igor only had her best interests at heart and no reason to want to keep her sedated.

As she continued to listen, it took Nadia a moment to realize that she wasn't falling asleep on her feet. How could that be? She'd swallowed the damned pill and the effect was usually instantaneous. Unless…?

Unless being sick she'd brought it up with her lunch before it dissolved.

She certainly felt better than she had for a while. Semi-alert and energized. But more confused than ever about what was happening to her. She pressed her ear closer to the door and gasped when she heard her sister's name. Why on earth would they be discussing Kara?

Cold fingers of fear gripped her, and she thought her legs were going to give out on her after all. Forgetting all about why she was wide awake, she gripped the door handle in an effort to remain upright and struggled to keep up with the conversation.

SEVEN

"Why, Mum?" Kara gaped at her mother, her words barely coherent. "Where did she go and why did you condone it?"

"She went because she wanted to get away from *him*."

"Dad?"

"Of course, who else? Just like you and Brett. Neither of you could wait until you were old enough to get away either."

"What changed?" I asked. "Why was she so desperate to get away that she abandoned her education? Was he abusing her?"

"No, nothing like that."

"Then what?" This was like getting blood out of a stone.

"I honestly don't know." She blinked, unable to meet my gaze, and I knew she was lying. "They fell out bigtime over something and Jas wouldn't even look at him after that, much less talk to him. The atmosphere was terrible. You were too young to know much about it, Kara, but Brett picked up on it and took his sister's side." She looked down and fiddled with a loose thread on the sleeve of her cardigan. "I was stuck in the middle, as always."

"I gather your husband was strict with the girls, but

that's surely not enough to make one of them take flight and for you to condone it."

"Jas was going whatever I said." Mrs. Webb glared at me, defying me to criticise her. "And I didn't blame her." She let out a deep sigh and lit yet another cigarette. "She met a woman at the Island Sailing Club who offered her a job as a hostess on a super yacht and she made up her mind she was going to take it."

"And you let her go without checking it out first?"

"I'd have gone with her if I could." She gripped her coffee mug with both hands and stared off into the distance.

"Un-fucking-believable," I muttered under my breath.

"You have no idea what it's like," she said. "You wouldn't be so quick to judge if you did. We were living under a dictatorship, scared to open our mouths for fear of saying the wrong thing and putting him in one of his moods."

"What was the name of the yacht?"

"I don't know."

"The woman's name?"

"Angela Smith," she said. I snorted. "That's the name she gave when I met her after Jasmine told me about the job offer. I liked the woman and it seemed a good opportunity for Jas so I didn't oppose her when she said she'd made up her mind to go."

"But you didn't know anything about the boat, the woman's background or who owned the yacht? She was an attractive girl, Mrs. Webb. Didn't it occur to you that she might have been targeted because of her looks?"

"Oh, she was well aware of her looks and what they could do for her, young as she was. She was streetwise and well able to take care of herself. Besides, it was the woman who insisted we meet, to put my mind at rest. She'd hardly do that if she wasn't genuine." She lifted her shoulders. "Anyway, if I'd said Jas couldn't go, it wouldn't have made a blind bit of difference and I would have lost her altogether. This way was better."

"But why the subterfuge? Why pretend she'd gone missing when you knew where she was all the time?"

She glared at me as though I was a few cards short of a pack. "Because *he* would have tried to bring her back if he knew where she'd gone. Not because he wanted her back necessarily, but because he couldn't have the world thinking there was contention within his perfect family unit."

"She's right," said Kara with obvious reluctance.

"Jas didn't want anything more to do with him, and that's why I didn't ask for more details about the job. That way he couldn't get any information out of me if he found out I knew. All I insisted upon was that she keep in touch by phone and let me know she's all right. If she needs to come home, she knows I'll send her money or go and get her, no matter where she is."

"Well, that's all right then." I glanced at Kara, wondering how she was taking all this. Her expression was stunned, which was hardly surprising. I was having trouble believing her mother's offhand attitude myself, and I'd been half expecting it. "So where is she now?"

"I don't know. I've never known. She phones me occasionally, just to let me know she's okay, but I never know when I'm going to hear. Sometimes it's once a month, others times it can be more than three before she gets in touch." She briefly shrivelled beneath my ballistic glare but quickly rallied. "She's well out of it, that's all I know."

"Is she married? Does she have children? Is she happy?" I rattled off the questions but Mrs. Webb merely shook her head.

"We don't talk about anything personal."

"What, you mean you don't want to know if you're a grandmother?"

"She wouldn't tell me if I *did* ask."

"So what do you talk about?"

"Nothing of consequence."

I gave up. "And she's never been back to see you all these years because…"

"Because of her father, obviously. Whatever they fought about, she still doesn't feel inclined to forgive and forget."

"You let Brett and me worry all these years." Kara stared at her mother as though seeing her in a completely new light. "You didn't encourage us to talk about her and I can see why now, but surely you must have realized what her disappearance did to us? How it tore us apart." Tears squeezed out of the corners of her eyes and trickled down her face. She dashed them impatiently aside. They made me want to pull her into my arms and make the hurt go away but Mrs. Webb seemed patently unmoved by her daughter's distress. "How could you, Mum?"

"It was for the best."

I kept quiet as Kara tried to get an explanation out of her mother that would make some sense to her. She was never going to succeed but it would take her a while to realize that. I kept Mrs. Webb in my line of vision as she spewed out reluctant halfhearted excuses, clearly anxious to get the conversation over with, not caring about anyone's feelings other than her own.

"Have you spoken to her since Brett died? Does she know?"

I waited for what seemed like an eternity for Mrs. Webb to respond. I stared fixedly at her, willing her to lie if necessary and say *yes*. Then surely Kara, disillusioned, would give up her search for her sister.

"No, she hasn't called since it happened."

I swore beneath my breath. Seeing disillusionment and then the start of an inchoate anger spreading across Kara's face, I decided it was time to leave.

"I think we're done here, Kara." I threw a withering glance in her mother's direction and stood up.

"But I need to understand—"

"Later," I said. Mrs. Webb knew more than she was saying but I sensed she'd never let on what it was whilst Kara was there. "Come on, let's go."

I almost frogmarched her from the room and she was still too stunned to put up much of a protest. I took her keys and pushed the driving seat back as far as it would go to accommodate my legs before starting the engine. We travelled for some distance in silence and I was content for it to be that way.

"You okay?" It was a stupid question but we were almost back at the marina, and she was still in a catatonic state, staring straight ahead, and her silence was starting to concern me.

"How did you know?"

I shot her a look. "That your mother was holding back?" She nodded. "I didn't for sure but her attitude didn't ring true at the time Jas disappeared so I played on that hunch."

"What's going on, Charlie?" She swivelled in her seat to look at me, eyes brimming with fresh tears she didn't bother to swipe away this time.

I didn't respond immediately. Instead I concentrated upon negotiating the tight bends in the marina car park as I searched for a free space. Finding one on the third floor, I applied the handbrake and turned off the engine.

"That's a very good question but I think it would be best discussed over something stronger than tea. Come on." I placed my hand beneath her elbow and steered her towards the nearby Wetherspoon's pub. "It's past midday so I guess it's allowable. Besides, you've had a shock so in your case an infusion of alcohol definitely qualifies as medicinal."

I opened the pub door and found a small table that overlooked the quaint but somewhat dilapidated floating Chinese restaurant. The tide was low, and the growth of seaweed and barnacles clinging to its waterline highlighted its neglected state.

"Now, what's it to be?"

I forced a vodka and tonic upon her, not letting on that it was a double. Then I sat back, sipping at my Guinness as I waited for the spirit to do its work.

"Come on, Charlie," she said when she'd consumed half her drink in record time. "You know more than you're letting on, so give."

I shrugged. "I know as much as you do."

"But you have your suspicions."

I offered her a guarded half smile. "I'm still a detective at heart."

She opened her eyes wide. They were touchingly full of faith in my abilities.

I only hoped that if it came to it, I'd be able to deliver. "The only thing I know for sure is that Jasmine is in contact with your mum, so she'll find out about Brett that way, if she doesn't already know."

"So you think I should give up looking for her, is that it?"

"Well, you did only want to find her to tell her about your brother."

"No, it wasn't only that. I need to understand, now more than ever."

"Yes, I'm sure you do."

"Will you still help me?" She didn't look at me as she asked the question. Instead she watched several children on the veranda throwing bread to a pair of swans gracefully treading the murky water below.

"Yes."

Her head snapped away from the swans and she met my gaze. "You will?" I nodded, almost tempted to smile at her incongruous expression. "But I thought—"

"You thought I'd try and talk you out of it."

She fiddled with a spare drip mat on the table in front of her. "Something like that."

"I would have done, had it not been for the threat to Harry."

"Ah yes, there's that of course." She was the one who actually smiled. "I'm sorry I got you into this, Charlie, and endangered your son. That was never my intention."

"I know that." I took a draught of my beer in order to avoid looking at her. Right now she seemed so vulnerable, so damned attractive, that I was having trouble keeping my mind on the job in hand. "So, let's think about what we now know. Jasmine left with your mother's blessing to take a job on a super yacht."

"Yes, if the woman she went with was telling the truth."

"I think this does have something to do with the sea," I said.

"Yes, I said that at the beginning. But why do you think the woman wanted Jasmine?"

I'd been asking myself the same question. "Well, I think we must assume she and whoever she was working for knew a great deal more about your sister than she let on."

"What, you mean they knew she was dissatisfied and wanted to leave home?"

"Very possibly. But don't overlook the fact that if Jas wanted to disappear and remain hidden, then she needed to have your mother on her side."

"But Dad was the one who—"

"She was angry with him, remember, and didn't care if she hurt him." I toyed absently with the menu card. "Jas would happily have left him to stew but didn't want your mum wondering what had happened to her for the rest of her life."

"But she obviously didn't care about Brett and me."

"We don't know that for sure." I briefly covered one of her hands with mine. "I think it was more a case of her being too taken up with her own problems to give either of you much thought. She was still very young, remember."

"You make her sound selfish and self-centred, which is not how I remember her."

Not surprising if I am, I thought, given that was how I was starting to think of her. "That wasn't my intention." I paused to take a swig of my beer and gather my thoughts. "I'm just trying to put myself inside her head. But anyway, I'll bet she's given a lot of thought to you both since she started her new life. Bear in mind she was determined to disappear but still allowed herself to be photographed with your brother. She wouldn't have taken such a risk if he didn't mean something to her."

"I suppose." She looked directly at me. "But she knew Dad wielded the power in our household. Okay, so Mum knew she was safe, but how would that prevent Dad from continuing to look for her?"

"Whatever she said to him during that phone call she made did the trick there. His attitude changed completely after that."

"Yes, I wonder what it could have been."

I shrugged.

"I don't have a clue. What I keep coming back to is where this mysterious woman materialized from." I stared at the water below us as I mulled the question over. The swans had been joined by a dozen or more ducks, and a feeding frenzy was going on. "You said your father kept her under close control when you raced. So presumably she only crewed on his boat."

"Yes…no, wait a minute." Kara lapsed into thought. "That last year she'd started crewing on a sixty-footer that was skippered by a woman. It had an all-female crew." She looked annoyed with herself. "How could I have forgotten that?"

"Because you didn't think it was significant. Can you remember the name of the boat, or the name of its owner?"

She wrinkled her brow. "I think the boat was called

Laissez-Faire, but I can't remember who owned it. I don't think I ever knew."

"No worries. I dare say the Small Ships Register will be able to tell us everything we need to know. Was the boat on a British flag?"

"Sorry, I don't know that either. But I do know someone who works at Lloyds Register. Perhaps she'll be able to look it up for me."

"Okay, I'll leave that to you." I paused to assimilate my thoughts. "It would explain why she was targeted by a woman for a plum job on a super yacht, of course. If she'd been seen crewing competently on a large yacht with a load of other women, I mean. We both know jobs on those gin palaces are highly sought after. The last thing the owners need to do is go on hunting expeditions for suitable crew."

"So why did they?"

I paused again, my attention on the squabbling ducks as I tried to decide if I ought to say what was on my mind. "Well, perhaps—"

"It's all right, Charlie, I know what you're trying to say. Perhaps my first thoughts when I heard she'd gone off with a woman were right." She took a large sip of vodka. "Okay, so what next? When do we go to Weymouth?"

"After you've checked out the ownership of that yacht. The likelihood of it being in the same hands after all this time is remote but it's still a good starting point." It was our only starting point but I didn't bother to say so. I also didn't mention that I intended to revisit her mother and Ramsay one more time before we set off.

We had another round of drinks and I polished off

a steak pie. Kara merely toyed with some nachos, still deeply shocked by her mother's duplicity.

"I wonder if Jas ever asks after me when she speaks to Mum?"

"I'm surprised you didn't ask her."

"Perhaps I don't want to know." She shook her head. "But what I can't figure out is why Brett didn't tell Mum he'd made contact with Jas. After all, Jas must have told him she still phones home, so why all the secrecy?"

"We don't know that. Your sister's been playing her cards very close to her chest."

"True, and I suppose if she wants to keep her life compartmentalised she might have asked Brett not to mention they'd met to Mum."

"Yes, that's probably what happened. After all, he didn't even tell you. You only found out when you came across that picture."

She sighed. "We aren't going to find any answers sitting here. Come on, let's get back to the boat and get to work."

Pleased to see some of her old spirit returning, I drained my glass and stood.

"I'll get onto my friend at Lloyds right away," she said as we left the pub. "What will you do?"

"Before or after I've taken Gil for his constitutional?"

I left Kara aboard the *No Comment* trying to track down her friend at Lloyds Register. Gil and I set off for our usual afternoon ramble along the beach on the eastern perimeter of the marina. It was usually quiet there. Gil was able to chase the seagulls to the water's edge and charge after the sticks I threw for him without upsetting the local busybodies who consider dogs, even on rocky unused beaches, to be health hazards.

After half an hour I whistled to Gil, and as I turned towards home I waved at a familiar figure approaching.

"Joe, what brings you here?"

"Thought this was where I'd find you. I went to the boat but the Webb girl said you were out with Gil."

"Well, you know me, mate," I said, surprised Joe hadn't made some comment about Kara getting all cosy on the *No Comment*. "I'm a creature of habit."

"Not all of them savoury."

But there was none of the usual humour in my old partner's voice. I frowned. He looked terrible and I wondered if he'd picked up some sort of bug. Or worse, if he was getting all territorial about Kara being in my domain when he had such high hopes for Sarah in that respect. Whatever the reason, something had happened to seriously piss Joe off. The deterioration in his appearance since our fishing trip a few days previously was astonishing. He looked wild, his hair and clothes unkempt, his face haggard. He was plagued with high blood pressure and I hoped he hadn't received bad news about his health.

"What's up, Joe? You don't look too good."

"No, I don't suppose I do." He ran his hand through his short thin hair. It stood up in spikes where he ruffled it, making him look as though he'd just stuck his fingers in an electrical socket. "I need a word. Can we sit down somewhere?"

"Sure." I left Gil to torment the seagulls and steered Joe to a nearby bench. "What's on your mind, mate?"

"Well, the thing is, Sarah told me Harry wasn't at school today. Is he okay?"

I didn't try to hide my surprise. "Yeah, he's fine. He's gone off with Emily to Spain to stay with her parents, that's all."

"But I thought they were going at the end of term."

"Their plans changed. Nothing much happens during the last couple of weeks of the summer term so it doesn't make any odds."

He let out a long breath. "No, I suppose not."

I looked at Joe askance. "What's this all about, mate? You're not looking like death warmed up because my son's missing a few days of school, that's for sure."

Joe expelled another laboured breath and stared at his feet. "Thank God he's okay."

"Joe?" I frowned at the unpleasant sensation seeping through my bones. "I think you'd better tell me what this is all about."

"Christ, don't you think I want to? That's why I'm here." He finally lifted his gaze from his feet and looked at me. "But before I say anything, I just want you to know that I never intended Harry to get involved."

"Involved in what? You're not making any sense. Has this got something to do with Sarah and Amy?"

"God, no! This is all about me being a bloody idiot." He stared off into the distance. "I'm so sorry, Charlie, but it was me who put that note in Harry's bag when I went to pick Amy up from school the other day."

NADIA HEARD THE door from Igor's study to the corridor open and scampered back to bed. The meeting must be breaking up, and in all probability her husband would come to check on her. She trembled at the thought of his reaction if he caught her eavesdropping. For the first time in her life she was afraid of him. He engendered that sensation in others. She'd seen tough men reduced to quivering wrecks when they'd done something to displease him, but he'd never treated her with anything other than love and tenderness.

Provided she did as he asked, of course.

How had that thought crept into her brain? Why was she only just realizing how comprehensively he controlled every aspect of her life, right down to taking the pills he forced upon her? And more to the point, when had she stopped asserting herself and allowed it to happen?

She pulled the covers up to her chin and curled her knees up to her chest in a defensive ball, disciplining herself to take deep, calming breaths as she waited for her heartbeat to return to normal. Repeatedly she tried to deny the words she'd overheard. Her Russian wasn't fluent—she'd obviously got it all wrong.

But Nadia knew in her heart of hearts that she hadn't. Igor was furious with his daughter, and with Viktor too. They had bungled something, exceeded their authority, which was never a wise thing to do with Igor. Nadia sensed the return of all the uncertainties she'd experienced when Brett died. Igor knew more about his death than he was letting on. But what had Kara to do with it, and who was the person called Hunter they were linking her name with? Why were they shouting at one another about her family? None of it made any sense.

The connecting door opened and Nadia heard Igor's soft footfalls traversing the thick carpet. She screwed her eyes tight shut but was convinced he must be able to hear the crashing of her heart against her rib cage.

She could sense him looming over her and, when his hand gently brushed the hair away from her cheek, she didn't know how she stopped herself from leaping with fright.

She let out a long breath when she heard him leave the room again. He wouldn't be back for a while. She'd heard him tell Viktor to bring the car 'round. They had business elsewhere. Nadia sat up, wondering what she ought to do about what she'd overheard. Should she do anything? Dare she?

Yes. She felt some of her old determination returning. She'd spent fifteen years living by Igor's code, ignoring his activities and trying to coax him into legal pursuits. But this time he'd gone too far. If Igor was involved with the death of her brother then she needed to find out how. And why.

She couldn't possibly confront him directly, and everybody in this house was unswervingly loyal to her husband. Everybody except one, possibly.

Nadia showered and dressed carefully and then went downstairs and played with the children. Olga told her Igor wouldn't be home for dinner. Excellent. She was unsure if she'd be able to face him right now and needed to follow up on her half-formed plan to get at the truth before her courage failed her.

"Then I shall eat with the children and put them to bed myself," she said. "You can have the evening off, Olga."

The woman looked as though she wanted to argue but in the end she settled for a frosty, "As you wish, madam," and left the room.

Having read the children a bedtime story, Nadia closed their door and went in search of Anton. She found him alone in the library, working on a laptop. He was an ace with computers and kept electronic track of her husband's business activities—a sort of online accountant, she supposed. He looked up when she walked in, smiled in his shy manner but didn't say anything.

She returned his smile, told him she was going for a walk and slipped out of the room, leaving the door ajar. As she anticipated, Anton followed her into their extensive rear garden and fell into step behind her. It wouldn't be safe to talk to him in the house. There were too many people about who'd report it to Igor. But there was nothing more natural than for her to take a stroll in the garden on a lovely summer's evening. And nobody would think anything of Anton accompanying her. After all, that was part of his job.

"It was you, wasn't it, Anton?" she said after they'd strolled some way in silence.

"It was me, what?"

"You left the newspaper with the account of my brother's death where you knew I'd see it." She watched his face as he struggled to decide what to tell her.

"Yes," he said. Nothing more, just "yes." She knew him to be a man of few words but felt she deserved more of an explanation than that.

"Why? You didn't tell my husband when we met that time, did you?"

"No. But I knew when your brother was reported dead that you should know. Mr. Kalashov, he say not to tell you, but I don't think that was right."

"Thank you, Anton." She touched his hand, and his face flooded with colour. "What else can you tell me about how Brett died?"

"Nothing." He looked away and she knew he was lying.

"I know you weren't involved, Anton, but I need to understand what happened to Brett."

"I know nothing about it. Perhaps I shouldn't have let you see that paper after all. Mr. Kalashov was right, it has upset you."

"No, Anton, I'm not upset, I—"

They heard the sound of tyres on gravel. "They're back early," he said, looking nervous as he faded into the shrubbery.

Damn! Nadia had lost her chance.

EIGHT

JUST FOR A moment I was tempted to laugh. This had to be some sort of sick windup. But one look at Joe's stricken features and I knew it wasn't. Still, it took a moment for my sluggish brain to assimilate his admission. It could only mean one thing, and I wasn't ready to believe that of my mentor and friend.

"I think you'd better explain," I said, aware of the tension in my voice.

"I wish it was that straightforward." Joe leaned his elbows on his thighs and dropped his head into his hands.

"I'd say it was pretty straightforward. You put a threatening letter in my son's bag because some scumbag you're involved with told you to." I felt my anger rising. "And didn't give a toss about putting Harry in danger."

"No, Charlie, you don't understand."

I balled my fists to prevent myself from grabbing Joe by the collar and throwing him in the sea. "You've got that right. I don't."

"Being reduced to putting that note in Harry's bag made me realize what I'd become. That's why I'm here."

I snorted. "It's a bit late to develop a conscience."

"If I can't hold my head up in the presence of my best mate, then what's left for me?"

"Perhaps you should have thought about that before you acted."

"That's easy for you to say because you've still got your self-respect. I lost mine a long time ago." He sighed. "But enough is enough. I don't care what happens to me anymore."

"Tell me," I said, tight-lipped.

"Well, it started when I was new to the force. I've always had a taste for the gee-gees, you know that."

I nodded, already wondering if this was something to do with a gambling scam. But if it was, how could it possibly involve Jasmine Webb, and why was it so imperative that she remain hidden?

"Well, I was just about keeping my head above water, losing more than I could afford, but I was a single bloke, under pressure in the job. We all have to have some form of release, you know that, and mine is the thrill of a punt."

"But you got in over your head?"

"Yeah, and if the brass had found out, it would have been curtains for my career. But still I thought I'd be able to sort it." He shook his head. "And I would have, except I met Barbara and fell for her. Heavily. At first I gave up gambling, I didn't need it anymore because I had her."

"Did she know?"

"Yeah, and she was supportive. Said she understood. But she didn't know how badly in debt I already was. I didn't dare explain and risk losing her. We had two incomes so I'd work it all out without her having to know."

I nodded. It was true what Joe said. The demands placed upon policemen were extreme and almost all of us had to have something to compensate so we could do our jobs effectively. Some drank too much, others womanised, some gambled. I was one of them. A regular face in the nick's poker school. Most managed to keep their addictions within the bounds of acceptability but there were always one or two who self-destructed. I would never have pegged Joe as one such and was almost sympathetic. Until I remembered what he'd been reduced to.

"You'll have me in tears in a minute," I said in an icy tone. "Just get to the point."

"I was about to." He ran his hands through his unruly hair. "Christ, Charlie, this is hard." I didn't trust myself to speak. "I would have worked it out. I stayed away from the bookies, was the first to volunteer for overtime and gradually made inroads into the debt."

"With the bookie?"

"Well, no." He couldn't meet my gaze.

I groaned. "You weren't in with a loan shark?" When Joe said nothing I almost lost it. "Jesus, I don't believe I'm hearing this!"

"It would have been all right. I had it under control and the end was in sight." He paused. "Then Barbara fell pregnant. We weren't planning to start a family for a few more years and I would have been straight by then."

"And so you started gambling again."

"Yes."

I didn't think it was possible for Joe to drop his head any lower but somehow he managed it.

"You have to understand, I was desperate."

I took a deep breath, attempting to quell my disgust. "How did they turn you?"

"I was approached one day in the bookies by a man I'd never seen before and never have since."

"Name."

Joe shrugged. "Like he was going to tell me."

"So what did he say?"

"That he knew all about my debts. He did too. He named the exact amount and said he could make it disappear permanently."

I glowered at him. "Did you really think it would be that easy?"

"No, but it was that or be thrown out of the job. And possibly out of Barbara's life too."

"What did he want you to do in return?" I held up my hands. "No, don't tell me, let me guess. To make certain *problems* disappear. To give advance warnings of raids on gaming establishments." I glared at my former partner with open contempt. "And you've been in their pocket ever since."

"I didn't realize what I'd got myself into until it was too late to do anything about it."

"Oh, pleeease!" How often had I heard that one?

"No, straight up, I—"

"You know, Joe, throughout my career I did everything I could to measure up to you but never thought I'd be half the copper you were." I shook my head, stood and paced towards the beach, wrestling with my disillusionment and growing anger. Only when I thought I had my temper under control did I sit again and speak without looking at him. "Tell me everything you can remember about the man who contacted you."

"It was nearly thirty years ago."

"And you've forgotten?"

"I don't think I'll ever be able to." Joe shuddered.

"But even if he's still alive, he'll have changed beyond recognition by now."

"Let me worry about that. Just tell me."

"All right." Joe threw his head back and closed his eyes. "He was over six foot tall, dark hair, heavy moustache, well-built, menacing. East European accent."

"Russian?"

"Possibly. How would I know? But I'll tell you something, he scared the shit out of me and I don't scare easily."

"So this Robin Hood got you out of the mire with the loan sharks out of the kindness of his heart. How often did you see him after that?"

"Never. They phone if they want anything. Little things at first, like they were testing me. Then long gaps and a slightly bigger favour." Joe looked directly at me. "If nothing else it brought me to my senses and I've not been near a bookie's since."

"Yet you live near the racecourse."

"That was Barbara's idea and I've always looked upon it as the ultimate test."

I attempted to remain detached as I learned all I could from Joe. If I let this get more personal than it already was, then I'd lose all sense of perspective. "How did you contact them to let them know you'd done what they wanted?"

"I didn't. They made contact with me and they seldom had to phone twice. I was more scared of them than I was of losing my job. They always knew when I'd done what they wanted and then left me alone, often for years at a time." He rotated his shoulders and sighed. "When I retired I really thought it was all behind me."

"But they got in touch again."

"Yeah, two days ago I got a call. That same cold, heavily accented voice that I'd hoped never to hear again." Joe shivered. "It shook me rigid, I don't mind telling you. He said he knew I picked Amy up from school on Tuesdays."

"Christ!" This was some organisation, keeping tabs on a bent copper no longer in the job, to the extent they were familiar with his routine. I wondered what the hell I was up against and had the good sense to experience a moment's fear. Organized East European crime families made the Mafia look like Walt Disney.

"Yeah. They said they knew we were still mates, so talking to Harry would be a natural thing to do. I was to slip the note in his backpack and that would be the last I'd ever hear from them."

"And so you did it, just like that."

"Actually, I told them to piss off."

My expression must have reflected my surprise. "But you did it anyway in the end."

"He said if I didn't, then someone else would be placing notes on Amy, or maybe visiting Sarah late at night. They quoted her address and know she lives alone with Amy." Joe shook his head. "What else could I do?"

"You could have tried acting like a man."

"Easy for you to say. If it was just me then I'd have stuck to my guns. I don't care what happens to me anymore. But I knew their threats towards Sarah and Amy weren't empty. These people are ruthless. They said it was just to frighten you and nothing would happen to Harry." He shifted his position and fastened his eyes on his shoes. "And so I did it."

"And now you're telling me about it, expecting me to forgive and forget."

"No, Charlie, I know you'll never do that."

Even so, I noticed hope flare briefly in his eyes, only to diminish when I didn't contradict him.

"When Amy said Harry wasn't at school today, my blood ran cold and I had to know he was all right."

"And you think they won't know you've spoken to me?"

Joe shrugged. "I suspect they're counting on it. If their threat against your son didn't put you off, I reckon they think me telling you how tough they are and how far their network stretches will be enough to make you back off this Jasmine Webb thing."

"Were you involved with that?"

"No, I had nothing to do with it."

"Well, at least that's something."

"What will you do now? I know you don't think much of me right now but I'm here because I care."

"It's a little late to develop a conscience."

"I mean it, they don't fuck about. Listen to me!" Joe placed a hand on my arm but I shook it off. I couldn't bear to be touched by him. "What's Jasmine Webb to you that you should risk your life for her? Make no mistake, that's what we're talking about here."

"I'll bear that in mind."

"I suppose her little sister's got you thinking with your prick. I can see why that might have happened, but is she worth dying for?"

I stood and turned away from him. "I'll let you know what I'm gonna do when I've made up my mind. That way you can tell your owners when they ask."

"No, not anymore. Charlie, just think about it—"

I whistled to Gil and walked away, leaving Joe slumped on the bench. I didn't look back.

"HI." KARA SMILED when I got back to the boat. "You've been a long time. Joe was here looking for you. Did he find you?"

"Yeah, he found me." I reached into the cabinet where I kept the booze and poured myself a hefty measure of brandy.

"Charlie, whatever's the matter?" She hovered 'round me, frowning. "You look terrible. Has something happened?"

I knocked back half the contents of my glass without replying.

"Tell me what's going on. You're frightening me. You look like you're ready to kill someone." She took my hand and dragged me across to the seating area. I allowed myself to be dragged because I didn't quite know what else to do and sank down heavily beside her. "Come on, out with it."

"I thought nothing could surprise me after all I've seen in the job over the years but this one's a real bummer."

"What's happened?"

Between numbing mouthfuls of brandy I told her everything Joe had said.

"That's awful." She was still holding my hand and gave it a heavy squeeze. "How could he have put Harry at risk like that?"

"They own Joe. That's the trouble with getting involved with people like them."

"Well, if they threatened to harm his daughter and

granddaughter, it must have made things difficult for him."

"My heart bleeds." I looked at her without seeing her, my brain in overdrive. "But what really concerns me is that I've made matters worse. Before he poured out his black heart, Joe asked me where Harry was. And I stupidly told him."

"But surely they can't get to him in Spain?"

"I don't think they actually want Harry but I wouldn't put anything past them."

"What will you do?"

I shrugged. "Get to them before they start targeting my family again, I suppose."

"I agree, *we* must. But what's it all got to do with Jas?"

I shook my head. "I just don't know but she's obviously mixed up with Eastern Europeans who'll go to great lengths to prevent anyone from trying to find her."

"But you still intend to look for her?"

"Someone's got to stand up to these thugs, but I think you'd better leave it to me after all. These people obviously don't muck about."

"Oh no! I got you into this."

"Somehow that's what I thought you'd say." I tilted her chin with my forefinger so she was forced to look into my face. "Do you have any idea how dangerous this might turn out to be?"

"My brother's dead, Charlie. Does it get any more dangerous than that?"

I shook my head. "No, it doesn't."

"His death was no accident, was it?"

"Somehow I doubt it."

She gulped twice. "Okay, so what do we do next?"

"What did your friend find out about the *Laissez-Faire?*"

"No sixty-foot sailing boat under that name was registered under a British flag fifteen years ago. Nor has one been since."

"Well, that makes sense, if the people are East European. Probably on a Panamanian or South American flag, which means they're keeping a low profile. We can check it out online later but I'm not holding my breath. Anyway, it doesn't matter, it was a long shot." I stood up and reached for my biking jacket.

"Where are you going?"

"There's something I have to do."

"I'll drive you."

"No, you stay here and keep the door locked. I won't be long. Don't let anyone on board, whoever they say they are. And if they insist then set Gil on them." I turned back to face her. "But, for God's sake, remember to tell him to attack, otherwise he'll lick them to death."

"You're scaring me."

"Scared is good. That way you'll stay alert." I gave her a quick peck on the cheek and squeezed her waist. "I won't be long, and when I get back we'll talk some more. I'll have a plan, of sorts, by then and we'll decide whether or not you're going to stay involved."

"That decision's already been made."

"We'll see."

I stood on the pontoon and watched Kara lock the main doors behind me. Then I got on the Harley and headed in the same direction I'd taken that morning with Kara. Back to her mother's house. The time for pussyfooting about was long past. The thugs had upped the ante when they threatened Harry and used Joe to do it. I fully intended to fight back, but in order to do that, I needed to extract a few honest answers from Mrs. Webb.

NADIA SPENT THE next few days in a permanent state of frustration. She managed not to ingest any of the pills Igor still insisted upon feeding her. He watched her take them, and sometimes she had to hold them under her tongue until he left the room and then dash to the bathroom to spit them out. She was feeling much more clearheaded, had more energy and found it tough acting as though she was still a walking zombie. Igor had heard about her putting the children to bed from Olga. Big surprise! It was something she hadn't done since Brett's death, and Igor probably wondered where she'd found the energy.

Now convinced she was pregnant again, Nadia had an added reason not to take narcotics. She hadn't told Igor the news, nor would she until she got to the bottom of the business with Brett. Igor seemed genuinely concerned about her and stayed closer than ever. He cancelled a lot of his appointments, or arranged for people who had business with him to call at the house, and she hadn't had a chance to corner Anton again about her brother's accident.

It was almost a week later when she finally got that chance. She needed to go shopping for the children, refusing to let Olga choose their clothes. On other trips she'd made during the preceding week, Igor had accompanied her himself. When he was busy, the taciturn Viktor took his place. He was being extra-vigilant, like he was expecting someone else to accost her at any moment. But at last, today, Igor had left the house with Viktor and so Anton drove Nadia to the shops.

He seemed edgy and Nadia attempted to put him at ease by chatting about nothing in particular. She bought several pretty summer dresses for Saskia and a pair of pink dungarees that she'd love, even though the colour would clash with her hair. For Sergei she sought out trendy shorts and T-shirts from Kids' Gap.

Anton carried her purchases and, when she said she was in desperate need of coffee, he steered her to the nearest café. Quelling her impatience, she waited until they'd been served before questioning him.

"I need to know." Her imploring gaze clashed with his implacable expression. "About my brother, I mean."

He shook his head. "There's nothing I can tell you."

"You, of all people, understand the importance of family."

"I also understand the importance of staying alive. Leave it alone! You have no idea what you're dealing with."

She touched his hand. "Please! Brett was my only brother."

He looked away. "I can't help you."

"It was no accident, was it?" Nadia increased the pressure of her hand on his. "Anton, please, at least tell me that much."

Looking miserable, he closed his fingers around hers and slowly shook his head. "No," he said, "it was no accident."

NINE

Mrs. Webb hadn't struck me as the type who had a busy social life and so I took a chance on finding her at home. She answered the door at my second knock and didn't seem that surprised to see me standing there.

"Oh, it's you. I had a feeling you'd be back." She shuffled towards the kitchen, which I took as an invitation to follow her. "What do you want this time?"

"I thought there might be something else you wanted to tell me. Something you'd prefer to get off your chest without Kara hearing it."

"I told you everything I know." She slumped into the same chair she'd occupied that morning and lit the inevitable cigarette.

"I haven't got time to ask nicely, Mrs. Webb, so we can handle this one of two ways. Either you tell me everything you know, or I'll see if your husband's willing to reveal what he argued with Jasmine about."

I took the chair opposite her and fixed her with a penetrating gaze. She glared back with an expression bordering on dislike. Well, I could live with that. I'd become immune to attitudes like hers whilst in the job. Besides, in this case, the feeling was entirely mutual.

"Why can't you just leave it alone?" She glowered at me. "There's nothing to be gained from raking over the past."

I glowered right back at her. "It's too late for that."

I thought of Harry's irrepressible smile and had to resist the impulse to shake the truth out of her. "This is now personal."

Something in my expression obviously convinced her that I wasn't leaving until she opened up. "If I tell you what happened, you'll only tell Kara and, trust me, she's better off not knowing."

"That depends upon what you have to say."

"Believe it or not, I'm trying to protect her," she said. I made a scoffing sound at the back of my throat. "I know it might not look that way, but in this dysfunctional family of ours that's about as demonstrative as we get."

I sat opposite her, sensing she believed what she was saying. "You're just gonna have to trust me to decide whether or not it's something Kara needs to know. She's hell-bent on finding Jasmine, and the only way to stop her is to shed as much light as possible on the reason for her disappearance."

Mrs. Webb lit another cigarette as she contemplated my ultimatum. "I expect Kara's told you all about her dictatorial father," she said after a prolonged silence. I nodded. "Well, she doesn't know the half of it. I learned just what a control freak, what an all-round fraud he was, soon after Brett was born. But it was too late for me. I was trapped. I hated the man I'd once loved but had nowhere to escape to." She stared through the window, speaking in a smoker's low rasping voice about a period in her life she'd obviously prefer to forget. "So I stayed and tried to make the best of it. What else could I do?"

"Didn't you have parents who'd take you in?"

"With two small children in tow?" She dragged her

eyes away from the garden and focused them on my face. "They worked hard all their lives, made all sorts of sacrifices for my sake, and were proud when I married Alan. They thought I'd gone up in the world." She dragged hard on her cigarette. "Much they knew. Still, I had to keep up the pretence or they would have got upset, so how could I suddenly admit everything wasn't wonderful?"

"Wouldn't that have been their call?"

She shook her head. "I couldn't risk it. Alan would have made life hell for us all until I returned to him. My parents weren't young and my father had a weak heart."

"You could have gone to a women's shelter."

"If you knew what Alan's really like you wouldn't even suggest it." She shuddered. "He'd have found us, and I'd have lived my life looking over my shoulder until he did."

It wasn't the first time a cowed wife had said those words to me. "What's all this got to do with his row with Jasmine?"

"I'm getting to that." She blew smoke rings at the ceiling, delaying the moment. "On the surface Alan's all sophistication and charm, the life and soul of every social gathering, but underneath he's nothing more than a tyrant and a bully."

"He hit you?"

"Worse. He liked kinky sex, and if I didn't feel like giving out then he just took what he wanted." She drew a deep breath. "Kara was born as the result of marital rape." She nodded in response to my stunned expression. "Now perhaps you understand why I can't warm to her the way I did my other two. I've tried. You can have no notion how hard I've tried, but every time I look at her I remember the foul things he made me do that night."

"That's hardly Kara's fault."

"I pleaded with him to stop," she said, speaking over my interruption. "But, of course, that's what he wanted, I can see that now. He got turned on even more when I begged."

"I'm sorry." It sounded inadequate but I couldn't think of anything else to say. "But why are you still living with him? Brett and Kara left home years ago. You'd have still been young enough to get a job, and the courts would have awarded you something from your joint property eventually, whatever he did to put a spoke in the works."

"I stayed," she said, enunciating each word with exaggerated care, "because of why he argued with Jas."

I sat straighter, sensing we were getting to the crux of the matter at last, but she lapsed into an uneasy silence again. "Mrs. Webb?"

She let out a long breath. "Jas found out her father was abusing Brett."

"Oh, shit!"

"Yes, when I said he liked kinky sex, what I'm really telling you is that he liked to violate me anally. The night Kara was conceived he was out of control. Couldn't seem to get enough. I was bleeding and begged him to stop so he took me the conventional way." She looked at me through dead eyes. "Well, conventional for him anyway."

I stood and swiped the hair away from my eyes. Mrs. Webb had just confirmed my suspicions. I was pretty sure it had to have been domestic violence or sexual abuse that had driven Jasmine away. That's why I'd wanted to talk to her without Kara present.

"I honestly never knew about him and Brett. I knew of his proclivities, so I suppose I should have suspected, but I didn't think even he would sink that low." She lifted her shoulders and lit another cigarette. "I let him carry on doing it to me, thinking that would keep him satisfied. But one day when I was out in the afternoon, Jas came home from college early and found him and Brett together." She exhaled loudly. "She loved her brother but never had much time for her father. As you can imagine, she went wild. She physically attacked Alan. Threw everything she could lay her hands on at him. Then she wanted to go to the police and expose him for what he'd done to Brett."

"But you stopped her?"

"Yes, for Brett's sake." A tear ran down her wrinkled cheek. "I felt responsible, you see. I should have known!" She was trembling. "A mother ought to be able to sense these things, but I didn't have a clue." She fixed watery eyes on me. "What does that say about me?"

"It's not uncommon, believe me. No woman likes to think the man she married is capable of such perversion."

"Yes, but still." She fell silent for a moment. "Anyway, if it all came out, it would have been even worse for Brett and I couldn't put him through that."

"They protect the identity of the victim."

She cast me a withering glare. I probably deserved it. "Do you think that really works? The local rag would have had a field day, seeing such a respectable pillar of society up on a charge of paedophilia. It wouldn't take a rocket scientist to link Brett to it all, and can you imagine how he'd have been treated at school after that? He already felt confused and guilty for letting it happen, thinking he was somehow to blame. Having to relive it through the courts would have crucified him."

I knew she was right and conceded the point with a nod. "But how could you be sure it wouldn't happen again?"

"By frightening my husband rigid with the knowledge I then held against him. That's when the balance of power within this family finally swung in my favour. Appearances are everything to Alan, and I knew he wouldn't risk touching Brett again. All I had to do then was reassure Brett and somehow make him realize it wasn't his fault. Alan had told him he was special, it was their secret…the usual crap these perverts spout to allay their guilt. Brett was such a sensitive child, he actually believed what they were doing was normal because his father said it was." She paused, anger radiating from her in waves as I forced her to relive the nightmare she'd buried with her son. "I've often thought that's why Brett was never able to have a proper relationship with a woman. He didn't seem to have any sex life at all, thanks to that bastard." She pulled hard on her cigarette and glowered at the table-top. "Perhaps he's better off dead."

"Didn't you worry about Alan finding another child outside the family?"

"No, he wouldn't have risked that. Besides, I made it my business to always know where he was back in those early days. In his line of work he mixes with plenty of men but has no reason to come into contact with children. I didn't care what he did with consenting male adults, just so long as he left the kids alone."

"So you stayed to protect Brett and Kara?"

"Oh, he wouldn't have touched Kara. It was the boys he preferred. But yes, I stayed to protect Brett. I moved out of the bedroom and told him if he ever laid so much as a finger on Brett, or any other child again, then I'd go to the authorities and get Brett to tell them all he'd done to him. I meant it as well and he knew it." She looked up at me, her expression malicious. "So now you know our dirty little secret. Happy now, are you?"

I was far from happy, and no further forward in understanding what had happened to Jasmine, even if I now understood why she'd left. "Thanks for telling me. It helps."

"I don't see how. Will you tell Kara?"

"I can't see what that would achieve."

"Good. Jas was adamant that she didn't need to know, even when she was old enough to understand. Her way of protecting her little sister, I suppose."

Kara would be gratified to know Jasmine had cared enough to make that stipulation but I couldn't let on without telling her the rest of it. I thanked Mrs. Webb and left the house, anxious to catch Ramsay again before college finished for the day. I was in luck and only had to wait ten minutes before he emerged into the car park.

"Another word," I said, cutting him off before he reached his car.

"What now?"

"Two things. Describe the man who approached you in the pub about Jasmine."

"It was fifteen years ago."

"And you haven't forgotten a thing about him. Not if you loved Jasmine as much as you'd have me believe."

"All right." He screwed up his eyes. "He was short and stocky. Muscular, like he worked out. Light-haired, blue eyes, very tough."

Not the same man who'd approached Joe then. "Accent?"

"East European, I think. Possibly Russian or Romanian."

"I see."

"You said you had two questions." Ramsay glanced at his watch.

"Yes. They didn't ask you for just any girl, did they?" I moved to within inches of him and looked directly into his face. "They specifically asked for Jasmine."

Ramsay, who'd been waving over his shoulder to a colleague, turned sharply to look at me. "How did you know?"

"I'm a detective. Presumably you were told to give her a specific message that would make her feel it was safe to go to a meeting."

"No, I was to tell her Angela Smith wanted to talk to her and give her a number to call."

"And nothing else."

"Yes, if she indicated she didn't intend to ring, I was to mention her sister seemed to be shaping up as a good little yachtswoman, as well."

I hadn't been expecting that and it threw me completely off balance. Jasmine had been coerced into meeting with this Angela Smith in order to protect Kara. Why was a seventeen-year-old English girl so important to these Eastern Europeans that they'd resorted to such underhanded tactics to entice her away? It just didn't make sense.

"And she went?"

"Presumably. She was very tight-lipped after that, in a perpetually bad mood, and wouldn't tell me anything. But after a while she became very excited. We got away from here early on a Wednesday afternoon and went back to my place. I've never known her so athletic in bed. It was incredible." He looked up at me. "But it was her swan song, I realized afterwards, her way of saying goodbye. I never saw her again after that."

I gave a contemptuous snort and walked away.

When I returned to the boat I was greeted by appetising smells coming from the galley. The bar was laid for two, complete with wineglasses and napkins. Gil was dogging Kara's every footstep so closely that I was surprised she didn't trip over him. I wasn't sure if I enjoyed the domesticity or felt threatened by it but had too much else on my mind to spare it much thought.

"Hi, that's good timing. It's just about ready."

I opened a bottle of Chablis and poured us both a glass. Only when we'd finished eating and cleared away did I answer some of the questions she'd been peppering me with throughout the meal.

"Ramsay wasn't quite honest with us," I said, having no intention of being completely honest with Kara either. She didn't need to know she'd been the catalyst that had forced her sister to attend the initial meeting with Angela Smith. She didn't need to know about her father and Brett either. "It was specifically Jasmine he was told to point in the direction of Angela Smith."

"Oh, I see." Kara took this latest revelation more calmly than I'd anticipated. "Actually, I don't see at all." She rubbed her forehead as though she'd suddenly developed a headache. "I don't understand why this woman didn't just ring Jas at home. Why all the sub-terfuge?"

"I don't get it either." But I had a good idea. Jasmine didn't want to buy whatever these people were selling but they wanted her badly enough to apply pressure. "I guess we'll just have to ask her when we find her."

"Who, Angela Smith?"

"No, idiot, your sister."

"So you still want to go through with this?"

"I don't see that I have any choice."

"There are always choices in life, Charlie."

"I'll back off if you will," I said, using her own words against her.

"That's not fair!"

I winked at her. "No, I don't suppose it is."

I picked up my mobile and dialled Joe's number. "You can report back on a successful mission," I said without introducing myself. "I've got better things to do with Kara than go looking for sisters who don't want to be found so I'm taking her to Cowes tomorrow instead."

I cut the connection before Joe could respond.

"Cowes?" Kara frowned. "Why would we want to go to Cowes?"

"We don't, but seeing as how your sister's keepers have eyes everywhere we can hardly turn up in Weymouth in the *No Comment*. My bet is they've been watching us all along and will know where we're headed before we get beyond Portsmouth."

"Yes, but I still don't see—"

"These people are rattled by our questions. They'll know Joe and I spoke this afternoon and, although he says they never check back with him, I'm betting they'll do so on this occasion."

"Yes, that's possible, but how will being in Cowes make things any easier than being here? Presumably they can watch us just as easily there."

"Sure."

"And what did you mean when you said you have better things to do with me than going to Weymouth?"

"Well." I permitted myself a rare smile. "Joe seems to think you and I are an item. It wouldn't do any harm to perpetrate that myth, just to put them off the scent." I let out an overdramatic sigh. "Do you think you could bring yourself to indulge in a spot of playacting?"

"Blimey, you don't ask much, do you." Her expression was martyred but she seemed to be having problems keeping her lips straight.

"We'd only need to act in public, be seen together all lovey-dovey for a day or two, and then I think they'll back off."

"Okay." She eyed me speculatively, as though weighing up my request and trying to decide if it would be worth it. "Sacrifices must be made for Jas's sake, I suppose. But there's still the question of getting to Weymouth."

"Well, that's why we're going to Cowes. I know someone there who just might be persuaded to lend me another boat."

ANTON ONLY TOLD Nadia what she'd been expecting to hear but the pain, the brutal reality of her husband's actions, still made her dizzy with regret.

"Are you all right, Nadia?" Anton reached across

the table and took her hand. "You look very pale. Here, take a sip of water."

She drained the glass he handed her. "Yes, thank you, I'm hanging in there. But I'll be a whole lot better if you tell me what happened. The truth can't be any worse than the thoughts that keep running through my head."

He shrugged. "I don't know very much. I make it my business to mind my own business."

"Then tell me what you do know."

"Well, after you saw your brother that time, I think he must have started asking questions about you."

"He wouldn't have gotten very far. He didn't know what name I use now, or where I live, or anything that would help him."

"No, but he had that picture I foolishly took of the two of you. Mr. Kalashov has spies everywhere, and word would have got back to him."

Nadia frowned. "In that case he must have wondered how that picture came to be taken in the first place. Did he ask you about it?" Anton shook his head. "Good, I'm glad it didn't get you into trouble. But he didn't mention it to me either. That's strange, don't you think?"

"Once your husband knew your brother was looking for you, he would have been on the alert for any sign of him in Weymouth."

"Perhaps, but to kill him, I can't imagine—"

"If it helps, I don't think the intention was ever to kill him, just to frighten him off. But Mr. Kalashov was out of town when Brett came back." Anton's expression clouded. "So Viktor dealt with the situation his way."

"Ah, so that's what they were arguing about."

"Who?"

"Never mind." Nadia's hand was still in Anton's. It felt good there and she made no attempt to remove it. "Anton, what has my sister to do with all this?"

"Nothing." He released her hand. "I've told you what you wanted to know. We should get back now."

"In a minute." She drummed her fingers on the table, thinking hard. "Anton, I heard my husband, his daughter and Viktor arguing. Something about Kara. I have to know."

Anton moved his face to within an inch of hers and stared into her eyes. "Your husband is a dangerous man when crossed, and I've already said too much. Just leave it."

"But he would never hurt me."

"Perhaps not, but he wouldn't hesitate to hurt me if he thought I was being disloyal."

TEN

KARA HADN'T WANGLED her way on board under false pretences. She could indeed cook and, not accustomed to such fine cuisine in my bachelor existence, I appreciated her efforts. Perhaps that's why I found it easier to force the events of the day to the back of my mind than I'd thought would be the case. She was an easy person to relax around, keeping the conversation flowing whenever I became distracted. I could see that putting her lonely hearts at ease would come naturally to her.

I invited her to join me when I took Gil for his late-night run. As a rule it was my thinking time and I didn't usually crave company, but somehow it seemed like the natural thing to do. Besides, I rather enjoyed being seen with her. As we strolled along the walkway full of people spilling out of the restaurants and bars to enjoy the mild summer evening, she certainly made heads turn. Something else I liked about her was that she didn't feel the need to fill the silence between us with banal chatter. Unlike most women, she knew when to keep her mouth shut and only spoke when she had something to say.

As we walked past a particular bar, "Jungle Line" was belting out of the speakers.

"Herbie Hancock's arrangement," I said.

"Come again."

I stopped walking and stared at her. "Don't tell me you've never heard of Herbie."

"Sorry. Should I have?"

"Philistine!"

"Guilty as charged," she said, and I sensed a smile in her voice. "So who is this Herbie character and why should I have heard of him?"

"Only one of the greatest jazz pianists of recent times, that's all."

"Ah well, that explains it then. I don't know anything about jazz."

"'Jungle Line' was a Joni Mitchell song." I looked down at her, horrified. "Please tell me you've heard of Joni."

"Of course, even if she was before my time. Something about putting up a parking lot, wasn't it?"

I didn't dignify that with a reply. "Herbie was fascinated by Joni's songs," I told her. "He dissected the lyrics of some of her most famous ones and did new arrangements to express the emotions behind them. But he still managed to stay true to the original melodies. Many consider the album *River* to be a masterpiece."

"You included, it would seem," she said. "You obviously like jazz."

"I like *good* jazz, which rules out a lot of it."

"How did you get hooked?"

"My mother was a musician."

"Was? Is she dead?"

"Yes."

I whistled to Gil and turned back towards the boat, belatedly regretting that I'd invited her to join me. How had our conversation veered in this direction? I didn't talk about my mother to anyone.

But either Kara didn't notice my reticence or she was thicker-skinned than I'd realized.

"How did she die?"

I pretended not to hear the question and made more of a thing out of unlocking the boat than was necessary.

"Sorry," she said when I failed to respond. "I didn't mean to pry."

I lifted my shoulders like it was no big deal, even though it was.

"Do you play an instrument yourself?" She lifted one of my hands and examined my long fingers.

"The piano, in a previous life. I haven't played for years." I glanced at my fingers, cut and bruised from countless battles with the boat's engine. Brendan, my former music teacher who still doggedly kept in touch and tried every trick in the book to get me playing again, told me he wept buckets every time he saw them. A pianist was supposed to protect his fingers more jealously than he guarded his bank balance.

"Oh, that's a pity. Demands of the job, I suppose."

"Time for bed." I had no intention of being drawn into this particular conversation. "I'd like to get away early in the morning. There's a regatta at Cowes this weekend so the marina is likely to be full."

"Yes, and they don't usually take advance bookings when there's something on."

"Right. It'll be first come, first served, which is why I want to get away early."

"Good plan." She smiled at me and turned towards her cabin. "Good night, Charlie."

"Good night."

I had a nightcap and pondered the events of the day whilst I waited for her to use the head. My bruised fingers absently tapped out the harmonic content of "Jungle Line" on the galley surface. I could hear the bass register flirting with the tenor chords. Syncopated variants flooded my mind in spite of my best efforts to ignore them, and I was horrified to find myself improvising on my imaginary keyboard, asking myself what, if anything, I'd have done differently from Herbie to enhance the melody. I stopped abruptly when my actions registered in my brain, deciding Miss Webb had a lot to answer for. With Gil at my heels, I held that thought as I too turned in.

THE WEATHER WAS fine and the *No Comment* behaved perfectly in the choppy force five that accompanied us all the way to Cowes. We arrived in the middle of the afternoon but the marina was already almost full. We were lucky to get a berth on the inside of the outermost pontoon.

"Any later and we'd have been stuck on the outside," I remarked as Kara efficiently made the last of the lines secure.

"You stink-boaters are all softies." She leapt agilely back on board. "There's nothing wrong with being on the outside, or on a mooring buoy either, for that matter."

"Yeah, as long as you don't mind being in the direct firing line of all the ferries and hydrofoils. And at the mercy of all the weekend grotty-yachties who don't have a clue what they're doing."

She poked her tongue out at me as she helped set up the shore power.

"Come on," I said when we were finished. "Let's give Gil a run."

We walked down the floating pontoon towards the quaint semi-pedestrianised high street. It had retained its character and had changed little over the years, if one overlooked the fact that shops once frequented by the locals had given way to expensive chandler's, Indian restaurants and fancy boutiques.

I took Kara's hand and she shot me a quizzical look. "We're acting, remember."

"Oh yes, of course. How could I have forgotten?"

I rolled my eyes. "Very easily. Obviously."

"Do you think anyone is actually watching us, Charlie?"

"I haven't noticed anyone but they're hardly going to advertise their presence, are they? Let's just assume they're out there and give them something to talk about."

We strolled along Cowes seafront, skirted behind the Royal Yacht Squadron and headed towards Gurnard. I let go of her hand at one point and draped my arm around her shoulders instead. She leaned into my side and laughed at some inane comment of mine, as though I was the wittiest person on the planet. Her laughter rang in my ears and made me feel good. The pressure of her body against mine made me feel even better.

I kept half an eye on the people 'round about, trying to decide who, if anyone, was watching us. I thought I saw the same gangly youth on a couple of occasions but he took no particular interest in us. Then there was a couple throwing bread for nonexistent ducks, which was being swooped upon by the seagulls instead. They turned away very quickly when they saw me looking at them, which aroused my suspicions. It also gave me an excuse to pull Kara a little closer. Just in case.

When we got back to the boat, the outside of the pontoon was rapidly filling up.

"Told you so," I said smugly.

"What do you fancy for dinner tonight?" She opened lockers in the galley and started rummaging around.

"Why don't we give one of those fancy Indian restaurants something to do?"

"Sounds good to me."

And so we did. Cowes Tandoori offered a bewildering array of dishes but I'd learned the hard way that they're usually variations on a basic theme, disguised with different sauces. To be on the safe side I order chicken madras, which was okay. Kara went for prawns in a mild sauce.

We lingered over our wine and walked slowly back to the marina, arms entwined. It still felt good. Too good. I wondered now if this was such a clever idea but had no time to dwell upon the deeper implications of our playacting, because as soon as we set foot on the boat I knew something wasn't right.

"Stay there!"

Kara was about to swing a leg over the gunwales but paused to look at me quizzically. "What's wrong?"

"I don't know. Something. Where's Gil? Why isn't he on the other side of that glass door wagging like crazy?"

"You're frightening me."

In spite of my telling her to stay on the pontoon, she'd come aboard and was standing at my shoulder.

"Come inside, Charlie," said a familiar-sounding male voice from the salon. "We've been waiting for you."

"What the—"

The door slid open a foot or two, enough for me to see Gil rolling on his back and having his stomach scratched by the elegantly manicured hand of my un-invited guest. My mind was whirling with possibilities. Gil was a soft touch but not to the extent that he'd allow someone he didn't know into his domain and then lap up the attention. He didn't even get up when he heard my voice. Hopefully that meant the intruder was one of the good guys, but I still couldn't place his voice and it was too dim to make out his features. With no alternative open to me I walked into the salon. Kara was right behind me.

My old boss, Chief Superintendent Gerry Monk, had made himself at home on the seating unit and was the one responsible for scratching Gil's tender spots. He had a reputation as a snappy dresser. I'd never seen him in anything other than a suit and tie before but even dressed casually, in chinos and a polo shirt bearing the logo of an upmarket designer, he managed to portray an image of satirical elegance. His salt-and-pepper hair, still thick and wavy, was combed neatly across one side of his scalp. The expression in his intelligent brown eyes as he looked up at me was sardonically amused.

"What the fuck are you doing here?" My relief that the chief super was responsible for the break-in mani-fested itself in an outburst I'd never normally have di-rected at a man who'd always enjoyed my unreserved respect.

"Close the door, Miss Webb," he said calmly. "And it'll be all right to put a light on now you're back, Char-lie. I dislike sitting in the dark. One never knows what surprises might be lying in wait when one can't see the hand in front of one's face."

"This is my ex-Chief Superintendent, Kara," I explained, flicking on the lights. "And since he obviously knows who you are, there doesn't seem much point in making an introduction."

"Obviously not," she agreed, shaking Monk's outstretched hand.

"What *are* you doing here, sir?" I asked, rephrasing my original question a little more politely.

"Why, I'm out for a weekend's sailing and happened to see your boat."

I raised a sceptical brow. "And felt the need to break in?"

"Oh, I'd hardly call it that." He waved the suggestion airily aside. "I was curious to see what you've done to it, that's all."

The chief super had left the local force about a year before I resigned, destined for some mysterious post in London. No one knew quite what he'd moved on to and he wasn't saying. But he'd heard about my resignation and made a point of coming to see me, spending a gratifying amount of time trying to get me to change my mind. That's when he'd got to know Gil.

"I see." I regarded him levelly, not deceived. His sangfroid attitude caused colleagues and villains alike to underestimate his fierce intellect, but I'd learned early in my career that little got past him. Twenty-four hours ago I'd have trusted him without reservation, but since Joe's revelations I was no longer sure whom I could place my faith in. Why was he here? And how come he knew who Kara was? There were many questions he needed to answer but those two were in a class apart.

"I work for Her Majesty's government in an unspecified role nowadays," he explained.

"What the hell's that supposed to mean?"

"Let's just say I'm employed in an advisory capacity wherever I'm needed. Your name came up recently, linked to Miss Webb's, and, well…here I am." He stretched, looking totally unperturbed when I glowered suspiciously at him. "Got anything decent to drink on this tub?"

Wordlessly I poured him a neat scotch, and then one for myself. I had a feeling I was going to need it. I looked at Kara but she shook her head. Before I could get my next questions out, a man I'd never seen in my life before emerged from the direction of the cabins and shook his head at my ex-governor. He was fairly short but lean and muscular, and looked as though he could take care of himself. He had close-cropped dark hair and eyes that appeared to miss nothing.

"This is James Levine. He works for Interpol."

The man flashed his ID, which I took from him and studied carefully before handing it back. It looked genuine enough but these things were so easy to forge nowadays, especially if, like me, you didn't know what the kosher document was supposed to look like. I took my time, looking between him and the plastic card in my hand, endeavouring to harness my anger. This man had been rooting around the boat, sticking his nose into my personal effects, and presumably Kara's too. I don't take kindly to that sort of intrusion.

"Find what you were looking for?" I asked him in a voice loaded with sarcasm.

"Just making sure no one's planted any listening

devices." His laconic tone suggested bugging was an occupational hazard he'd learned to take in his stride.

I frowned. "What's this all about, guv?" I asked. I had a pretty good idea but wasn't going to make it easy for him.

"You've obviously lost your touch since leaving the force, Charlie. You used to be one of my most astute officers."

"Sorry to disappoint you." I leaned on the galley counter, sipping my drink, still playing dumb. "Since I'm not answerable to you anymore, I guess you'll just have to get over it. And perhaps, if it's not too much trouble, you'll tell me in your own time why you're trespassing on my property and why you're so paranoid about people overhearing us."

Monk shot me a look. "Well, obviously, it's about Miss Webb's sister."

"Jas!" Kara's face lit up. "You know where she is?" I wanted to warn her that if Monk was involved, it wasn't going to be that straightforward.

"Oh yes, we've known exactly where she is for a long time."

"And you didn't bother to let her family know?"

"By the time she showed up on our radar she was of age." He lifted his shoulders in a what-could-we-have-done sort of gesture. "She hadn't broken any laws so it was up to her whether or not she got in touch with her family."

I felt Kara's frustration and squeezed her hand. "Why are you, Interpol that is, so interested in Jasmine Webb?"

"She's not Jasmine Webb anymore. She's been known as Nadia for years now."

Kara frowned. "Why?"

"A very good question, Miss Webb, but I'd hazard a guess that it has something to do with her being married to a Russian gentleman by the name of Igor Kalashov."

"Who?"

A few more pieces fell into place in my brain. The Eastern Europeans who'd strong-armed Ramsay into giving Jasmine up and Joe into threatening me through Harry. An organisation sufficiently well placed to know what Kara and I were up to every step of the way. The Russian Mafia. I'd known it all along, of course, but still felt a slight chill at the prospect of tangling with such brutal thugs.

"Yes, that's right." Monk had been watching me closely and obviously realized that I'd figured some of it out. "I'm afraid your sister is mixed up with some rather dangerous individuals, Miss Webb."

"Do you know where she is now? Is she in Weymouth?"

"Yes. Her husband has homes in Russia, the south of France and Weymouth, but your sister spends a lot of time in this country because her children go to school here."

"Children?" She shook her head as though on information overload. "Am I an aunt?"

"Yes, Nadia Kalashova has two children. A boy called Sergei who is seven and a little girl, Saskia, who's four."

"I think I'd like that drink now please, Charlie."

"Sure." I poured a hefty measure of brandy and handed it to her.

"So, what's your interest?" I asked Monk.

Levine answered the question. "Kalashov is former KGB. He's fifty-two—"

"A lot older than my sister then."

"Yes. He's a Muscovite, from an ordinary working-class family. But even as a young man he had brains, charm and ambition, and the KGB was the perfect organisation in which to hone all three. He'd risen to the rank of captain by the time the KGB broke up."

"But," Kara said, shaking her head, "that's a different world from Jasmine's. How could she have—"

"The fall of the Soviet Union in 1991 had been widely anticipated," Levine said, ignoring Kara's interruption, "and an intelligent man like Kalashov couldn't fail to appreciate the opportunities it presented. He certainly took advantage of the widespread corruption that prevailed. Poverty and distrust of authority was common, and it became a case of the survival of the fittest." He shrugged. "I suppose it was inevitable that someone of Kalashov's ilk would become involved in organized crime—"

"Oh God!"

Kara dropped her head into her hands whilst Monk took up the narrative.

"Kalashov got involved in drugs, prostitution, gambling, smuggling of precious metals. In other words he was a fixer. He had all the contacts, was and still is barely on nodding terms with his conscience and supplied whatever anyone was willing to pay top dollar for. He ruthlessly wiped out any competition and established himself as a force to be reckoned with. He was suspected of arranging contract killings in the early days, and sometimes even carrying them out himself, but was never arrested or even questioned about those crimes. He now hides behind a wide network of inter-mediaries, and Interpol hasn't been able to pin any-thing on him."

"But how did Jas get involved with him?" Kara asked.

"We're not altogether sure, but we're able to make an intelligent guess. He loves yachts and your sister crewed on a boat for him—"

"The *Laissez-Faire*."

Monk's eyebrows shot up. "You knew that?"

"We didn't know who owned the boat."

"Well, we think Kalashov saw Jasmine crewing and wanted to get to know her. Our understanding is that his feelings weren't reciprocated, which was the start of his obsession with your sister. He's a good-looking, rich and charismatic guy who isn't used to being rejected."

"Which is why he was reduced to manipulating Jas-mine?" I surmised.

"What do you mean?" Monk asked.

I was about to tell him, then I remembered all the people who'd been corrupted by Kalashov's organisa-tion, and hesitated. Could I trust him? Was he only here to find out how much we knew?

"If I was with them, Charlie," he said softly, "why would I be telling you all this?"

"Yeah, I suppose." I was in over my head and wouldn't be able to get near Jasmine or Nadia, or what-ever the fuck her name was nowadays, without profes-sional help. Besides, I had to trust someone. I made up my mind it might as well be Monk so I told him how Ramsay had been forced into giving Jasmine up.

Monk nodded. "That fits in with our scenario. Kalashov wanted a fling with Jasmine but he was married and Jasmine didn't do married men."

"So what changed?"

"Well, as I said, we think the more she rejected him, the more obsessed he became with her," Levine said. "He tried everything but she remained unimpressed by his ostentatious display of wealth. In the end he offered her a prime job on his personal yacht, just to keep her close to him. If it helps you any," he added, nodding at Kara, "I think she was unaware of the true nature of his activities, at that time anyway."

"I don't doubt it," Kara said. "She wouldn't knowingly involve herself with such people. I dare say she just wanted to work on the boat."

"I'm sure you're right. Anyway, a year after giving her a job, Kalashov's wife died, supposedly after a long illness, but the circumstances are extremely suspect. As far as we've been able to find out from the few people of ours who've managed to penetrate his organisation, Jasmine was still refusing his advances and it was driving him crazy. He had to do something and for a man like him, getting rid of an inconvenient wife, well…" Levine shrugged, leaving his words dangling.

"Kalashov has three children from his first marriage," Monk said, taking up the story. "Two boys in their midtwenties. One is coordinating a building project for his father in Spain."

My head jerked up. "Spain?" My immediate concern was for Harry. I'd sent him there to get him away from these people. God forbid that I'd put him in the direct line of fire.

"Yes, is that a problem?" Monk looked mildly concerned.

"Probably not."

"Right, we'll tell you more about his interests there in a minute. The other son's in Russia. What his role is we're unsure but we think it has something to do with facilitating the goods Kalashov supplies."

"And his other child?" I prompted when Monk fell silent.

"The eldest is a girl called Monika, who concerns us most of all. She's thirty and a chip off the old block in all respects. She runs her father's escort agency in the West End with a fist of iron and we've been unable to get anywhere near her."

"Why should that bother you? The escort agency, I mean. It's not exactly on the same scale as supplying contraband."

"Well, yes, except we think a lot more goes on in that establishment than meets the eye and we'd love to be able to get through the doors."

I felt a quickening of interest. "You think she handles some of her father's other business activities?"

"Almost certainly." Monk executed another of his elegant shoulder lifts. "It's the perfect cover. All the girls in the agency are Eastern European and it's natural enough for visiting businessmen from those countries to call there."

"Can't you raid the premises?"

"Certainly, if we could get a warrant." Monk looked harassed for the first time. "But even if we managed to find a reason to apply for one and got there before Monika was tipped off, I'm willing to bet a year's pay that we wouldn't find anything to help us. This lot are too well organized to leave a paper trail."

"I still don't understand what you want with Kara and me. What can we do?"

"We've been looking for a weakness in Kalashov's organisation for years."

"But you said you had people infiltrated—"

"Neither of them has been heard from for months."

"Ah, I see."

"Your sister, Miss Webb, is Kalashov's weakness," Levine said. "His only weakness. He still worships the ground she walks on and, for her sake, is legitimising his business affairs. The development in Spain I mentioned is a major project. An hotel, golf course, upmarket houses overlooking the sea, shopping complex. A whole town being built from scratch on farmland north of the Costa del Sol. Even Kalashov doesn't have sufficient funds to finance it outright, doesn't want to take a partner and is doing one last major deal to raise the capital."

"What sort of deal?" I asked. "It must be something heavyweight to attract the sort of money he'll need."

"Yes, you're right about that and we think…no, we know, he's behind a plan to supply Hamas with rocket launchers and bulk military equipment." Monk's eyes drilled into my face like lasers. "And his clients are the Iranians."

ANTON REMOVED HIS hand from Nadia's but she snatched it back.

"Do you care for me at all, Anton?"

"You know I do." His expression was anguished. "When I think of you with him, when I hear you together, I can't—"

"Then please, tell me what I need to know. I have

to understand. Why was my husband talking about my sister?"

"Nadia, I can't tell you these things. You know how he is about loyalty. He wouldn't hesitate to kill us both if he even suspected."

"Then why do you work for him? You're not like Viktor and the others." Nadia couldn't bring herself to say he wasn't like Igor. She'd been forced to see her husband in a very different light recently but still couldn't think of him as a cold-blooded killer. "Why do you stay?"

Anton finally lifted his eyes to meet hers. "You know why I stay. And as for why I first agreed to work for Mr. Kalashov…" He looked away again. "It was an opportunity too good to pass up. There was nothing for me in Russia. You've seen for yourself how it is for the ordinary people there. I wanted more than I'd ever be able to achieve in my homeland. Your husband needed someone with my expertise in the field of computers, I was recommended to him and jumped at the opportunity to prove myself. Like you, I soon learned to pretend everything was all right and to keep my mouth closed." He paused. "Then he asked me to accompany you sometimes, and by then it was too late. I could never walk away from you and the children."

Nadia, moved by Anton's straightforward sincerity, couldn't think of anything to say. Instead she reflected upon the hopelessness of her situation, gradually becoming aware of Jasmine's fighting spirit reemerging from where it had been crushed deep within her. The essence of the person who'd kept the mighty Igor Kalashov dangling for so long was clamouring to be heard, telling her to protect her baby sister and keep the children safe, regardless of the cost.

Jasmine's determination gave her fresh hope. It was time to stand up for herself again.

"Tell me about Kara," she said.

He sighed. "She's trying to find you."

Nadia gasped. "Why, after all this time?"

"She thinks you ought to know about Brett. And she wants to know why you disappeared all those years ago."

In spite of the enormity of the situation, Nadia smiled. How alike she and her sister were in so many ways. "How does Igor know?"

"He has people everywhere who report to him. Charlie Hunter used to be a policeman and he was assigned to look into your disappearance. Your sister approached him and asked if he would help track you down."

"They must be stopped. We must warn her." Nadia jumped to her feet. "It's too dangerous for her." She pulled her mobile phone from her bag. "I know where she lives. Perhaps I can get her number from enquiries."

"Don't use that!" Anton snatched the phone from her hand. "You'll leave a trace."

Nadia shook her head. "No, it's all right, it's a pay-as-you-go. There are no bills."

"You must still be cautious. If your husband were to click through the calls made, he'd realize what you were up to."

"Yes." Nadia was about to say Igor would never do something like that but quickly changed her mind. She no longer knew what her husband was capable of. "Then what?"

"If you insist upon doing this then we must find a public phone. But we must be quick. If we're not back soon we'll be missed. I caught your husband looking at me strangely the other day. I think he suspects something."

"He can't possibly." Nadia spoke with more confidence than she felt. "There's nothing to suspect."

"Perhaps I'm not so good at hiding my feelings." He took her arm. "Come now, we must hurry."

They found a bank of pay phones at the railway station and Nadia obtained a number for her sister from enquiries. She dialled it with trembling hands, rehearsing what to say over and over in her head, only to be greeted by an answering machine. The sound of her sister's cheerful voice asking her to leave a message temporarily deprived Nadia of the ability to think. Anton was indicating the time with his hands and gesturing for her to hurry, so she assembled her thoughts and cleared her throat.

"Kara," she said, after two false starts, "this is Jasmine. Please, don't look for me. You'll be in terrible danger if you do. I know about Brett," she added, her voice catching, "and I don't wish for you to finish up the same way."

Replacing the receiver, the courage that had galvanised her into making the call deserted her and she fell sobbing into Anton's arms. His hands stroked her back, soothing her.

"There could be a way out of this," she said, "but I need your help."

"What do you want me to do?"

ELEVEN

I RUBBED MY chin, procrastinating as I tried to conceal my reaction from Kara. This thing was way too big for me but I doubted whether she'd be deterred by anything as trivial as a spot of international terrorism.

"Iranian links to Hamas are no secret," I said, jumping in before Kara could formulate a question.

"Impressionable youths with nothing to lose are prime targets for those with wider agendas."

"We think the Iranians want to divert Israel's attention away from their nuclear programme by keeping it focused on the Palestinian problem," Levine said. "And what better way to do it than having the Palestinians lobbing rockets into their territory at regular intervals."

"If Iran achieves her nuclear ambitions it could be catastrophic for the rest of the world," Monk pointed out. "Which is why Kalashov needs to be stopped."

"So why come to me? This is way out of my league." Why did I get the feeling that Kara and I were being manipulated? "I don't think we can help, if that's what you've come for."

Kara opened her mouth again but I silenced her with a look. No way were the powers that be going to use us as sacrificial lambs.

"Like I just said, Jasmine, or Nadia as we think of her, is the only weakness Kalashov has and therefore our only way of getting to him."

"So you want me to talk to her." Kara ignored my warning glare. "See if there's anything she can do to stop her husband." She frowned. "Hang on, though. Even if she doesn't know what he's up to he *is* still her husband. The Jasmine I remember was pretty loyal."

If Kara knew how her sister had played Ramsay—I still remembered the look on his face as he described their last afternoon together—she'd be forced to amend her fond recollections. Whatever, I wasn't going to stand by and let Kara get mixed up in this mess. But I kept my mouth shut and waited to see what Monk and Levine had in mind.

"No, possibly not, but I doubt she'd be able to resist the opportunity to get one over on Monika. Kalashov's daughter hates your sister, never speaks to her if she can avoid it, and does everything in her power to drive a wedge between Nadia and her father." Monk's expression underwent a subtle change, becoming speculative. "I think she has suspicions about her mother's convenient death. She adores her father and wouldn't blame him for it, even if common sense tells her he must have been involved. But she'd have no trouble placing the blame at your sister's door."

"But Jas wouldn't know anything about it."

"No, but if we could find out about her refusal to get involved with Kalashov whilst he was married to someone else, Monika must know about it too."

"So you want Kara to feed her sister some disinformation about Monika." I could hardly believe the gall of the two men. "Forget it!"

"Don't I have any say in this?" Kara asked.

"No, you don't."

"Yes, you do, Miss Webb," Monk said smoothly.

"Fine." She returned my glare before asking Monk, "What do you want me to do?"

"Your sister never goes out alone. If she isn't with her husband, then one of his minders always accompanies her."

"God, poor Jas!"

"She seems to be used to it."

"How can I get to her if she's never alone?"

"Your niece and nephew attend Chapter House Preparatory School, one of the best fee-paying schools in Weymouth. It takes day children and boarders but the Kalashov children don't board. That would make them too accessible to their father's enemies."

Kara shuddered and I placed a hand on her shoulder. I was unable to say quite why I was trying to reassure her, when I'd much rather she be too frightened to go through with whatever Monk had in mind.

"However, it's their sports day next Wednesday, and we happen to know Kalashov won't be in the country. He's booked on a commercial flight to Moscow tomorrow and not due back until Friday."

"But Jas won't be there alone?"

"No, she'll have one of her husband's goons with her, but he won't be too close. If you and Charlie were there posing as prospective parents checking the place out, there's a chance you'd be able to have a few words with your sister without anyone noticing. It's bound to be chaotic, and it's only natural for the adults at these things to boast to one another about their offspring's sporting prowess."

"Yes, that would work, wouldn't it, Charlie?"

"Have you forgotten what happened to your

brother?" I asked with ruthless disregard for her finer feelings.

"That was an accident."

"No, Miss Webb, I'm sorry but it wasn't."

"What do you mean?" Kara gasped and sank onto the end of the seating unit. I took her hand and felt it tremble in mine.

"Much as I need your help, I'm not prepared to send you in there blind. You need to know all we do before you make up your mind."

I didn't imagine for one moment that they'd reveal anything more than they had to in order to get Kara involved, but I didn't see any point in saying so. At least not yet.

"But the postmortem, it said—"

"Your brother really did meet your sister by accident that first time. We always have someone watching the Kalashov family and so we knew about their encounter. We approached your brother after that and told him what we've just told you. He agreed to help immediately. We arranged for him to deliver that boat to Weymouth and kept him informed of your sister's movements so he could accidentally bump into her again and set up communications with her." Levine scowled. "We had a man in the same bar as your brother that night. I'm sorry, Miss Webb, but two men were waiting outside the bar for Brett, and there was nothing our man could do to help him. He reported the incident and that's the last we heard from him."

"Christ!" I handed Kara my handkerchief, ran a hand through my hair and glowered at Monk. "This just keeps getting better and better."

"We suppressed the fact that your brother was murdered and issued a false postmortem report because we didn't want to alert Kalashov."

"But why? If he killed Brett—"

"We don't think he ordered the killing. He was out of the country at the time and it was down to his right-hand man, Viktor Barayev, to handle your brother."

"Charming!" I was having increasing trouble keeping my temper in check.

"Kalashov might not have liked his wife being in touch with her brother again," Monk said, "but he loves her too much to order his murder. He probably just told Barayev to make sure they didn't meet again."

"Why did my sister's husband not want her to have anything to do with her family?"

"We can only assume it's because if the connection became known it would be another way for his enemies to get to him." Monk smiled at Kara. "He's an excessively cautious and private man. With good reason."

"So," I said, "let's see if I understand what you're saying. Brett Webb was killed by someone in Kalashov's organisation, simply because he spoke to Jasmine, and you want Kara and me to go waltzing in there and do what exactly?"

"Try and make communication." Monk was doing a sterling job of ignoring my sarcasm. "The sports day is an ideal opportunity. Too good to pass up."

"Even if I was tempted, which I'm not, don't you think Kara might stand out a little?" I lifted a lock of her bright red hair and my eyebrows simultaneously.

"Well, that could be remedied. On a temporary basis, obviously."

"And you're forgetting something else. We're pretty sure we were being watched in Brighton, which is why we came to Cowes instead of going directly to Weymouth. If the *No Comment* turns up in Weymouth, how long do you think it would take Kalashov to be aware of our presence?"

"Well, obviously, you couldn't go in this boat but perhaps we could do a swap." He nodded towards the Sealine S42 sports cruiser moored on the outside of the pontoon almost directly opposite us. "It has a top speed of over twenty knots, so it would help you out of any tight spots you might get yourselves into."

"How comforting."

"We'll do it," Kara said, not looking at me.

"We won't do it," I countered. "What we will do is talk about it and let you know what conclusions we've reached tomorrow."

"That's all I ask." Monk stood up. "I know you're anxious about your sister, Miss Webb, and I know Charlie's furious with me for even suggesting you contact her. I can understand that. This is exceedingly dangerous, I won't try to pretend otherwise, and if it weren't for the fact that we're desperate to stop Kalashov, I wouldn't even have suggested it."

"Well, that's all right then." I ignored my ex-boss's outstretched hand, opened the salon door and ushered the men off my boat.

"We'll hear from you tomorrow then, Charlie," Monk said.

"You will indeed, but don't hold your breath."

Once they'd gone neither Kara nor I seemed in any hurry to speak. I used the time to think how best to persuade her that this crazy scheme of Monk's was a nonstarter.

"Well, at least we know now where Jas is," she said.

"Yeah, we'll send her a postcard."

Kara paced the small salon, treating my flippant comment with the contempt it deserved by ignoring it. "I'm going to do this. I have to, you must see that. Will you help me?"

"No. Sorry, sweetheart, but I can't stand by and watch you get killed, as well."

"But Interpol will protect us."

I snorted. "Like they protected your brother?"

She winced. "That was different. They're better prepared this time. Charlie, please!" She turned, eyes brimming with tears, in my direction. "We're so close and—"

"And what? Even supposing you get to talk to your sister, what are you going to say to her?"

"Well, I—"

"Do you really imagine she's been with this man all these years and doesn't know how he makes his money?" I spoke with deliberate scepticism, pretty sure Kara had images stored in her head of her big sister being manipulated against her will by a ruthless Russian Mafia boss. She needed to face facts. "I don't think so."

"It's possible though. Perhaps he's tried to protect her from it all. Mr. Monk did say he's giving his old ways up for her sake."

"Yeah, he did." But I wasn't sure I bought that. Something told me Monk was just saying that to persuade us to help him. I wouldn't put anything past him. "All right, so you manage to tell her in a school full of people that she's married to a murdering thug who was, directly or otherwise, responsible for your brother's death. Then what?"

"Well, Mr. Monk's offered us a fast boat. We could take her with us and—"

"Wake up, Kara! She can't just walk out of there and come back to Brighton with us. We both know how far the tentacles of her husband's organisation reach. Besides, I doubt if she'd leave her children behind." I caught sight of my eyes, flat and hard, in the galley mirror as they bored into her face. "Give it up, Kara, and get on with your life. There's nothing you can do to help your sister."

"Mr. Monk thinks there is. Why would he have followed us here otherwise?"

"Monk isn't thinking about you. He only cares about stopping Kalashov and is prepared to use you, to put your life in danger, in order to get to him."

"Yes, but I still think we ought to—"

"Sorry, Kara, but no dice." I locked the salon door with a finality that deterred further discussion and dimmed the cabin lights. "Let's turn in. Good night."

She swirled away from me and headed to her cabin without saying a word. I'd upset her, but she'd get over that in time. Far better she was annoyed with me than harbouring unrealistic fantasies about saving her sister.

I lay on my bed, fully clothed, staring at the framed picture of my mother on the wall opposite as I waited for Kara to use the head. I wondered, as I always did when looking at Mum's image, what path my life would have taken if she'd lived. If I hadn't been walking beside her when someone blew her brains out. The Mozart sonata she'd played in concert on that final night of her life drifted unbidden into my mind. I tried to tune it out, but it obviously wasn't going anywhere—a sure sign that I was stressed.

"What have I got myself into, Mum?" I said aloud, pushing myself off the bed. Kara's door had just closed, not especially quietly, so I guessed she'd finished with the facilities.

Sleep was a long time coming that night. What would Monk do when I told him we weren't prepared to do his dirty work? I experienced a moment's guilt at the prospect of disappointing him. But no more than that. James Bond I wasn't. I'd leave the resolution of world terrorism to those better qualified to handle it in exchange for living long enough to see my son grow up.

Something woke me. It took me a moment to recognise it as to the sound of Gil's tail thumping against the teak floor of my cabin. I sat up and rubbed my eyes, wondering if we had more uninvited guests.

"What is it, boy?"

"It's only me."

Shit! I should have anticipated something like this. If nothing else, I'd learned over the past few days that Kara was no quitter. Something as insignificant as being bumped off by a gang of Eastern European thugs was unlikely to stop her from reaching out to her sister. And it was obvious she'd do whatever she had to in order to enlist my help.

She stood in the open doorway to my cabin, wearing nothing more than an oversized T-shirt with the picture of a kitten on the front of it. I knew that was all she was wearing because the light from her own cabin was immediately behind her, shining straight through the flimsy garment. Jesus!

"What is it, Kara?" *Bloody stupid question, Hunter.*

"I can't sleep. Are you still awake?"

"I am now."

"Sorry." She shivered. "I'm scared."

"No need to be. We'll go back to Brighton tomorrow and you can get on with your life. No one will hurt you if you leave Jas alone."

"I can't." Her expression defied me to argue and right now I was all out of arguments.

The cold was making her nipples stand up, pert and inviting against the fabric of her shirt. Somehow I couldn't seem to drag my eyes away from them.

"Don't you understand? I can't just walk away from her when she might need me." She moved to the bed, her bare feet soundless on the teak, and knelt beside me. "But I can't do it alone. Please, Charlie, come with me to that school. I just want to talk to her once, make sure she knows about Brett and see what she has to say. That's all I want to do." Her face was now inches from mine, determination and strength of character reflected in her expression. "If she says she's happy, then I'll leave it at that. I promise."

"Like you promised you'd give up the search once we'd spoken to Sally and Ramsay."

"Come with me." She reached out and touched my face. Her fingers were cold but seared my skin in the places where they made contact with it. "Please."

Her lips met mine and I was powerless to resist. Just one kiss, then I'd send her back to her cabin. I told myself I'd earned that much. But somehow my arms closed around her without my being aware of it, and before I knew what was happening I was kissing her back. One of us pulled the covers aside. I can't remember which of us it was. Not that it matters. The result was always going to be the same.

She finished up in the bed beside me. The physical attraction between us had been building for days and what followed was a foregone conclusion. I always sleep in the buff and she only had to glance down to see for herself just how pleased I was to see her.

Her T-shirt finished up on the floor, her breasts finished up in my hands, Bill Evans's interpretation of "My Romance" flooded my mind, and the rest, as they say, is history. Not that it surprised me. As soon as I started thinking with an organ situated farther south than my brain, it was inevitable that I'd agree to go to that bloody school with her.

WHEN IGOR RETURNED to the house for dinner, Monika was with him for the third time that week. Nadia's suspicions were aroused because she could think of no reason for his daughter to be in Weymouth. The Spanish delegation had gone home and Monika's business was in Chelsea. Something was going on and Nadia was determined to find out what it was. She withstood her stepdaughter's spiteful glares across the dining table, adopting a drowsy demeanour and trying hard to treat her husband the way she always had since he'd started feeding her narcotics. As soon as the meal was over, he insisted that she go to bed. Suspecting he had business he wanted to discuss with Monika, Nadia didn't protest and allowed him to support her up the stairs.

"Get some rest, my darling." He brushed the hair back from her face with a gentle hand. "I have to talk to Viktor and Monika and some other people whom I'm expecting. It will take a long time I'm afraid." He sighed. "It's very tedious. I would much rather stay here and hold you in my arms until you fall asleep."

Nadia snuggled beneath the covers, holding the pill

Igor had given her under her tongue and hoping he'd leave again before it dissolved. "Good night," she muttered sleepily.

"I shall try not to wake you when I come to bed." He kissed her brow. "You're so beautiful, Nadia, that sometimes it takes my breath away. I wish I had time to show you how much I love you."

Nadia mumbled something deliberately incomprehensible, wondering if she dared slip the pill from her mouth and hide it under the pillow. No, it was probably better not to risk it.

"Soon, my darling," he said, sighing, "all this will be behind us and I can have you to myself. Always know, everything I do is for you. I have to go to Russia on Monday..."

"Monday?"

"Yes, darling, just for four days. When I come back it will only be another week or two and then we can start making plans to settle in Spain."

"I don't want you to leave me, Igor," she said, knowing it was what he wanted to hear.

"Sleep well, my love."

The moment he slipped through the adjoining door to his study, Nadia sat up and spat out the remnants of the pill into a tissue. She sped across to the bathroom, gargled and cleansed her mouth of all traces of the medication. Then she cleaned her teeth, just to be sure. Locking the main door to the corridor to ensure that no one barged in on her, she sat close to the connecting door and listened. The sound of several voices reached her but she strained to hear what they were saying. Unlike last time, they were speaking in muted tones and it was next to impossible for her to follow what was being said.

Giving up and trusting to luck that Anton was faring better, Nadia returned to bed, wondering how Monika could be involved in Igor's plans. Was it anything to do with his need to go to Russia, something he seldom did nowadays? If Monika wanted more girls for the agency, Igor had an established method of smuggling them into the country that didn't involve his direct input.

Nadia flushed with guilt when she thought about the women who worked for Igor's daughter. It had been one of her first jobs, before she became personally involved with Igor, to help bring them in. She'd readily agreed, thinking she was being useful. A couple of women handling an ordinary-looking forty-foot sailing boat excited little attention, and they were easily able to conceal two or three girls in the cabins until they made shore. When darkness fell, Igor's men came to take them away. Looking back, Nadia found it hard to credit her naïveté. She had believed Igor when he said the girls were being brought to England to start a better life. They would learn the language and get good jobs. Perhaps she believed it because the girls themselves did.

Monika spitefully told her the truth when it became obvious that her best efforts to keep her father and Nadia apart had failed. Nadia had been appalled to think of the bright, enthusiastic girls she'd met being forced into prostitution, and she tackled Igor on the subject. He'd been furious with Monika but overcame Nadia's objections by taking her to the elegant premises in Chelsea where Monika ran the operation. It certainly didn't resemble her mental image of a brothel. Igor explained it was merely a centre of operations from which dates were arranged for the girls.

Nadia spoke to a couple of the ones she'd brought in herself and they seemed happy enough with their situation. Igor told her the girls accompanied rich businessmen to dinners, the theatre and so forth. Anything else they chose to do was up to them, and there was no question of coercion. Nadia believed him because she wanted it to be true. She couldn't live with herself if she thought the girls she collected from Igor's luxury yacht anchored off the Italian coast were being forced to do anything they didn't want to.

She drifted in and out of sleep, aware of the soft hum of voices coming from next door but no longer trying to eavesdrop. She was woken from a deep sleep by the fierce rattling of the door to the corridor. Sitting bolt upright, she glanced at the digital clock and covered her mouth with her hand to prevent herself from crying out in terror. She'd ruined everything.

It was almost three in the morning. Igor thought he'd left her in a drug-induced sleep, and now the door was locked from the inside.

TWELVE

I AWOKE AT first light. Kara was still fast asleep beside me. The sight of her luscious body rekindled my ardour with a vengeance. She must know I wouldn't go back on my word to take her to that school, so I was interested to see if she'd still be as keen on the physical as she had been the night before.

She was.

We lay side by side afterwards, limbs entwined, her fingers twisting the hairs on my chest and tugging them gently.

"Is that your mother?" She nodded towards the framed photograph on the wall opposite.

"Yes."

"You look like her."

"Thanks, I'll take that as a compliment." I tensed, anticipating her next words.

"It was meant as one. What happened to her?"

"She died."

"Charlie!"

"She was murdered," I said after a long pause.

"Oh God, I'm sorry!"

"It's okay."

"No wonder you understood about Brett. You've been through the agony too. Did they get who did it?"

"No."

"Is that why you became a policeman?"

I raised a brow. She was the first person ever to ask me that question. "Yes. At sixteen I couldn't understand why the police seemed to have stopped looking for the people who'd taken away the centre of my universe." Answers were what I needed and I hadn't given up hope of getting them. Not even after all this time. "I thought if I became one of them I'd be able to carry on looking from the inside." I let out a mirthless laugh. "Much good it did me."

"What happened?" She was leaning up on one elbow, looking directly into my face, seemingly unaware of her breasts dangling over my chest, brushing against it. "Why would anyone want to murder your mother?"

I paused, waiting for my brain to shut out her intrusive questions and sympathetic expression. I couldn't handle sympathy in connection with my mother's death. To my surprise, instead of closing down and changing the subject, I found myself answering her.

"That's what I've been trying to find out for over twenty years now," I said, looking up at the ceiling. "My mother was a concert pianist."

"Ah, that's why you played. And let me guess. You gave up when your mother was killed and took to sleuthing instead."

Her refreshing lack of tact was cathartic. "Yeah, to my teacher's enduring regret." I chuckled. "He still hasn't given up trying to get me to play again. When he heard I'd left the force, he plagued me for days. Even the sight of my battered fingers didn't deter him. He helps out at a place for underprivileged kids and has one who shows great potential as a pianist. He wants me to help bring him on."

"You must have been quite a player for him not to have given up on you."

"Evidently he thought so, but he's wasting his time. I'm too old to make a career out of it, even if I wanted to. Music isn't part of my life anymore."

"Isn't it?" She grinned, like she thought she knew more about it than I did. "Then how come you sing jazz in the shower?"

"That's hardly the same thing."

"Of course it isn't." She kissed the end of my nose. "Tell me about this kid he wants you to help."

"Brendan found him on the Whitehawk estate, of all places. I took my life in my hands and went there to hear him play."

"And is the kid as good as Brendan said or is it all just a ploy to get you near a piano?"

"You have no idea! When I heard that scrawny black kid playing an old Bill Evans number on an acoustic piano, I got pretty excited. His jazz chord voicing isn't something you hear every day, his right hand playing octaves in lockstep with the left like it's no big deal. But, trust me, it is. The scrawny black kid responsible for producing that masterpiece in syncopation couldn't have been more than twelve years old. There was no music on the stand and I got the impression that he wouldn't have known how to read it even if it had been there."

"So, will he keep it up?"

"Well, I think he wants to. There's no hiding that sort of passion. But he's being pressed by his mates to join their gang and he's torn between doing what he wants to do and being accepted." I sighed. "For the first time I understand why Brendan was so upset when I quit. Perhaps that's why he invited me there. Anyway, I've offered to help with the kid if I can. If he doesn't exploit his talent, he'll finish up living like the rest of them up on that estate, and that really would be criminal in all senses of the word."

"So, you're back into music then."

"No," I said emphatically, "I'm not."

"Have it your way." She offered me a mischievous grin, as if she knew something I didn't. "But you still haven't said what happened to your mother."

I took a moment to decide whether or not to answer her. "She was soloing with a regional orchestra at the Fairfield Halls, Croydon, on the night she died. I was with her and so was Jarvis Goldsmith, her manager. I liked going along and soaking up the atmosphere, even though I'd decided classical music wasn't for me and that I preferred jazz."

"Did that upset your mum? I imagine she envisaged you following in her footsteps."

I considered the question. "No, I don't think it did. My father was the one pushing me in that direction. Mum rather enjoyed jazz too and thought I had more chance of making a living that way. She knew how hard it is for concert pianists to make the grade."

"A pragmatic lady then."

"Yes, she was. She believed that children should find their own way. Unlike my father, she had no intention of achieving her own ambitions vicariously through me."

"Which is what your father was doing?"

"Yeah." I spoke with finality. It seemed I was ready to talk about Mum but no way was I getting onto the minefield that was my father. "Mum played Mozart the night she died." I closed my eyes and let both the haunting melody of the sonata and the memories I usually blocked out flood my mind. "There was something about her performance that made me sit up and take notice, some edge I suppose I'd not been astute enough to notice before. It was as though some secret was inspiring her. Anyway, I obviously wasn't the only one to pick up on it because she took six curtain calls."

"What happened after that?"

I didn't realize my words had trailed to a halt. Obviously I was subconsciously debating whether or not to tell her more. I glanced in Kara's direction. Her eyes, soft with sympathy, and the gentle feel of her fingers dancing over my chest, decided me.

"We left the concert hall at about ten thirty by the stage door. We were in a gaggle with the orchestra, who were getting onto buses. The three of us were going to walk the short distance to East Croydon station and were just saying our goodbyes when a scooter screeched along beside us and the pillion opened up with a gun."

"My God!" She covered her mouth with a hand.

"Jarvis was closest to the gunman, with Mum next to him. Being on the inside probably saved my life," I said in a matter-of-fact voice. "Jarvis was hit in the shoulder and Mum had her brains blown out all over me."

I could see she was shocked, both by what had happened and the bland voice in which I'd related the incident, but none of the inadequate expressions of sympathy I'd come to loathe, and which usually prevented me from speaking about my mother's murder, were forthcoming. Instead, Kara merely rested her head on my shoulder and sighed. I felt her tears sliding onto my chest and knew I'd confided in one of the few people who actually understood how I felt.

"There must have been a murder enquiry."

"Of course. But how many random shootings can you think of that have been solved? Unlike in crime novels, unless the perpetrators are known to the victim, it's virtually impossible to track them down. Trust me, I know about what I speak."

"Was it random?"

"The police thought so. Wrong place at the wrong time, and all that." I wasn't about to tell her that the gunman was reportedly a hit man hired to kill an Iranian dissident, a lady similar in height and appearance to my mother, who played third violin in the orchestra. There was such a thing as information overload.

Monk knew, of course, which is probably why he'd told me about the Iranians being Kalashov's paymasters, hoping I wouldn't be able to resist having a dig back. It irked me to acknowledge he was right. Kara's seductive methods were only part of the reason why I'd agreed to go to Weymouth with her.

"They were unable to find any reason why anyone would want to kill either my mother or Jarvis," I said.

"Why did you leave the police force when you were still so young?"

"Disillusionment about the way the job was going. All that paperwork, unrealistic targets and pressure to meet them. And then my marriage broke up, my uncle died a year later and left me this boat, and it seemed like the ideal time to get out and try something else."

"How long ago was that?"

"Six months. And I was forty at the time, to save you asking."

She giggled. "Ah, the old midlife crisis. That would account for the Harley."

"Wash your mouth out, wench!" I tickled her into submission.

"How did your father take your mother's death?" She gulped. "Oh God, I can't believe I asked that question. Sorry, that was insensitive."

"Actually, it wasn't. My parents met when Mum started making a name for herself. He played violin for a second-rate regional orchestra she toured with for a while. Dad wasn't half the musician Mum was but love blossomed, as they say, and they married. Dad gave up the orchestra and became Mum's manager—"

"But I thought you said—"

"I came along late in their lives. Dad wasn't much of a manager. He didn't have the necessary charisma, wasn't thick-skinned enough to take the rejections, and was jealous of any male who spoke to Mum, which didn't exactly help. So when I was born Dad was cast in the role of babysitter and Mum got herself a new manager."

"Did your father resent being demoted?"

"I think there was a lot of tension between them. They argued a lot. He was jealous of Mum's talent and success. But not to the extent that he'd arrange to have her killed."

"And her new manager was the man who was with you when she died?"

"Yes. She'd known Jarvis for ages. He'd tried to entice her away from Dad, managerially speaking, and when he eventually did so her career took an upward turn almost overnight."

"Which couldn't have done much for your father's bruised ego."

"No, I guess not, but when I showed some musical ability Dad invested all his interest in me. Made me his project, if you like. When Mum died he wanted me to carry on playing the piano like nothing had happened, if you can believe it." I felt myself scowling. "He didn't seem to think having my mother's brains splattered all over my face would affect me in any way."

"Not exactly the empathetic type then."

"You could say that. Anyway, I rebelled and haven't touched a keyboard since."

"That's terrible! Your father's attitude, I mean, not your rebellion. Didn't anyone get you professional help, after what you'd been through?"

"It was offered but unbeknownst to me my father refused on my behalf, saying he'd look after me and we'd get over the loss together."

Kara stared at me in bald disbelief. "And I thought my father was insensitive."

"My father doesn't exactly qualify as the ultimate role model. We're not so very different in that respect."

"Does yours still live in Brighton?"

"No, when I wouldn't play the piano anymore and joined the police, he lost interest in me. He married a trombone player a year after Mum died. They run a B&B in Yorkshire."

"Was he suspected of involvement in your mother's death? Not that he could have had anything to do with it if he wasn't there, but isn't the husband always the first person the police look at?"

"Yes, they pulled his life apart but never found any reason to suppose he was involved. Not only was he not in Croydon at the time but he also had a cast-iron alibi. He was in a pub full of people and had dozens of witnesses to prove it."

"And you've been trying to find out what happened ever since." She smiled at me. "No wonder you understand what I'm going through. About Brett, I mean. I've always been able to sense a sort of empathy between us. Now I understand why."

"I suppose." I couldn't think of any reason to postpone the inevitable. "Monk will be waiting for us to get in touch. Are you sure you want to go through with this?"

"Absolutely! And you promised you'd help me." She looked at me intently. "Charlie, is something wrong?"

"I don't know. It's just that something doesn't feel right but I can't put my finger on what it is. I'm hardly an expert on terrorism but it all seems a little too trite. How come Monk knows so much about what your sister's husband is supposedly about to do?"

"Charlie, he's involved with Interpol. They must have ears to the ground, informants everywhere."

"And a better way to get on the inside than sending lambs like us."

"You heard what he said about that."

"Yes, I heard." I sat up, trying to arrange my thoughts into some sort of coherent order without the distraction of her delectable body draped all over mine. "But this is big, Kara. It's risky, and with so much at stake it ought to be handled by specialists, not you, me and a soppy dog."

"Perhaps they won't suspect ordinary people like us."

I didn't bother to say what I thought of that suggestion. "Is it feasible to expect your sister to spill the beans? She's been married to the man for years and must feel something for him."

"If she knows he's responsible for Brett's death, who knows what she'd be prepared to do? Besides, there's only one way to find out."

"Yeah, if you insist."

"Come on, Charlie, think positive. Let's see Monk now, decide how we're going to play it and take it from there."

The voice of reason. "Yes, ma'am!"

"The shower's mine first." She threw back the bed-clothes and made a dash for it.

"There's room for two."

"And you'd know that, would you?"

"Sure." I overtook her and switched on the taps. "I designed the room myself."

She rolled her eyes but took no persuading to join me under the hot jets of water.

AN HOUR LATER Monk and Levine presented themselves on board, loaded down with a bagful of croissants and fresh orange juice. I was aware of Monk scrutinizing us carefully. I doubted whether the change in our re-lationship—Kara's swollen lips and a certain light in her eye—escaped his notice. He half-smiled but wisely refrained from comment.

"Good morning," he said. "I trust you both slept well."

I scowled at him and got straight down to business. "Against my better judgement we'll go to that bloody school and make contact with Kara's sister but, just so we're clear, that's as far as we're prepared to involve ourselves. This thing is too big for us."

"Thank you." Monk inclined his head towards us both. Kara, who was busy in the galley making coffee, merely smiled absently and told him he was welcome.

"When do you think we should leave?" I asked Monk.

"Well, the regatta starts today. Are you a member of the Island Sailing Club, Miss Webb?"

"Yes, and call me Kara."

"Okay, Kara, I think you and Charlie should make yourselves seen at the club today. Watch the racing and talk to as many people as possible so anyone watching can't fail to notice you."

"Is anyone watching?" I asked. "I thought I noticed a young gangly kid with dark hair."

"Yes, him and a couple of others."

"Yeah, I clocked those too."

"Glad to hear you haven't lost your touch." Monk took a bite of the croissant Kara placed in front of him. He was the only person I knew who could eat one without making a huge mess. I wanted to ask him how he did it but restrained myself. "I have a couple of people coming over today who'll take your place on the *No Comment*, just to be on the safe side, but I reckon after today the watchers will be called off."

"Let's hope you're right."

"We think we've noticed someone else watching the boat itself as opposed to you, so we'll know soon enough if he disappears," he said. I was impressed, not having seen anyone near the *No Comment* myself, but was damned if I'd say so. "If you take the Sealine, my couple will look after Gil and impersonate the two of you until you get back."

"Gil comes with us." I made it obvious from my tone

that the issue wasn't up for debate. I wasn't exactly sure why I was so insistent but something told me a large dog, even if he was a gentle giant, might come in useful at some point.

"As you wish." Monk must have realized how little provocation it would take for me to back out. "Can we rustle up another dog who looks like Gil?" he asked Levine.

"Shouldn't be a problem," he said nonchalantly.

"See to it then." He turned back to us, handing me an invitation to the sports day at Chapter House school, together with directions to the establishment. "You will be Mr. and Mrs. Christopher Higgins. You have a five-year-old son, James, whom you are thinking of enrolling at the school at the start of the new year."

I scowled at him again. "You seem to have arranged everything. What if we'd said no?"

He shot me an amused look that told me he'd known that wasn't going to happen. "I like to be prepared, Charlie," he said, taking another bite of his croissant.

"How do we keep in touch with you?"

He handed me a mobile phone. "This is a pay-as-you-go so it's untraceable. My number is programmed into it under 'George'." I raised a brow, since that wasn't his name. "Levine is under 'Joseph'. You'd better leave your own mobiles with me when you go, along with your credit cards and anything else that might reveal your true identities. Just in case."

I grunted, resisting the temptation to ask in case of what. Sometimes it was better not to know.

"Here's some money and a few bits and pieces to back up your new identities." He handed me an envelope stuffed with cash. "Not for a moment do I imagine you'll need them but better safe than sorry, what?"

"What exactly do you want me to say to Jasmine?" Kara asked.

"Whatever you say, it will have to be done very carefully. Don't forget she'll have one of her husband's men standing guard over her." Monk rubbed his chin. "Merely get close to her, let her see who you are and try to find out if she knows about your brother's murder. Other than that, I'll have to leave it to you to decide how much more it's safe to say in that environment. Hint, if you can, that her husband was involved in Brett's killing and see how she takes it." He spoke to Kara but his eyes rested upon me. "The vital thing is to establish a means of communication. A phone number where you can reach her, an arrangement for her to call you, anything at all."

"We'll see what we can do," Kara said.

"There are some wigs in this bag for you to try on, Kara. Choose one and wear it all the time, even when out at sea. And when at the school remember to wear sunglasses, both of you, and hats, if possible. If you speak to Mrs. Kalashova for long it will be noticed, and the less recognizable you are the better if will be for you both."

Kara shivered and I instinctively reached out a hand to cover hers.

NADIA TREMBLED AS her husband rattled the door handle. How could she have been stupid enough to leave it locked? He would be suspicious of her now, and she'd be given even less freedom than she currently enjoyed.

"Nadia, Nadia, are you all right?"

She detected underlying fear in her husband's voice and wondered if she ought to answer him. If she'd really swallowed her pill, would the racket he was making have woken her? She wasn't sure but settled for mumbling something and curling into a tight defensive ball. The sound of several pairs of feet rushing down the corridor outside reached her ears. Some of Igor's men had come to see what the problem was. The rattling stopped. An exchange of rapid-fire Russian preceded the connecting door to Igor's study flying open. She was aware of several people looming over her but kept her eyes firmly closed, concentrating on keeping her breathing even. She heard Igor quietly dismiss his men. Then his hand touched her shoulder and shook it gently. She opened her eyes and blinked at him, hoping she looked sleep-disorientated when in fact she was now wide awake.

"Igor, what's wrong?"

"Are you all right, my darling?"

"Mmm, sleepy."

"Why is the door locked?"

"Door, what door?" She shook her head, closed her eyes again and clasped her hands together under the covers to prevent them from trembling. Her heart was racing. Surely Igor must be able to hear its loud, irregular beat. "Come to bed, Igor."

"In a moment."

The tension had gone out of his voice. She heard him cross to the door in question and unlock it. Then he sat beside her on the bed and lifted the house phone. He spoke in Russian to whoever answered it. Probably Viktor, who never seemed to sleep. He asked if anything unusual had happened during the evening, to which he obviously received a negative reply. Had anyone been near his wife's room? No again. Had anyone been absent from their posts for any reason? Nadia's heart missed a beat when she heard the mention of Anton's name. He had supposedly been working online for Igor but had left the library twice. She breathed a sigh of relief when Igor concluded he must have gone for a smoke. As a purist he never smoked anywhere near his beloved computers.

But Nadia knew the real reason Anton had left the library was to try to overhear what had been going on in Igor's study. She knew because she'd asked him to do it. Her blood ran cold at the thought of his narrow escape. Of what Viktor would have done to him if he'd been caught eavesdropping. And all because she forgot to unlock a bloody door!

"I must have locked the door myself as a precaution before I went into the study," Igor said quietly into the phone, "and forgot doing it." He paused, listening to something Viktor said to him. "No, that's impossible, I gave her a pill myself. Besides, why would she? But be extra vigilant, Viktor, I don't like irregularities, especially now."

He hung up and Nadia could hear him shedding his clothes. The mattress sagged as he climbed into bed beside her. Aware that she must divert him from thinking too deeply about Anton's unexplained absences, she rolled towards him, mumbled as though in her sleep and snuggled against his side. As she knew he would, Igor wrapped her in his arms, holding her close. What she hadn't expected was that he would kiss her when he supposed her to be asleep. She hadn't been prepared for his hands to start roving over her body either, like he actually intended to make love to her. What the hell should she do? Respond or continue to feign sleep?

Deciding that sleeping through his actions would be more suspicious than coming to, she forced her eyes open and tried not to cringe as his hands continued to explore.

"Igor?" She blinked in confusion. "What time is it?"

"It is late, my darling, but I want you." He made no apology for waking her. "Close your eyes and let me love you. Loving you is all I seem to be able to think about when my mind should be elsewhere. And it's all your fault. You have my heart, and for you I would move mountains."

Nadia trembled at the fierce sincerity behind his words. She closed her eyes as passion gripped her, wondering with the section of her mind still capable of rational thought what Monika had been doing at the house. Wondering what Anton had overheard.

Igor was inside her, hard and insistent. Nadia gave herself over to pleasure, opening her legs wider as she lifted her hips to meet him, unable to stem the tears that slid from the corners of her eyes. Her last conscious thought before she climaxed was what to do about the new life she was convinced was growing inside her.

THIRTEEN

EARLY MONDAY MORNING, before it was light, Kara, Gil and I sneaked across the pontoon and took control of the Sealine. Kara was sporting a fetching short dark wig. A man of about my height and build, a woman with long red hair, and a dog that bore an uncanny resemblance to Gil exchanged places with us on the *No Comment*. Where did Monk find these people—to say nothing of dogs—at such short notice?

The Sealine's engine room checks had been completed by Monk, who informed me the tanks were topped up with marine diesel and the fridge fully stocked. With no reason to hang about, Kara let the lines go and we were away. Quite what lay in store for us was anyone's guess, especially since I was convinced Monk hadn't told us everything he knew.

I sat at the double helm seat and steered the boat slowly out of the marina, careful to avoid the buoyed channel reserved for the ferries from Southampton. Kara tidied away the fenders and lines and then slipped up beside me, her face lifted to the wind. There was a slight chop as we cleared the mouth of the Medina river, but once we were clear of it I opened up the throttles, hoping it wouldn't blow up any more. This boat might have more speed than the *No Comment* but she was much less likely to take rough seas in her stride. Gil curled up on the floor of the cockpit, taking up most of the limited space as he settled in for a snooze.

The weather didn't get any worse and I settled into a cruising speed of fifteen knots. We reached Weymouth without incident by late afternoon.

"One of the few good things about a sports cruiser is the lack of height restriction," I said as we bypassed all the flybridge cruisers and sailing boats waiting for the bridge to lift, and radioed to the marina to say we'd arrived.

We were directed to a berth in the inner harbour, where Kara handled the lines with economical efficiency. Once I was satisfied the boat was secure, we took Gil for a much-needed walk. By the time we returned to the boat he'd acquainted himself with all the lampposts along the esplanade. I phoned Monk on the mobile he'd given me to let him know we'd arrived.

"Keep a low profile, Charlie," he advised. "Stay on the boat as much as possible tomorrow." He chuckled. "I'm sure you'll be able to think of a way to pass the time."

I snorted down the line. "Are you still in Cowes?"

"No." He didn't say where he was and I didn't ask. "But you know you can always reach me. Oh, and Charlie, there's some clobber for you to wear to the sports day in one of the lockers on the boat. Jeans aren't quite the thing for such an occasion and I wasn't sure if you'd have anything more suitable to hand."

I hung up before telling him exactly what I thought of him. But I took his advice to heart. Kara and I only left the boat that night and the following day to walk Gil. There was no point in inviting trouble.

"WHAT DO YOU think, Mrs. Higgins?" I paraded before her on Wednesday morning in the well-cut grey slacks and expensive polo shirt Monk had supplied. Why wasn't I surprised to discover that they were a perfect fit?

"Very impressive."

Kara, wearing a printed sundress held up by thin shoulder straps, gave me a twirl. Her feet were thrust into high-heeled sandals and she was wearing her short wig.

"Likewise." I kissed her and was chastised for removing half her lipstick. "Come on then, let's see if we can get a taxi to this school. Ready?"

My tone was calm and decisive. Last night she'd been trembling at the prospect of confronting her sister but seemed to be holding it together now. I figured she needed manly strength and an attitude of professional detachment from me. I'd do my best to deliver. Simultaneously we donned sunglasses and I handed Kara her floppy hat.

"This is very impressive." Kara's hand was in mine as the taxi deposited us at the doors to the school. She looked up at the façade and nodded her approval. "Wonder how much it costs to send a child here?"

"More than I'd ever be able to afford for Harry." I treated her to one of my carefully rationed smiles. When I recalled how we'd filled the time over the last day or so I figured she'd definitely earned it. "Perhaps I ought to consider a life in organized crime."

"Don't you dare!"

She was laughing when a well-dressed woman came down the steps to greet us, hand outstretched. Unsure how much, if anything, Monk had told the woman about our real reason for being there, we played the part of wealthy parents keen to find the best education for our overindulged little treasure. Kara described our imaginary son in detail, her voice full of maternal pride. It took me a moment to realize she was actually outlining Harry's physical characteristics. Clever girl! We'd discussed how to handle every aspect of our meeting with Jasmine but, incredibly, hadn't given any thought to how we'd get through this initial part of the fiasco. Other things on our minds, I supposed.

After a tour of the building we were invited to take tea with the principal and then, at last, left to mingle with the other parents enjoying the sports day.

"Where is she?" Kara stood on her toes, trying to locate her sister.

"Shush, have patience. We'll find her."

It took a quarter of an hour. The place was packed with well-dressed, well-spoken parents who refused to keep still, which meant we kept coming upon the same people time and again. A sharp intake of breath from Kara told me exactly when she saw her sibling. Jasmine Webb, dressed in a plain yet elegant lemon sundress, was seated beside a tall dark man whose eyes darted constantly about. She laughed as she watched a gaggle of young children sprinting in crooked lines down a grass track, cheering and clapping when a little redheaded girl was first to break the finishing tape. She turned to the man seated beside her, her face glowing. He too was applauding.

Taking advantage of the general mayhem when the race finished, we moved closer to Kara's sister and grabbed two seats that had just been vacated immediately behind her. Kara's hand was trembling as she extracted it from my grasp. Before I could stop her she reached forward and tapped her sister on the shoulder.

Inwardly I groaned. What the hell did she think she was doing? We'd discussed this a hundred times. Jasmine wasn't alone and we had to assume the man with her was loyal to her husband. As though confirming my fears, he glared at us when Kara touched Jasmine, and he half-rose from his chair. I met his eyes and smiled as benignly as I could, digging Kara hard in the ribs at the same time. But it was like she'd forgotten everything I'd told her.

"Jas," she whispered. "Jas, it's me, Kara."

I glowered at her but the damage was already done. *When you find yourself in a hole, stop digging.* I lowered myself in my seat, trying to look as nonthreatening as possible as I waited to see what happened next.

Jasmine started violently at the sound of her sister's voice and slowly turned 'round to look directly at her. Kara had at least retained her sunglasses and floppy hat but I could hardly believe what I was seeing when she reached up to remove the glasses.

"No!" I snatched her hand away from her face. "Leave them on."

"Sorry, Charlie, but I—"

"Is it really you, Kara?" Jasmine's face, at first full of uncertainty, broke into a beatific smile. Tears trickled from behind her dark glasses. "I can't believe it!" She dabbed at her eyes with a tissue. "How did you find me?"

"It's a long story."

Kara seemed too choked up to say anything more, and for a long minute the two women simply looked at one another.

"You shouldn't be here," Jasmine said. "It's not safe for you."

The man with Jasmine was following the exchange closely. She didn't appear to feel inhibited speaking in front of him, which I took to be a good sign. I nodded at him and he cautiously returned the gesture.

"I had to come. Where can we go to talk? There's so much to say."

"It's better to stay here, Kara, in a crowd," I said.

"Yes, I suppose." Kara bit her lip. I sensed her need to embrace her sister and have a good heart-to-heart, but even she appeared to realize that was out of the question. "This is Charlie Hunter." Great, so now she was revealing my true identity when we didn't even know how things stood between Jasmine, her husband and, more expediently, the guy with the mobile eyes. "He's been helping me to find you."

"Oh, so you're the policeman."

So she already knew who I was. I was stunned. Stunned, and worried.

She must have sensed it because she explained. "I heard my husband talking about you."

Was that supposed to make me feel better? "In what respect?"

"This is Anton," Jasmine said, ducking my question. "You can say anything in front of him."

Just as well, since Kara had already blown our cover.

"That's such a relief." Kara was crying and smiling at the same time. "I want to know everything that's happened to you since you left, Jas."

"Narrow your questions down, Kara," I said. "We don't have long."

"Do you know about Brett?" Kara's voice trembled.

Jasmine nodded, crying again. "Yes, I know."

"But you didn't ring or anything." When she didn't respond, Kara got impatient. "Come on, Jas, we know you've spoken to Mum often enough over the years. Didn't it occur to you that she just might want to hear from you at such a time?"

"It was difficult, I didn't...that's to say, I wasn't sure—" She threw back her head and sighed, leaving me with the impression that she was weighing her next words carefully. "I've made so many mistakes, and anything I said would only have made matters worse. At least by staying away I could protect you, Kara."

Kara looked confused. "How do you make that out?"

"You see, I think...well, I think perhaps Brett was murdered, and my husband's business associates might have had something to do with it." She twisted her hands together in her lap. "It's not safe for you here, Kara. I tried to tell Brett that and look what happened to him. If anyone other than Anton had been with me today, it would have been disastrous." Her voice caught. "You must leave at once and never come back."

"And what about you?"

"There's no escape for me."

"You'd stay with a man who possibly ordered our brother to be killed?" Kara stared at her, as though seeing her in a completely new light. "Why?"

Jasmine, tears in her eyes, nodded towards a nearby gaggle of children. "I stay because of them. If I ever decided to leave him, he'd never let me take the children with me."

The little girl who'd won the race barged up to Jasmine, sporting a gap-toothed grin. "I won, Mummy, I won!"

"So I saw." Jasmine's brittle expression softened as she pulled the girl onto her lap and smoothed down her wayward hair.

"Hello," Kara said.

"Hello," the child responded. "My name's Saskia, what's yours?"

"Kar—"

I kicked Kara's ankle. Hard.

"Ouch!" She glared at me and then caught on. "Oh yes, it's Karen." She smiled as she regarded her niece for the first time, her eyes suspiciously moist.

"Whose mummy are you?"

"Our son, James, doesn't go to this school yet, but he might start next term. Do you like running?"

Saskia nodded. "I won my race."

"Yes, I saw you."

"I wish Papa had been here to see me, as well," Saskia said peevishly.

Anton stiffened. "He is."

I grabbed Kara's hand to prevent her from turning 'round. "Meet us tomorrow morning," I hissed in Jasmine's ear, leaning in close as I stood up. "The Prince Regent Hotel."

"I don't know if I can."

"Then you'd better try because Kara won't leave until she gets some answers."

"Then you must make her."

"Don't think I haven't tried."

Jasmine looked at me and sighed. "All right, I'll come if I can but I'm not sure when I'll be able to get away." Her eyes darted towards her husband, who was almost upon them.

"I'll take a room there under the name of Harris," I whispered.

I grabbed Kara's hand and moved away as a well-built man with a full head of grey hair, wearing a superbly cut suit, walked up to Jasmine and kissed her.

"Igor," she said in a commendably calm voice. "What a lovely surprise. When did you get back?"

NADIA DIDN'T KNOW how she was able to face Igor at a time when she was feeling so emotionally drained. Kara's appearance had totally floored her, and she was overwhelmed with a whole raft of conflicting feelings. Her delight at seeing her sister again warred with very real fears for her safety and brought the whole nightmare of Brett's death flooding back. If anything like that were to happen to her feisty sister, it would all be her fault and she didn't think she had the strength to withstand another such tragedy. Kara had her handsome policeman to protect her but he'd be next to useless when faced with her husband's army of thugs.

IGOR HADN'T ENTIRELY convinced himself that he was responsible for the locked bedroom door and had ordered her to be more closely watched in his absence. Nikolay, produced from the same mould as Viktor, had accompanied them to the school and stationed himself outside. Igor had never considered it necessary for her to have two minders before, which implied that he was suspicious of her. Did he know that Kara was here? The thought turned her blood cold. He'd come home from Russia two days earlier than anticipated, which meant he could hardly have been in the country for more than a few hours before turning 'round and coming straight back to England. And now he'd caught her in close conversation with two strangers, which would not please him.

"WHO WERE THOSE people?" Igor asked her. Paranoid as always about her safety, he didn't encourage her to get too friendly with other parents at the school. He'd promised her that soon, when they left England, she'd be able to live a more normal life and develop a circle of friends.

But Nadia didn't delude herself. Theirs could never be a normal existence, and the only friends she'd ever be able to have would be those approved first by Igor.

"I didn't catch their names. They're thinking of enrolling their son in the school and were asking me if our children were happy here."

"I see." His smile didn't trouble his eyes. "I wonder why they chose to quiz you about the school. Surely the Head would have given them a tour."

"Yes, I dare say." Nadia shrugged. "But they happened to sit behind me and I suppose they wanted to know what a parent had to say." She took his hand. "Sometimes you're too curious about inconsequential things, Igor."

"Perhaps, but—"

"Papa, Papa!" Saskia's tone was accusatory as she jumped from foot to foot, desperate for his attention. "I won my race but you didn't see me."

Igor smiled, properly this time, and scooped his daughter into his arms. "Well, of course you won!"

"I was second in the high jump," Sergei pointed out.

"I'm very proud of you both. Now, come along, let's

have some tea and perhaps we'll find your new friends and you can introduce me to them."

Still with Saskia in his arms, Igor ushered Nadia and Sergei towards the school building. Anton, his expression brooding, fell into step behind them.

Nadia thought back to the person she'd once been and marvelled at her guilelessness. Never once had she doubted her ability to right all the wrongs in her world. After all, hadn't she kept the mighty Igor Kalashov dancing to her tune for months? Only now did she realize just what a hash she'd actually made of everything.

FOURTEEN

KARA FELL INTO the taxi beside me with a deep sigh. I slipped an arm 'round her shoulders, feeling awkward but knowing better than to try to find the words to comfort her. I'd always known that she'd come away from the confrontation with her sister with more questions than answers rattling about inside her head. What she needed to do now was work through her feelings without me sticking my clumsy oar in.

We got back to the boat and received an enthusiastic greeting from Gil. This tub was too small for a dog of his size to be cooped up in for any length of time. He bounded between us with scant regard for anything that came within range of his wagging tail, hoping, as always, for an energetic game of tug. Kara absently rubbed his ears with one hand and blew her nose on a piece of kitchen paper with the other.

"Thanks for not saying you told me so." She dashed at fresh tears with the back of her hand before they could get past the corners of her eyes.

I shrugged in a manner that suggested I understood. "It's something you had to do." I found a bottle of white wine in the fridge and opened it. "The sun has to be over the yardarm somewhere in the world," I said, handing her a glass.

"Thanks." She offered me a watery smile and

plonked herself down on one end of the small seating unit.

I sat at the other end and examined her face. "Well, you've seen her," I said, stating the obvious. "So how do you feel about it?"

"To tell you the truth, I'm not sure." She sucked in a long breath. "I've looked forward to the moment for so long that my mind went a complete blank when I was actually face-to-face with her. There was so much I wanted to say, so many questions I wanted to ask her, but when I actually got my mind into gear we'd run out of time." She took a large gulp of her drink and lifted her eyes to mine. "I suppose, most of all, I want to understand what made her act so dramatically but I'm no further forward in that respect than I was before I saw her."

"It was probably something to do with her argument with your father."

"Yes, but I still don't know what they fought about. Perhaps I'd be able to understand better if I did." She shook her head. "Face it, Charlie, most kids fall out with their parents at some point during their adolescence but find a way 'round the problem without running away."

I didn't reply. Not being able to set Kara straight about what I knew didn't make me feel good about myself.

She stretched her arms above her head and yawned. "It's all been one big waste of time."

She drained her glass and reached for the bottle. Whilst she refilled our glasses, I used Monk's mobile, called enquiries, obtained the number of the Prince Regent Hotel and booked a room for the following day.

"What are you doing?"

"You want to talk to you sister, don't you?"

Her expression was priceless. "You arranged something? Is that what you were whispering with Jas about?" When I nodded, she uncoiled her legs from beneath her and threw herself at me. "I get to see her again? Charlie, I don't know what to say. 'Thank you' sounds kind of inadequate."

"Don't thank me yet." I slid my arms 'round her. "It may come to nothing but I mentioned we'd be in that hotel tomorrow and she said she'd try to drop by. Nothing's definite but I have a feeling she'll make it."

"But why? Why put herself in more danger if nothing can come of it?"

"There probably isn't anything we can do to help her, but I thought you'd appreciate the opportunity to talk to her for a while without anyone else around." I kept my tone deliberately offhand. "Who knows, perhaps there's something she can tell us that'll help us to—"

"For Monk, you mean? You're worried about those weapons."

"I don't give a flying fuck about Monk. I'm more concerned about your sister."

"Thank you." She kissed my lips and then paced the small cabin in a state of high agitation. Not easy, given the restricted space and Gil taking up most of it. "I think seeing her and yet not being able to be with her was worse than not seeing her at all." She stopped in front of me and touched my shoulder. "You were right about that."

"Well, if you ask me, she needs our help, whether she realizes it or not. I shall be in that hotel room tomorrow, and if your sister shows up, there's a few questions I want to ask her myself."

"You know I'll be there with you," she said with a flash of her old spirit. "But I don't see what good it will do. You can hardly expect her to betray her own husband."

"Did you notice her expression when she said she thought her husband's business associates might have been involved in your brother's murder? My instinct tells me the only thing stopping her from shopping him is the thought of losing her children. If we can somehow convince her that Monk can extract her and the kids and keep them safe, then I reckon she'll go for it."

Kara's face lit up. "But what if she doesn't know anything?"

"She's bound to. She must have heard stuff even if she doesn't realize its significance."

"But is it safe for her? That man who was with her, can we trust him?"

"Oh yes."

"How can you be so sure?"

"Come on, Kara. Didn't you see the way he looked at your sister?"

She shook her head. "No, I didn't take much notice of him."

"Well, if you'd seen the way he looked at Jasmine, you'd know that he's in love with her and will do anything to get her away from Kalashov."

"Oh."

The mobile rang, sounding unnaturally loud in the small cabin. I knew without checking the display that it would be Monk.

"How did it go?" he asked.

"We made contact but Kalashov appeared before we could say much."

"Kalashov? But that's impossible. He's in Russia."

"Not anymore he isn't."

"But we had people watching him all the time. I had no idea he'd left."

"Well, he must have known he was being watched and given them the slip for reasons of his own. Anyway, he can't have been in Russia for long so whatever he had to do there must have been pretty straightforward."

"I'll check out how he got back. He couldn't have travelled under his real name or we'd have been alerted."

Monk's inability to keep one man under surveillance didn't exactly fill me with confidence but I was in too deep now to turn back. "There's a possibility, but no more than a possibility, that we might see Jasmine again tomorrow," I said. "With Kalashov around, it won't be so easy for her to get away."

"Where?"

"In the shopping centre."

Don't ask me why I didn't tell him the truth. Perhaps, if he knew we were meeting in private, I suspected that he'd gate-crash and throw his weight around. My only interest was Kara, not world peace, and if Jasmine was frightened off then we'd probably never get another opportunity. Time enough to involve Monk if she confirmed she was looking for a safe out.

"What time and where?"

"Nothing definite. We only had a moment to suggest the plan before Kalashov appeared. We'll hang around in the morning, and if she appears we'll let you know what she has to say."

A long pause. We both knew I was lying but he decided not to push the issue. "All right. Fair enough." He paused again. "What were your impressions of her?"

"That she's disillusioned with Kalashov. But she's scared for herself and her kids. Leave it to us and we'll be in touch."

I cut the connection before he could argue the toss and refilled our glasses for the third time.

"Let's eat out tonight," I suggested. To hell with Monk's over-elaborate precautions.

THE NEXT MORNING we took Gil for an extra-long run. We couldn't take him to the hotel with us, and I didn't know how long he'd have to stay inside the small boat, so it only seemed fair to lavish some attention on the poor brute. At about ten o'clock we set off in the direction of the shopping centre.

"The hotel's in the other direction, Charlie." Kara pointed over her shoulder.

"Don't look now but we've probably got company."

She giggled. "It's like being in a spy film."

I took her hand as we sauntered along. "Come on," I said when we reached the shops. "Let's indulge in a spot of retail therapy with Monk's money."

Call it childish, but we did something I'd seen in films and have always wanted to try for myself. We went into a department store, bought clothes in different colours and styles from the ones we'd walked in wearing, went to the toilets, changed into our purchases and strolled out individually through different doors.

I watched Kara from across the road as she wandered into the Prince Regent and took a seat in the lounge. I let ten minutes pass by, during which time

I saw nothing to excite my suspicions, and then entered the hotel myself. I registered, paid with more of Monk's cash and took a key to a room on the second floor. Kara joined me at the lift. The second-floor corridor was empty and we made it to the room without anyone else observing us as far as I could tell.

"And now we wait," I said, putting the Do Not Disturb sign on the door.

Kara giggled. "They probably think we're here for a dirty afternoon."

I waggled my brows at her. "That's not such a bad idea."

"You're insatiable."

"You're the one that started on the seduction routine," I reminded her, not very gallantly.

"Humph, you didn't take much seducing."

Chuckling, I switched the television on and we both tried to concentrate on some inane daytime programme. Over two hours later our nerves were stretched to the breaking point. I was starting to think Jasmine wasn't coming when there was a gentle knock at the door. A glance through the spy hole revealed the man who'd been with her the day before. He looked better-built and more menacing in the narrow corridor but didn't have a monopoly on tough-guy attitudes.

I went on the offensive, giving as good as I got when I opened the door by staring him down. I felt mildly satisfied when he looked away first and ushered Jasmine into the room ahead of him. She and Kara looked at one another for a protracted second before stepping forward at exactly the same time and hurtling into one another's arms. I locked the door behind Anton and invited him to sit down.

"Thanks for bringing her," I said to him. "It means a lot to Kara."

"We can't stay for long. It's very dangerous."

"I didn't think we'd be able to come at all," Jasmine said, extricating herself from her sister's arms but still holding her hand and smiling through her tears. "But my husband received a phone call and dashed off to London."

I open the minibar and found a couple of small bottles of wine. Anton refused but I reckoned the rest of us could use a little Dutch courage. I'd readdress the thorny question of my increased alcohol intake when this was all over.

"All these years, Jas, and never a word from you." Kara spoke with curiosity rather than accusation in her tone. "Can you imagine how that made us feel?"

"I know, darling, and I'm sorry." She patted Kara's hand. "Brett said the same thing but, believe me, it was for the best."

"What happened? Why did you go? I've never been able to work that out."

"You don't know?" She appeared surprised.

"No, we know you argued with Dad but not what about."

Jasmine opened her mouth. I got the feeling she was about to bare her soul, which would be a seriously bad idea. Kara was too emotionally fragile to handle the truth. I caught Jasmine's eye and shook my head. She nodded once and simultaneously took a sip of her drink.

"I was just rebelling," she said. "I'd met a man he didn't approve of—"

"We know about Ramsay."

She blinked back her surprise. "You do?"

"Yes, Charlie's very good at persuading people to tell what they know."

"I'm sure he is." She transferred her attention to me for a moment, openly assessing me, before returning to her conversation with Kara. "Well, I just couldn't stand it any more. I was getting pressure from all sides. From Dad to concentrate on my college work and get good grades, from Colin to move in with him." She shrugged. "Everyone else seemed to think they knew what was best for me, and I was getting fed up with it. Things changed when I started crewing on the *Laissez-Faire*."

"Yes, we know about that too."

"Well then, I guess you've been able to piece the rest together for yourselves." Her eyes roamed 'round the anonymous hotel room. "Igor saw me on his boat and invited me to dinner. I'd been warned by some of the others that he probably would. He was charming and rich and exceedingly well-mannered but…"

"But it didn't happen?" suggested Kara when her sister's words trailed off.

Jasmine sighed. "No, not at once. I knew I wouldn't be able to wangle it because of Dad. I would have died if he'd seen us together and started laying down the law, so I thought it better just to decline." A half smile illuminated her face. "What I didn't know at the time was that nobody says no to Igor. By turning him down I'd inadvertently increased his interest in me. And the more I rebuffed him, the more determined he became to get me to change my mind."

"And when you still held out against him, he resorted to threatening you?" I said.

"Yes. I knew he was dangerous but that wasn't an

issue then. To a seventeen-year-old it seemed glamorous that he always had minders with him. It kind of added to his attraction. He kept sending me gifts, which I returned unopened." She giggled. "By all accounts he was furious. Anyway, eventually he made veiled threats against you, Kara—"

"Me!" Kara looked stunned. "But I'd never met him."

"No, but he found out about me, about my family, and knew where my weaknesses lay. He's very good at that sort of thing. Anyway, I agreed eventually to have dinner with him, just to get him off my back." She smiled. "He was charming and attentive, took me somewhere exclusive and ruinously expensive. Everyone there rushed to do his bidding and, well, I admit he made me feel special."

Kara smiled. "I can imagine."

"Anyway, my capitulation coincided with my argument with Dad, and when Igor offered me a job it seemed like the ideal solution to my problems. Ramsay was pushing me for commitment, my home life was a mess, and I was being offered the opportunity to do what I loved the most."

"Working on a boat."

"Yes, even if it was a gin palace without sails."

"But you could have said, Jas." Kara's expression was a combination of understanding and condemnation. "Just leaving us like that. It was cruel."

"I'm sorry, Kara." Jasmine squeezed her sister's hand. "I can see that now and, believe me, if I had my time over again—"

"Did you actually go to London when you first left?" I asked.

"Yes. Igor has a woman who runs his office in London. She was responsible for taking me under her wing, giving me somewhere to live and so on. I wouldn't have gone otherwise. I didn't want to be seen as Igor's bit on the side. Which I wasn't, by the way. I knew he'd soon lose interest in me, like he did all the others, now he had me where he wanted me. But I refused to get on in his organisation through any means other than my own skill."

"But he didn't lose interest?"

"No. I wouldn't go to bed with him, you see. He was a married man with a daughter who watched him like a hawk and reported all his activities to her mother. I might have gone with Igor just to spite Monika, but I have this thing about not breaking up families."

"But his wife died and he wore you down."

She looked down at her hands. "Yes."

"Were you aware what he did for a living?" I asked.

She shot me an exasperated look. "Well, I knew he was no Boy Scout, if that's what you mean. You have to bear in mind he's ex-KGB. When I met him the whole Soviet bloc was falling apart and it was every man for himself. And I was still only eighteen when we got married. I was swept along with it all, and I'm not ashamed to say I was seduced as much by the glamorous lifestyle as I was by Igor." She looked off into the distance, a reflective expression on her face. "I gradually found out a few things, but he protected me from it as much as possible. As I didn't really want to know, it was easier just to pretend that I didn't."

"Is that why you changed your name?" Kara asked.

"Yes, he said it would help to protect my family."

"I don't understand why he's so paranoid about you seeing us," Kara said.

"He's obsessive about me." Jasmine's modest tone made it apparent that she couldn't understand why. As a man I only had to look at her and his reasons were immediately obvious. Kara was good-looking but her older sister was in another league. "Even now, after all this time, he's still like that about me, and his enemies, of whom he has any number, are aware of it. That's why I can't ever go anywhere alone, in case they get to him through me. If they knew my true identity, then my family would also become a target."

"A target for his enemies, not for him," Kara said, a tremble in her voice.

"Yes, I don't understand that myself."

I did. Brett Webb had, just like us, been acting for Monk. With all his connections, Kalashov would have known that. How long would it be before he rumbled us? If he hadn't already.

"Is your husband aware that you know of his involvement in your brother's death?" I asked.

"No, but I did question him about it and ever since then he's been feeding me pills that make me drowsy."

Kara bridled. "Why on earth would he do that?"

"Presumably so I don't ask him any more awkward questions. And he's guarding me more closely than ever."

Kara peered closely at her sister's face. "You don't look drowsy."

"No, because I realized what he was doing and stopped taking the pills. I'm all right during the day. He makes sure I'm escorted everywhere and his men won't tell me anything. But he feeds me the pills at night—"

"So that when you're alone with him you can't force the issue."

She shrugged. "I guess. And now I have to pretend to be drugged up even though I'm not."

"That's awful." Kara regarded her sister with a genuine expression of sympathy. "Why on earth is he doing it?"

"I'm not sure." She wrinkled her brow. "But something's going on, that much I do know. He's never usually away as much as he has been recently. I think he wants to keep me quiet until it's all over so that I don't distract him."

"Something to do with supplying arms to terrorists?" I suggested mildly.

She didn't bat an eyelid. "I don't know anything about that." But the suggestion clearly didn't surprise her.

"No." The sound of Anton's voice startled us all. It was the first time he'd spoken since entering the room, and I'd almost forgotten he was there. "It has nothing to do with arms."

"Then what?" I asked.

"Have you ever heard of the Russian Business Network?"

"Can't say that I have."

"They are a multifaceted cybercrime organisation."

"Ah, I see." And I was beginning to. "Identity theft for resale, hosting illegal or dubious businesses, that sort of thing."

"Yes, and child pornography, spam, even phishing."

"Phishing?" Kara looked baffled.

"Yes, you know, e-mails from far-flung African countries offering you a percentage of millions of dollars if you give them your bank details so they can transfer the money to you." I rolled my eyes. "You'd be astonished how many people fall for it."

"Why would Jas's husband get involved in that sort of thing?" Kara asked.

"Yes, why?" But far from looking as confused as she sounded, Jasmine appeared to be struggling to contain a smile, as though a great weight had been lifted from her shoulders. Her reaction wasn't what I'd been expecting, and it got me wondering.

"If he's involved, I'd say it's because it's almost impossible to trace the hosts." I looked at Anton and he nodded. "It can all be controlled through obscure locations and there's no hardware involved. Not like with the supply of weapons or drugs."

"Mr. Kalashov has gradually been giving up all his other activities in order to concentrate on this. He sees more profit for less risk."

"Anton, why didn't you say something about this before now?" Jasmine looked at him in bewilderment but her eyes were sparkling, as though a lot of things she'd been unable to fathom suddenly made sense.

"It was better you didn't know."

"Why did he go to Russia this week then?" I asked Anton. "And why did he return sooner than planned?"

"This I don't know. I merely look after his legal business affairs and don't concern myself with anything else. It's better to know as little as possible about what he does."

"Where does he run his cybercrime organisation from? Do you know that?"

"I think his daughter controls it."

"Monika." Jasmine opened her eyes wide. "But she just runs an escort agency."

Anton smiled acidly. "She's a very intelligent woman, more than capable of doing two things at once."

"That must be why she's been meeting so often with Igor recently," Jasmine said. "Now it's all starting to make sense."

It sure was and I didn't like it one little bit. I knew now what I'd suspected all along. Monk had deliberately lied in order to get me involved, and if there was one thing I couldn't abide, it was being manipulated.

"Would you be willing to talk to some people I know?" I asked Jasmine, playing into Monk's hands in spite of myself. "They could protect you and your children in return for any information you could give them."

Jasmine emphatically shook her head. "No one can protect me from Igor. Anyone who crosses him, especially me, can expect no mercy. He rates loyalty above everything."

"Yes, but—"

"He has eyes and ears everywhere." Jasmine's voice trembled. "It's impossible to evade him for long. Besides, even if I did manage to disappear, he'd still be able to get to me through Kara and Mum."

She was right but I couldn't leave it without giving it one last try. "Look, there's no harm in just talking to these people. If I can arrange it for tomorrow, will you at least hear them out?"

Jasmine thought about it for a long time and finally nodded her head. "Very well. Anton and I will try to come here at the same time tomorrow but we can't guarantee anything."

She abruptly stood up, looking far from happy with the arrangement, kissed her sister, nodded to me and left the room in Anton's wake. I gave her fifteen minutes to get clear of the hotel and then rang Monk. He answered immediately.

"The Prince Regent Hotel, room 207," I told him.

Monk hadn't admitted to being in Weymouth but I wasn't the slightest bit surprised when he and Levine knocked at the door less than ten minutes later.

NADIA'S HANDS WERE trembling as she followed Anton from the hotel. Her brave, beautiful sister was putting her life on the line to try to help her, and Nadia knew she didn't deserve such compassion. She also knew Kara's efforts were doomed to failure. She was beyond help. Charlie Hunter seemed to think there was a way out for her and her children but he was underestimating her husband's influence. Igor would find them no matter where they went.

"Come." Anton gently steered her towards the car. "We've been out for too long. Olga spies on you and tells your husband everything."

"I know, but it doesn't matter." She smiled through her tears. "Thank you for taking me to see Kara, Anton."

He started the engine but didn't move away from the curb. "You know I could never deny you anything." He took her hand and kissed the back of it. "But I don't think we should go to that hotel again. You're right, there's nothing that can be done to extricate you from your marriage, and I'd rather endure the agony of seeing you with him than put your life at risk."

"Oh, Anton!" Nadia was overwhelmed with the desire to kiss him but resisted the temptation. Igor really did have eyes everywhere. "Perhaps it will be better when we go to Spain."

"I won't be going to Spain with you."

"But you must. You can't leave me now."

"I have no wish to leave you, Nadia. It's your husband. He told me yesterday that when you move to Spain, I will be needed at the escort agency."

"Helping Monika." She paused, totally confused. "But why?"

Anton shrugged. "I don't know."

"Why is he doing this now? You've always been with us. I like having you with me. The children are comfortable with you." Nadia, in a highly agitated state, absently rubbed her stomach. Talking of her children unconsciously made her consider the welfare of the one she was now carrying. "I'll talk to Igor about it."

"No! That will only make him suspicious."

Nadia grasped his arm. "But there must be something we can do. Anton, please, I can't cope without you."

He looked at her for a long time, considering her words, making Nadia regret the emotional blackmail she was employing. She ought to put Anton's safety before her own and not interfere with Igor's plans. She could sense the battle raging inside his head. To keep her safe or risk everything on the outside chance of their finding a way to be together.

"All right." He ran a finger down her cheek and arrested the progress of a tear. "We'll meet with your sister's friends tomorrow but I don't think there's anything they can do to help us."

FIFTEEN

I OPENED THE door to Monk and Levine and they stepped inside. Monk looked around, obviously hoping to find Jasmine still with us.

"She's hiding in the bathroom," I told him, deadpan.

"Shame she's left." He seemed unconcerned by my sarcasm. "I should have liked to talk to her myself. Did you get anything from her that might help us?"

"With her husband's *terrorist* activities?"

"Ah, I see." He nodded several times, not quite able to hide his satisfaction at the turn our conversation had taken. "So she knows what he's really up to then?"

"And so have you, all along." I stood up, towering over Monk. He'd arranged his long limbs as elegantly as always in an upright chair beside the window, and my posturing was having no discernible effect upon him. His sangfroid attitude irritated me and I made no effort to keep the anger out of my voice. "Why did you lie to me, guv?"

"Oh, you know how it is, Charlie." He flapped a hand as though it was a stupid question. "In our line of work it's sometimes necessary to be economical with the truth in order to get results."

"You seem to have forgotten that I'm no longer in the job."

"You can get out anytime but you can never leave, to coin a phrase."

I snorted. "I was planning on coming to Weymouth with Kara anyway. You didn't need to make up stories about Iranian paymasters in order to induce me."

"Charlie?" Kara was staring at me with open curiosity. "Why would the thought of Iranian terrorists keep you involved with Jasmine?"

"You haven't told her then?" Monk appeared to be enjoying his role of provocateur.

"It's nothing to do with her."

"It's a matter of public record."

"My mother's death," I said to Kara succinctly, my eyes still glued to Monk's face. "It was assumed she was shot in mistake for someone else by an Iranian hit man."

"Good God!" Kara stood up to join me and glared belligerently at Monk. "I thought you had standards."

He shrugged. "Terrorism tends to focus minds, especially in these uncertain times. And your brother-in-law is a world-class terrorist, Kara, make no mistake about that."

"So he might be but that doesn't mean you can—"

"The majority of people don't yet understand the full implications of large-scale cybercrime," Monk said, talking across Kara's interruption. "And those who do mostly don't give a toss." His eyes fell censoriously upon me. "I guess I can count you amongst that lot, Charlie."

"Perhaps, but you should have had the balls to tell me the truth."

"Would you have become involved if I had?" Monk asked mildly. I glowered at him but couldn't hold his gaze. He was right and we both knew it. "Because cybercrime happens electronically it doesn't feel personal, until someone has their identity cloned, that is."

"Well, we're involved now whether we like it or not, so I guess you'd better tell me everything." I paused. "And how about starting with who you work for?"

"Fair enough. I am attached, loosely of course, to the U.K. National High Tech Crime Unit. It's an organisation that does precisely what it says on the tin and fights an uneven battle against, amongst other things, cybercrime. In case you didn't know it, cybercrime is the fastest-growing major criminal network in the world and, as always, the good guys are way behind the perpetrators. Naturally I'm doing my humble best to redress the balance."

I snorted. "Of course you are."

"Levine here is with Interpol, working in conjunction with the Botnet Task Force, a body set up by Microsoft to try to help combat this type of fraud."

"Okay." My temper was cooling in the face of his annoyingly temperate manner. "But why is Kalashov so important that you'd risk involving first Brett Webb and now Kara and me?"

"A few years ago an eleven-man international gang stole almost fifty million from a well-known High Street chain by breaching their computer systems."

I whistled softly. "I don't remember that hitting the headlines."

"You wouldn't because it never became public knowledge. A lot of the target companies choose to keep quiet and take the hit rather than risk public humiliation and loss of customer faith. They simply tightened up their computer security and tried to make sure it didn't get breached again." He lifted his shoulders.

"That's one of the beauties of cybercrime. Apart from being almost untraceable, it also embarrasses the targets into keeping stum."

"Sounds as though it beats working for a living."

Monk ignored my interruption. "Kalashov was widely supposed to be the boss behind that big scam but we were never able to prove it. The anonymity of cybercrime is a huge attraction to the perps, you see, as is the phenomenal growth of the world wide web. Just about any transaction you care to name can be carried out electronically nowadays. That makes it the perfect tool for stealing and—here's the neat bit—equally useful to the criminals when it comes to laundering their ill-gotten gains."

"Surely there are ways of tracing the culprits?"

"No, not really. Cybercrime outfits bear uncanny resemblances to organized crime families. A boss, in this case almost certainly Kalashov, heads the organisation. He operates as a business entrepreneur and doesn't commit cybercrime himself. Beneath him is an underboss—"

"Kalashov's daughter, Monika," Kara muttered.

"Very likely." Monk shot her a look. "If that's what your sister told you, it confirms our suspicions."

Kara frowned. "If you already knew it, why haven't you raided her premises?"

"Presumably because he has no grounds for a warrant," I said. "Suspicion alone isn't sufficient reason to harass the daughter of a wealthy entrepreneur."

"Precisely. Monika Kalashova operates a legitimate escort agency. The business is properly registered, she pays her taxes on time and does everything by the book. She runs the thing from her home address, which is in a residential area, but applied for and received business use on the premises, so we can't get her there."

"How was that approved if you suspect her of illegal activities?"

Monk snorted. "Her father has influential friends in high places. He contributes a lot of cash to both major political parties, so they feel obliged to throw him the odd favour."

"So Monika's the underboss in the cybercrime thing," I said, steering Monk back on track.

"Yes, she acts as second-in-command and manages the operation. She provides the trojans and manages the command and control of them."

"Trojans?" Kara frowned.

"Malware that appears to perform a function you need but in fact allows unauthorized access to the host machine," Levine said.

"Monika Kalashova will have several lieutenants operating beneath her, heading their own sections," Monk continued. "Their campaigns usually enable the criminals to operate in markets highly sensitive to location, language and regional economic trends. Each attack incorporates a crime wave tool kit, trojans and command-and-control servers. It enables them to divert traffic from a specific region, with specific characteristics, using trojans designed for targeting selected businesses."

Kara pulled a face. "It all sounds pretty technical."

"It's like everything else, easy when you know how. And make no mistake, these people sure know how."

"We think Monika Kalashova's lieutenants are several of the highly educated and very attractive women employed at the escort agency," Levine said. "The last people you'd expect to be involved but who are, in fact, at the hub of Kalashov's latest scam."

"That's clever," I remarked. "They have legitimate reasons to be at Monika's premises and, let's face it, when you think of large-scale crime, it's usually men you suspect. It hadn't even occurred to me that women might be involved, which is a pretty chauvinistic view because there's no reason in the world why they shouldn't be."

"Exactly. None of the girls live permanently at Monika's, unless they're new in town. She does keep a few rooms to put new recruits up until they get places of their own, but that's all."

"So, what's the organisation up to that's got you so worked up?" I asked.

It was Levine who answered. "We think they're about to target one of the U.K.'s leading banks and take them for millions in order to finance Kalashov's grandiose building plans in Spain."

"Yes," Monk agreed. "He's going back and forth to Russia, tidying up the last of his business interests there. What's frightening about that is the crime families have stopped killing one another and started cooperating. Kalashov is selling off the last of his stockpiles of contraband to his once deadliest rival. For a return on the profits, naturally. He doesn't seem to be able to turn his back on it altogether." He grimaced. "You can take the thug out of Russia…"

"If you know the fake transactions are emanating from Monika's house, can't you trace them electronically from there?" I suspected it wasn't that straightforward but felt the question needed to be asked.

Monk raised a cynical brow. "Hardly. They're routed through a dozen different servers in various countries simultaneously. That's why it's so difficult to prosecute the culprits and make charges stick, even if we do manage to catch them."

"So why bother?" I stared out of the window and stretched my arms above my head. "Why not warn all banks to be especially vigilant and leave it at that?"

"Because they'd simply identify an alternative target and we'd be back to square one. At least we have some idea where to start looking this time, and if we can trace their activities we stand a good chance of prosecuting successfully. A high-profile guy like Kalashov in the dock would act as a deterrent to others. We have a team of computer specialists who can unravel the trail and specialist lawyers standing by ready to take the cases to court, but in order to do so—"

"In order to do so you need access to one of the machines from which the scam is operated," I finished for him.

"Precisely."

"But Jasmine wouldn't be able to get to one," Kara protested. "She knows nothing about it."

"No, but if she's no longer kindly disposed towards her husband, you might be able to persuade her to spend some time in town with Monika—"

"Wouldn't work. They don't get on."

"Perhaps not, but when she goes to town with her husband they sometimes stay in Chelsea with her. Monika may not like her stepmother but I doubt that she mistrusts her." Monk cast a speculative glance in my direction, as though an idea had just occurred to him. Knowing him as well as I did, I wasn't taken in by it. "Who knows what she might come up with if she snoops about a bit?"

"You're clutching at straws, guv," I said. "Jasmine seems to resent her husband now but he controls her and her kids absolutely, and she'd never do anything that would separate her from them."

"Ah, but if she was in London, willing to help us, we'd find a way to protect her children and get them to her."

"How?" I glared at him, annoyed at the hope that flared in Kara's eyes. "The children are guarded by his goons, who probably carry guns and aren't afraid to use them."

"Oh, we aren't without a few tricks of our own up our sleeves." Monk straightened the already razor-sharp creases in his trousers. "This suspected raid on a U.K. bank wouldn't only be embarrassing but also one liberty too far. So I have carte blanche to do whatever it takes to stop Kalashov, and almost limitless means at my disposal with which to do it."

"But not a search warrant, apparently."

"Oh, I don't know, Charlie." He stretched his legs in front of him, looking almost amused by my words. "I dare say I could fabricate a reason to issue one, but the ink wouldn't even be dry before Kalashov got to hear about it. Computers can be wiped clean or moved within minutes and the trail would go cold."

"Jas might come back here tomorrow—"

"Kara!" I threw her a warning look. Too late. Both Monk and Levine swivelled their heads and focused their attention on her.

"I agree she's in an almost untenable position, but I think she should listen to what Mr. Monk has to say and decide what she wants to do for herself," Kara said defensively. "It's not up to us to make up her mind for her."

"Thank you, Kara, that's all I ask." Monk inclined his head. "But what's your take on the guy who was with her, Charlie? You said he was a computer expert. Do you think he's in on the scam?"

"No." I rubbed my chin, trying to put into words something that had been bothering me. "And Jasmine seemed pleased when he explained what was going on."

"I think she was surprised, that's all," Kara said.

"Yeah, possibly."

"Perhaps this Anton could throw some light on matters. Point us in the right direction."

"I doubt it. He deals with the legitimate side of Kalashov's operation. But he *is* stuck on Jasmine so I reckon he'll follow wherever she leads."

"Well, we'll just have to see where that takes us then, won't we." Monk stood, indicating to Levine that it was time to go. "We'll catch you here for breakfast in the morning and take it from there. Thanks, Charlie, I appreciate your help. And yours, Kara."

The room seemed very quiet without them. I looked at Kara, for once at a loss for words. She tossed her wig aside, walked across to me, wrapped her arms around my neck and rested her head on my shoulder.

And suddenly words didn't seem to matter.

We went out for dinner again that evening. Monk's expense account was taking a hammering but it was no less than he deserved for using us. We were drawn by unspoken agreement to the lounge in the Prince Regent for an after-dinner drink. A pianist was crucifying Gershwin, which wouldn't have been so bad if the instrument he was playing hadn't been of such fine quality.

"We could go somewhere else," Kara said, wincing.

"No, it's all right. Just don't applaud and encourage him, that's all I ask."

She smiled, looking down at my fingers, which were unconsciously tapping out the chords on my thigh. I realized what I was doing and abruptly fisted my hand.

"Why don't you show us how it ought to be done," she said when the hapless player left the instrument and wandered towards the bar.

I shook my head but for a moment was sorely tempted. That bothered me. Brendan's best efforts had failed to get me in the same room as a piano for more than two decades. Now this green-eyed hussy thought she could tempt me by humming the familiar melody of "It Don't Mean a Thing If It Ain't Got That Swing," which was playing softly in the background.

"Go on, Charlie, I dare you!"

"Nope. You've already got me into enough trouble."

"Trouble?" Her eyes sparkled. "You don't know the meaning of the word."

With that she slid across the seat we were sharing, plonked herself on my knee, draped her arms 'round my neck and kissed me. A full-frontal assault, tongue-down-the-throat sort of kiss. I could hear the disapproving tuts coming from the staid couple seated opposite and tried to remain detached from her efforts. But we could both feel my boringly predictable response, and I had to suppress the urge to laugh. Tipping her off my knee, I shrugged and headed towards the piano, my mind a deliberate blank. Sometimes you just had to go with your instincts.

I sat on the stool and flexed my fingers, waiting for common sense to intervene, but it seemed to be taking a vacation. Tentatively I ran my fingers over the keys, feeling awkward, expecting them to hit all the wrong notes.

They didn't.

The melody I produced sounded as sweet and fresh as though I'd practised it just yesterday. I played along with the piped music, and no wrathful hand of God yanked me off the stool, asking me what the hell I thought I was doing, breaking my promise to my mother. I'd vowed never to play again until I solved the riddle of her murder and yet here I was, showing off because a pretty girl had stuck her tongue down my throat in a public place. I tried a few variations I had no recollection of learning. They sounded good, causing me to wonder if Mum had intervened from wherever she now was to tell me it was all right to get on with my life.

I became absorbed, barely aware that a small crowd had gathered in the lounge to listen. Kara stood at my shoulder as I played and led the applause when the number ended.

"That was amazing, Charlie," she said. "You haven't lost your touch. No wonder your old teacher is so keen to get you to play again. He'll be delighted to hear that you have."

"I haven't." I stood up and shut the lid with a decisive clunk. "That was a one-off, to stop you showing me up."

"Oh, is that what it was!"

My audience wanted more but, already regretting my impulsive action, I drained my glass, settled our bill and led Kara out of the hotel. Annoyed that she'd bent me to her will so easily, I intended to exact revenge as soon as we were alone.

"Someone's been on board." I stiffened as I unlocked the boat and was greeted by a subdued, cross-eyed Gil.

"How can you tell?"

"I can smell cigarettes. Unfiltered, foreign cigarettes. Whoever came aboard wants us to know they were here, obviously."

"What do you mean?"

"Even the densest of villains would know the smell of cigarette smoke lingers. If they hadn't wanted us to know they'd been here they wouldn't have lit up."

"Yes, I suppose you're right. But why didn't Gil stop them?"

I shrugged. "You know Gil. Besides, by the looks of him, they drugged him." I hunkered down to take a closer look at the poor chap, furious that these nameless cowards would treat a harmless dog in such a cavalier fashion, just to make a point. As far as I could see, he wasn't in any great distress but that wasn't the point. "We'll keep a careful eye on him."

"Oh no, poor baby!" Kara crouched down and cuddled Gil, who wagged his tail halfheartedly, as though he knew he'd failed in his duties, and licked her face. "Thank goodness he seems to be okay."

"Yeah, but at least now we know they know we're here." I shrugged. "So much for Monk's elaborate precautions." I took a quick look 'round. "As I thought, nothing seems to be missing."

"Then why did they break in?" Kara was still fussing over Gil and didn't look up as she spoke.

"To intimidate us, that's all. And make sure there's

nothing on board that could harm them." I grimaced. "Like we'd be stupid enough to leave any evidence we might have lying around."

I didn't sleep well, concerned about Gil and worrying that our uninvited guests might make a return visit. I felt drained and tired in the morning but at least Gil appeared to have slept it off and was back to his normal boisterous self. We met Monk and Levine in the hotel dining room and told them about the break-in.

"I'll have someone keep an eye on the boat. But after today, whatever happens, you'll be able to return to Brighton with the grateful thanks of Her Majesty's Government, and I doubt you'll be troubled by these thugs again."

"That's what we intend to do."

"Do we, Charlie, I wasn't thinking we'd need to—"

"Yes, Kara, we're finished here. Come on, let's get up to the room and see if our visitors decide to join us."

They did, earlier than they had the day before, which was just as well because I was tired and on edge. Something told me we weren't just going to sail away into the sunset and get on with our lives, and I had a bad feeling about how things were going to pan out.

Kara and Jasmine hugged one another, introductions were made and Monk made his pitch. Jasmine heard him out in silence.

"I've been thinking about things a lot since we spoke yesterday. I know he's planning something big," she said. "And, from what Anton said yesterday, I suppose it might be to do with computers." She paused, tilting her head in a compelling manner that made her look fragile and vulnerable. I also felt it was contrived, as though she knew precisely what effect it was having on the men in the room. "It's funny, but that would never have occurred to me. It's rather sophisticated for Igor. Still, it explains why Monika has been around so much recently. And Igor's at her place in Chelsea now."

"Can you do anything to help us, Mrs. Kalashova? We would protect you in return and create new identities for you and your children so you can start again somewhere new."

She shook her head. "I would like to but there's nothing you can do to stop my husband."

"You don't need to steal the computer. Merely copy the hard drive."

"But that would take hours, wouldn't it?" I asked.

Monk grimaced in a most un-Monk-like manner. "Yes, unfortunately it would. But if the computers are left unattended, say, in the evening, it just might be possible."

"But hugely risky," Kara said. "And what about passwords? Presumably they wouldn't be left switched on."

"No, but there's a way 'round that. You could put your own Linux CD into the computer and boot from that, then do the hard drive copy."

"What's Linux?" Kara and I asked together.

"It's the operating system of choice for today's cybercriminals."

"All right," I said, holding up my hand to halt Levine's explanation, aware that I'd never grasp all the technicalities. "Why would using a Linux CD be an advantage?"

"Because it would allow you to get 'round the password and give you control of the machine." Levine's face fell. "But, alas, it's not instantaneous so there would be a chance of your being caught, Mrs. Kalashova. But if you steal a computer it would definitely be missed in no time."

Jasmine gave an apologetic little shrug. "I'm not very technically minded, I'm afraid."

"I realize it's asking a lot but if you were to—"

"She said *no*." Anton moved to place himself behind Jasmine's chair. "It's too dangerous. Mrs. Kalashova must think of her children as well as herself."

"I must also think of you, Anton." She covered the hand that was resting on her shoulder. "Anton's life wouldn't be worth a cent if my husband even suspected him of disloyalty. I'm sorry, but I think it better if we don't meet again."

She hugged Kara for a protracted moment, shushing her protests, smiled just once at me and followed Anton from the room without a backward glance. Kara fell into a chair, covered her face with her hands and quietly sobbed. Which was why, unlike me, she didn't observe Anton and Jasmine emerge from the hotel a few minutes later, to be intercepted by Igor and two of his henchmen.

"Igor!"

Nadia tried to hide her fear at his unexpected appearance. She'd thought him to be safely ensconced in London. Otherwise she wouldn't have risked coming to the hotel and endangering Kara. Damn, she should have anticipated this. Her heart hammered against her rib cage when she caught sight of the steely set to Igor's features. She actually trembled when she glanced at Viktor and Nikolay standing at his shoulder, their expressions impassive.

"What were you doing in that hotel with my wife?"

"Igor, we were—"

"I wasn't talking to you."

Nadia thought her legs would give way. Never, in fifteen years, had Igor used that tone with her before. She could explain, of course, but was damned if she did, damned if she didn't. If she told him the truth about Kara, her sister might well finish up like Brett. Which meant Igor, jealous at the best of times, would assume she and Anton were having a physical relationship.

"Mrs. Kalashova was feeling unwell and so we stepped into the lounge for coffee."

Igor nodded at Nikolay, who disappeared inside. He returned a few minutes later, shaking his head. Wordlessly, Igor steered Nadia to a car. His car, not the one she usually travelled in with Anton. Igor climbed in beside her and Viktor got behind the wheel. Both were grim-faced. Neither of them spoke a word.

"Where are we going, Igor?" she asked, when she could bear the silence no longer. "Home is in the other direction."

"We're going to London."

"But the children, I—"

"Olga will look after the children. That's what she's paid for."

"But I don't understand, I—"

"Nor do I, Nadia, but I intend to extract some answers from you before the day's out." The granite set to his features turned her stomach. "How could you, Nadia? How could you deceive me with the likes of him?"

"I didn't deceive you, Igor. I would never do that."

"I've given you everything in life a woman could possibly ask for. I worshipped you. I would have given my life for you. I didn't believe Viktor when he told me. I thought he was being spiteful and was prepared to give you the benefit of the doubt." Without warning he lashed out and struck the side of her face, drawing blood from the corner of her lip. "I've told you often enough what will happen to you if you betray me, and you're about to find out that I don't make idle threats. But first," he added in a musing tone, "you might like to watch and see what's going to happen to your lover." He nodded out the back window and Nadia noticed the other car, being driven by Nikolay, Anton's head just visible in the backseat.

Nadia felt the colour drain from her face. She'd been so concerned about herself and the children that she hadn't spared a thought for poor, loyal Anton. Somehow she managed to hold on to consciousness, determined not to give Igor the satisfaction of seeing her keel over. But her insides were twisted into tight knots because she knew, whatever her husband had in store for her, for Anton it would be ten times more brutal.

SIXTEEN

"WHAT THE HELL!"

I turned to Monk, who was standing beside me at the window. He took in the situation at a glance, pulled his phone from his pocket and hit speed dial. "I've got a man stationed outside. Perhaps he'll know what's going on."

Kara came up behind us. "What's happening?"

By then Kalashov's cars had disappeared and I didn't immediately answer her, waiting to see what light Monk's man could shed on the situation first.

"They're taking them to London." Monk grimaced as he pocketed his phone. "My chap overheard Kalashov's instructions to his driver."

"No!"

Kara caught on and her face crumpled. I felt for her. This was my fault as much as Monk's, and there was sod all I could say to reassure her.

"We have to do something, Charlie." Kara was tugging at my sleeve.

"I'm afraid there's very little you can do right now," Monk said in a measured tone.

"But we put her at risk by—"

"No, Kara." For once Monk's face showed a little animation. "Your sister put herself at risk by getting involved with a man like Kalashov. We have no grounds to interfere in their domestic dispute."

Monk was putting my own thoughts into words. It sounded harsh, but there was nothing more we could do to help Jasmine.

"It's more than *domestic,*" Kara said hotly. "She took a big chance in coming to see us. You were happy enough to make use of her but at the first sign of trouble you abandon her." She flashed him a disgusted look. "How do you sleep at night?"

"Very well, thank you."

I attempted to take Kara's arm but she shook me off and walked away from us both.

"We've done everything we can here," Monk said, apparently unaffected by Kara's justifiable anger. "Why don't you go back to the boat, both of you, collect your stuff and I'll drive you back to Brighton? Someone else can bring the boat back."

"Have I got a home to go back to?" I asked.

"Yes, the *No Comment* is back in her berth in Brighton."

"Okay, that sounds like a plan. Come on, Kara."

I put an arm 'round her shoulders and steered her towards the door. This time she let me touch her but barely spoke a word when we got back to the boat and gathered our things together.

The two of us and Gil met Monk, who was waiting for us in an illegally parked BMW at the entrance to the marina. I left Kara in Monk's care whilst I sorted matters at the marina office. When I returned she was in the back of the car, cuddled up to Gil, dried-eyed and tight-lipped. I'd have preferred arguments and some more of her crazy suggestions to help Jasmine. But all I got was an accusatory silence.

I'd done everything I'd said I would, and more. I'd

known all along it was a bad idea to try to help someone
who didn't want to be helped, but still I'd gone along
with it. Kara hadn't uttered one word of criticism and,
up until today, had repeatedly expressed her gratitude
for what I'd done. So why did I still feel so shitty about
letting her down?

Monk pulled up outside Kara's flat. I got out of the
car too, heaved her bag out of the boot and deposited
it at the front door.

"Well," I said, feeling awkward. "I guess this is
goodbye."

"Yes, I suppose."

"Will you be all right? Do you want me to stay?"

"I'll be fine. You've already done more than
enough." She stood on her toes and gave me a linger-
ing kiss. "And thanks for…well, for everything."

"Take care, Kara. I don't want to scare you but your
sister's husband seems to know every move we make
before we make it."

"He won't harm me. Not if I keep out of his business."

"Precisely!"

"Warning heeded."

She inserted her key in the lock, picked up her bag
and disappeared from sight without looking back. I
walked slowly back to Monk's car and slid into the
passenger seat.

"All a bit of a mess, eh, Charlie?" He flashed me
an assessing glance as he manoeuvred the car through
heavy traffic and headed towards the marina.

"Yeah." I kicked at the mat in the footwell of the
car, wondering what if anything I could have done dif-

ferently. "Where do you suppose Kalashov will have taken them?"

"Oh, to his daughter's house off the Fulham Road, I should think. Cathcart Road, to be precise. Do you know it?"

"Yes, I know the area. I'm a Chelsea fan."

"Well, there you are then." He pulled up in the marina car park. "Thank you, Charlie." He offered me a firm handshake. "On behalf of Her Majesty's Government, I'd like to express my thanks for all you tried to do."

He handed me the keys to my boat and drove off, leaving Gil and me standing there. I watched him go, wondering quite what it was I'd done to earn his gratitude.

The boat was spotlessly clean, which was something to be grateful for. I filled the rest of the day doing all the odd little jobs that boat owners do, trying to keep busy. The fridge was full of food I didn't recall buying so I cracked a few beers that night, cooked a basic meal and tried to put the events of the past week behind me. But even the CD of Art Tatum playing "Tiger Rag" couldn't stop me thinking about all the things that had gone wrong. I phoned Spain and spoke to Harry, hoping the sound of his voice would cheer me up. He seemed to be having a rare old time and even Emily sounded less fractious than usual.

In spite of being reassured about my son's safety, I still tossed and turned all night, feeling lonely. I'd got used to Kara sharing my bed remarkably quickly and was loath to admit that I missed her. I thought she might have phoned but I hadn't heard a word from her. She was obviously getting on with her life. Doing the sensible thing by forgetting all about her sister.

Which was what I ought to be doing. But since when had I been sensible?

For the first time ever, Nadia was unable to reach her husband. She racked her brains as they drove to London, trying to think what she could say to calm him down. He'd never struck her before, not once in fifteen years, and that in itself revealed the extent of his jealous rage. She held a handkerchief to her cut lip, aware of Viktor's expression of smug satisfaction as he darted frequent glances at her in the rearview mirror. He'd always resented Igor's devotion to her and was making no attempt to hide his satisfaction at her spectacular downfall.

Several attempts on her part to engage Igor in conversation were met with stony silences. In the end she gave up trying, leaned into the farthest corner and closed her eyes in weary resignation, no longer caring what happened to her. She was unsurprised when the car drew up outside Monika's house in Cathcart Road. She got out without waiting for Viktor to open her door and ascended the front steps with her head held high. Igor was at her side, supporting her arm, with every appearance of husbandly concern. Monika came to greet her father, frowning when she saw Nadia with him.

"I wasn't expecting you both," she said, kissing her father on both cheeks and pointedly ignoring Nadia.

"Nadia needed a change of scenery. And you have another guest." He indicated Anton who, ashen-faced but as yet seemingly unharmed, was escorted into the house by Nikolay.

"As you wish," she said frostily.

"Put him in the top room at the back," Igor said to Nikolay. "Go with them," he added to Viktor.

Viktor grunted and headed for the stairs.

"Come, my dear," Igor said to Nadia with a flash of his old-worldly charm.

For a moment Nadia was encouraged by the change in his attitude but soon realized he was putting on a show for his daughter's sake. He wouldn't wish Monika to know he'd been cuckolded by the wife she despised and had advised him against marrying. Viktor and Nikolay would know better than to enlighten her.

They reached the first floor and Igor opened the door to the room kept for him whenever he visited London. A sumptuous apartment with a far-reaching view but, her mind focused on the forthcoming confrontation with her husband, the splendour of her surroundings was lost on her. She felt herself trembling as Igor closed the door behind them with considerable force.

"Now then, my dear." He strolled towards her, speaking with a casualness she could tell was entirely feigned. There was a pulse working beneath his eye and a thin layer of perspiration on his forehead that gave him away. "Perhaps you'd care to explain what you were up to today."

"But there's nothing to explain, Igor, I've already told you, I—"

She didn't see the blow coming, and it knocked her clean off her feet. She fell heavily, winding herself. Instinctively she curled into a tight ball, fearful that Igor might kick her, and wrapped her arms 'round her head to protect herself.

"Igor, please!"

He loomed over her, his immaculately shone shoes close enough for her to touch.

"Don't hurt me. Think of our baby."

His arm arrested midswing. "Baby? What baby?"

And for a fleeting moment he couldn't disguise his joy.

I WRENCHED OPEN the door to my clothes cupboard, seeking out the one suit I still owned, which would have passed muster even in the rarefied atmosphere of Monk's sartorially elegant circles. Charcoal grey, well cut and ruinously expensive when purchased three years previously, I kept it to remind me what I was escaping from. And for weddings, funerals and the particular destination I had in mind for that evening. I showered and shaved carefully, slicked my long hair severely back with some goopy stuff I dashed out to buy in the local Asda, and donned a pair of horn-rimmed glasses with clear lenses. Wearing the suit over a white shirt and blue silk tie, I barely recognized myself when I looked in the mirror.

Gil was treated to an extra long run and left to guard the boat. I stopped by on the next pontoon, hailed my fellow live-aboards, Tessa and Mike, threw them the keys to the *No Comment* and asked if they'd mind giving Gil his evening run. It was a favour they'd done for me once or twice before, and I reciprocated by helping Mike sometimes in his engine room.

"Sure." Tessa gave me the once-over and grinned. "Hot date?"

"Something like that. And if I get lucky I'll probably be late."

Mike laughed. "Not that cute little redhead that's been hanging around?"

"Now, Mike, you know better than that." I wagged a finger at him. "A gentleman never kisses and tells."

"That lets you off the hook then."

"Fair point."

I treated myself to a taxi to the station and caught a fast train to London just as it was about to depart. Arriving at Victoria I found a bank of pay phones and called the number I'd obtained from enquiries that morning. A well-modulated female voice, with a slight accent, answered on the second ring.

"All-Bright Escort Agency. 'Ow may I 'elp you?"

I explained what I wanted and was given directions to the house in Cathcart Road. I took the tube to Fulham Broadway. In seemed strange to be in the area and not heading for Stamford Bridge, but I had no time to dwell upon the misfortunes of my favourite team. Instead I concentrated upon finding the house in question and had to admit to being impressed when I succeeded. If this was Kalashov's daughter's place, then she sure lived in style. Four stories of immaculately maintained terraced house. The sort of place that went on the market for five million quid or more. I looked up at the façade, wondering if Jasmine Webb was behind one of those spotless windows and, if so, how she was being treated.

I rang the bell and a disembodied voice echoed through a grill, asking me my business.

"Joe Longthorpe," I said. "I phoned earlier."

"One moment, Mr. Longthorpe."

The door swung open on silent hinges. Feeling as though I was entering the dragon's den, I stepped into a chequered, marble-floored foyer, trying to look as though I belonged.

"Mr. Longthorpe?" A fashionably dressed, very attractive woman was there to greet me. She extended a hand that sported a manicure as immaculate as her clothes. "You found us all right?"

"Yes. Your directions were very precise."

"And 'Ow can we 'elp you?"

"Well, like I said, I'm down from Yorkshire on business for my company." I briefly described the town where my father now lived. Nothing like a bit of local colour to add flesh to a story. "I, um, well, I find myself at a bit of a loose end tonight…" I ran a finger 'round my collar and tried to look uncomfortable, like I'd seen any number of suspects with stuff to hide do when being interrogated down the nick. "The thing is, the business dinner I was supposed to attend has been cancelled and I just, well, I wondered, er…I wondered—"

"Of course." The woman had obviously heard it all before and didn't have time to listen to the excuses of a randy businessman hoping to get his end away and charge it to expenses. "Perhaps if you'd come this way I could show you some pictures. I feel sure we'll be able to satisfy your needs."

She led me into an anteroom, comfortably and elegantly furnished, and offered me something to drink. I was tempted to ask for a beer but suspected there was no place for such lowly beverages in this establishment and amended my request to a gin and tonic. I wondered if this woman was Kalashov's daughter. My curiosity was satisfied when she returned with my drink and a large album of photographs and invited me to address her as Vera.

"Why not relax after your journey and see if you like any of these girls? I will come back later to see what you think. Ring the bell if you need me."

And she was gone. Smiling face after smiling face greeted me as I flipped through the book. Beautiful as they were, to me they looked like so many clones with no individuality. I sighed, still wondering quite what I hoped to achieve by being here. My idea of dating one of the girls and cross-questioning her about the setup seemed pretty dumb, now that I'd actually arrived. Okay, so I'd got through the door, but that was as far as I was likely to get. Any hopes of finding Jasmine or locating the computers used for cybercrime were as remote as Chelsea's chances of winning the Premiership next season. No actual entertaining of clients took place here and anything of interest would be on the upper floors. Well out of bounds to the likes of me.

I continued to examine the bevy of lovelies available to me for a few hours in exchange for an astronomical fee and questioned the quality of Monk's intelligence. This house seemed to be on the level and was the most unlikely location imaginable from which such a scam would be run. But then again, surely that was the whole point?

Vera returned, all smiles, and asked me if I'd made a choice.

"Well, it's just so hard, I don't really know—"

The sound of voices—of one especially familiar voice—caused me to turn my head sharply towards the entrance hall. I could only hope my acute interest in the owner of the voice hadn't aroused Vera's suspicions. My training as a policeman kicked in, helping me to tamp down my surprise at seeing Kara, her hair now a light shade of brunette. She shook hands with another woman and carried a very familiar-looking hold-all towards the stairs. Some sort of sound must have escaped my lips because she turned in my direction, her expression one of abject shock. But to her credit she managed not to blurt out my name. Vera was observing me closely and thankfully mistook my shock for admiration.

"This is Isabel," she said, indicating Kara. "She's only just joined us today. She's very beautiful, is she not?"

"Oh yes, and it's much easier to choose a girl in the flesh, so to speak. Perhaps, if…" I stared at the floor, at pains to project the image of a married man having second thoughts about being unfaithful.

"Of course." Vera took control. "Isabel, why don't you go and change? Margarita will show you to your room. And when you're ready, this gentleman would like to take you out to dinner."

"How nice!" Kara flashed a blistering smile my way and followed Margarita up the stairs.

"Now then, Mr. Longthorpe, how would you like to pay?"

She named the sum I'd be required to part with for the pleasure of Kara's company. I tried not to wince, even though I was paying with Monk's money, which hadn't yet run out. Vera didn't raise an eyebrow when I told her I preferred to deal in cash. She freshened my drink and excused herself to go and deal with another punter.

I was left alone again with ample time to curse my stupidity in assuming Kara would quit whilst behind. But in spite of the danger she'd put herself in, I had to admit to a sneaking admiration for her courage. Her chances of finding anything out about Jasmine whilst living under this roof were ten times better than my own inept attempts. But still, the moment I got her alone she was in for a severe tongue-lashing.

"Ready, Mr. Longthorpe?"

I'd been so lost in thought that I hadn't heard Kara enter the room. I glanced up at her and did a rapid double-take. She was wearing a simple black dress, which finished just above the knee and had those thin shoulder straps I'd admired on her once before. Her hair tumbled down her back and she wore the minimum amount of makeup. She looked simply stunning. I stood and almost knocked my drink over in my haste. I was vaguely aware of Vera standing behind Kara, trying to hide her amusement at the way my tongue must have been literally hanging out.

"Err, yes, right, Isabel, is it?" My nervousness was not altogether a fabrication. "If you're ready, shall we go?"

"Shall I call you a taxi, Mr. Longthorpe?" Vera asked.

"Yes, that would be good."

I waited for the taxi to deliver us to an upmarket watering hole I knew of but had never patronised before I said anything to Kara. But as soon as we'd found a table and ordered our drinks, I laid into her.

"Just what the fuck do you think you're playing at?"

She smiled sweetly. "I could ask you the same question."

"This isn't about me but, just so you know, I stopped by on the off chance to see if there was anything obvious I could do to help your sister."

She rolled her eyes. "Oh, so you just happened to be passing, all suited and booted." She fingered the lapel of my jacket. "Very nice," she added, grinning.

"Kara!"

"We're just thinking alike, Charlie." She leaned towards me, her eyes alive with determination. "You didn't imagine I'd simply abandon Jas, did you?"

"Jasmine made her own bed," I said harshly. "She knew the score when she married Kalashov."

"Don't be so heartless. She couldn't have known what her husband was really like or she wouldn't have married him. She said herself she didn't know what he did in Russia."

I made a scoffing sound, which she ignored.

"There was so much I wanted to say to her, Charlie." She stared at the tabletop. "All these years I've been thinking of the questions I'd ask her if I ever saw her again, but I never got the chance because you and Monk took over." She finally looked up at me, making no effort to wipe away the tears that were brimming. "I feel responsible for what happened, and I couldn't live with myself if I didn't at least try and help her."

"Has it occurred to you," I said, enunciating each word carefully, "that by enrolling at that bloody place, you've laid yourself open to having strange men pawing you and…" I was too angry with her to carry on talking and fell into a disgruntled silence.

"It's a good job you came along then," she said sweetly. "I don't mind you pawing me."

"Do you know how much they charged me for the privilege of your company?" I held up a hand. "No, don't answer that. What I mean is, the men that go to those places, they expect more than just dinner and good conversation. A lot more. And they might get nasty if you don't give out."

"It's not like that. Monika—I met her by the way, she interviewed me—told me how much of your lovely money I'll get for putting up with your company, and that anything else I do is entirely up to me. I also have a number to call if I get into situations I can't handle."

"I doubt it'll be that straightforward."

"You're starting to sound like my dad. I'm quite capable of taking care of myself. What's more, since I've just arrived in the big bad city and have nowhere else to stay, I've been given a room at the Cathcart Road house. Don't you see what that means?"

I did, but my frosty attitude remained firmly in place.

"I'll be able to explore at night when everyone else is in bed. And if I don't find Jas, at least I might be able to locate those laptops and copy whatever's on them."

I groaned. "Please don't tell me you have a portable hard drive in your luggage." I leaned across the table and glared at her. "Hasn't it occurred to you, in your misguided attempts to help your sister, that your belongings are probably being searched even as we sit here? The only thing you're likely to do is make trouble for yourself as well as her."

"I'm not entirely dense you know." She opened her bag and waved a gizmo under my nose. "It will never leave my person."

In spite of everything, I felt my lips twitching in reluctant admiration. "All right, I guess it's pointless trying to talk you out of this madness."

"Madness, you call it. Remind me again what it was you expected to achieve."

She had me there.

"Okay, but before you go charging in to do your female impersonation of James Bond, just bear in mind that those computers are hardly likely to be left unguarded. If no one's manning them, you can bet your life there'll be a camera or alarm of some sort in the room with them, alerting whatever passes for security in that house that someone has intruded. You'll be rumbled within minutes."

She looked crestfallen, as was my intention. "Oh, I hadn't thought of that."

"It makes sense. If they're planning some big scam, they aren't going to skimp on security."

"Yes, but still, I might be able to find something to help."

"Promise me you'll only stay there for a couple of days."

"Oh, I don't know." She absently played with her bottom lip. "I might get to date the man of my dreams who'll keep me in the style to which I intend to become accustomed."

"Kara!"

"Yes, all right, Charlie, I promise. If I haven't found anything out in that time, then I doubt I ever will."

"Good girl. Okay then, let's go and get something to eat. I'm starved. And," I added, helping her with her jacket, "you can pay out of the money I just forked out to be with you."

She pulled a face. "That's not how it's supposed to work."

"It does tonight.

"How did you find out where the agency was, by the way?" I asked her over dinner.

"Oh, Mr. Monk told me."

I frowned. "No, you mean you asked him to tell you."

"No, he volunteered the information yesterday when you were sorting things at the marina office. It sort of planted the idea in my head to come and have a little look-see."

I sensed the manipulating gloved fist of my ex-boss at work here. "The crafty bastard!"

"What's up, Charlie? You look furious again."

"He told me where it was, as well. I did ask him, mind you, but if I hadn't, I bet he'd have found a way to drop it into the conversation." I stared off into the distance, my brain whirling with the implications of Monk's actions. "We've been set up, darling. He fully intended us to get further involved but knew if he suggested it outright I'd put the kibosh on it."

"Well, if he set us up I dare say he's got his people looking out for us, so you have no need to worry about me anymore." She reached across, removed my glasses and slipped them into the top pocket of my jacket. "That's better."

"Don't change the subject."

"I'm bored with the subject. Mr. Monk was only trying to help."

I bit back a sardonic laugh. "Why are you always so willing to forgive? Do you like being manipulated?"

She drew a pattern on the back on my hand with her forefinger. "Depends upon who's doing the manipulating."

When I dropped her back at Cathcart Road I was again full of foreboding but knew it was pointless trying to get her to change her mind. I got out of the taxi and walked her to the door, aware of the discreet camera in the porch pointing directly downwards. Someone inside would be watching our every move. I wondered what other security devises there were about the place but didn't want to make it too obvious that I was looking.

"Smile," I told her, "you're on candid camera. No, don't look up! Pretend you don't know it's there. Just act naturally. We don't want them to capture our faces looking directly at them in case we're recognised."

"How does a professional escort act in such circumstances?"

I shrugged. "Search me."

"So you've never paid for company before then?"

"I'll be back on the boat before midnight. Ring me to let me know you're all right and do the same thing in the morning. We'll take things from there."

"You worry too much, Charlie."

"Just do it!"

I glared at her and then kissed her on the cheek, mindful of the security cameras recording our fond farewells. Then I got back in the taxi and headed for Victoria. It was only as I got on the train that I realized I hadn't put my glasses back on before seeing Kara to the door. Whoever was inside watching us couldn't have failed to notice that their myopic client had suddenly developed twenty-twenty vision.

SEVENTEEN

I GOT BACK to the boat by midnight and received a call from Kara soon after that. She spoke in a whisper but assured me nothing untoward had happened.

"Monika was around and seemed surprised to see me back so early."

"I told you that you were supposed to seduce me."

"I'm not that sort of girl, Charlie."

"No, of course you're not." I chuckled. "Anyway, did she cross-question you?"

"She only asked if everything had gone smoothly—"

"But what she really wanted to know was why you hadn't come back to my hotel."

She giggled. "I guess. I told her that you were too hung up about your wife to do anything more than hold my hand."

I could hear the mischief in her voice. "Get some sleep," I told her. "And make sure you ring me again first thing."

I turned in and slept better than I had for a while. I interpreted that as a good omen but when by ten the next morning I hadn't heard from Kara again, I figured my optimism had been premature. There could be any number of innocent reasons for her silence but that didn't prevent me from worrying. And blaming myself for letting her stay in that bloody house. I should have put my foot down and insisted she come back to the boat with me last night. She was a morning person, full of energy as soon as she opened her eyes, so why the hell hadn't she called?

I paced the salon, Gil's eyes following my every move, telling myself there was probably a simple explanation. Yeah, very simple! She'd been rumbled. Explanations didn't come any simpler than that. Gut instinct told me her crazy plan had gone pear-shaped and she was in danger. I was about to ring Monk and ask him what was going on, fairly sure he'd know, when my phone chirped into life. I breathed a mammoth sigh of relief.

Better late than never.

A quick glance at the display and my relief turned to puzzlement. It wasn't Kara calling. It was someone I hadn't heard from for years.

Jarvis Goldsmith. I experienced the familiar sense of loss as keenly as though it was yesterday. My mother's manager, who'd been with us the night she was killed. Jarvis himself was injured in the attack and had been inconsolable when my mother didn't survive. That ought to have brought us closer together, uniting us in our grief. But I rebuffed his attempts to befriend me, not always very politely. I was unable to explain that, irrationally, I held him responsible for what had happened. By the time I was old enough to accept that there was nothing he could have done, the rift was too wide to breach and we seldom spoke anymore. Wondering what it was that he wanted now, I answered the call.

"Jarvis, how are you?"

"Charlie, it's good to hear your voice."

I frowned. It wasn't good to hear his. If I hadn't been aware who I was talking to, I never would have known it was him. He'd been ill recently and I felt a stab of guilt at not having been in touch. Still, it was too late for self-recriminations. Besides, I was anxious not to tie the line up for too long in case Kara called so I cut to the chase.

"This is quite a surprise. What can I do for you?"

"Well, I was rather hoping that you'd be able to spare the time to come and see me. There's something I need to talk to you about."

"What, now?"

"Now would be good, if you can."

"Well, I've got a bit of a panic on at the moment and I'll probably have to go up to town. Could it wait a day or two?"

"Not really. I'd come to you but I'm not too mobile right now." His voice trailed off, as though the explanation for his immobility was too painful to articulate. The last thing I needed was the emotional turmoil of making polite, stilted conversation with Jarvis, and I was tempted to put him off. "I'm probably inconveniencing you and I wouldn't ask if it wasn't important."

I was about to make my excuses, but something in his tone made me hesitate. He'd never made any demands of me over the years, not even when Brendan tried to enlist his help to get me to carry on playing the piano. Kara would still be able to reach my mobile, and it might take my mind off her predicament if I had something else to think about.

"All right. Give me an hour."

For Jarvis home was a bungalow in Saltdean. It had been convenient for his wife, who'd been restricted to a wheelchair ever since I'd known her due to a freak reaction to an over-the-counter headache pill. She'd died a few years previously. Jarvis had contacted me at the time but like the coward I could sometimes be, I sent flowers and condolences but didn't attend the funeral.

I climbed onto the Harley and headed for Saltdean, trying to focus my thoughts on Kara rather than the confrontation that awaited me. It didn't work. Images of my mother's face, her features as clearly defined as if I'd seen her just yesterday, flooded my mind. I shook my head to dispel them. This was ridiculous, I was getting all worked up about seeing an old man, just because he'd occupied a special place in my mother's life. The villains I'd nicked over the years would laugh themselves sick if they could see the state I was in at the prospect of it. They had me pegged as a hard man, with good reason, and I owed it to their perception of me almost as much as I owed it to myself to get over my ridiculous hang-ups. Jarvis was harmless and my mother had been dead for more than twenty years.

It was finally time to put the past behind me and get on with my life.

I pulled the bike into the driveway of the neat bungalow I remembered. Except it was no longer quite so neat. The garden was overgrown and the house looked shabby and neglected. I took a moment to check my phone, making sure I hadn't missed any calls. Nope. I rang Kara's mobile. It was still switched off. Tamping down my growing concerns, I rang Jarvis's bell.

"It's open, Charlie," called the frail voice I recognised from the phone.

I turned the handle and walked in, wishing I could be anywhere other than here. The house smelt dank and was too warm. It was a hot day but Jarvis had the heating turned up full blast. The windows were all closed, and as I approached the living room the aroma of antiseptic I normally associate with hospitals almost knocked me sideways.

"You should keep your door locked, Jarvis," I said, entering the room. "There's lots of bad people about nowadays. Good heavens…" I caught sight of Jarvis, small and hunched, his skin deathly pale and paper-thin where it stretched across his protruding cheekbones, and was unable to hide my reaction.

"Hello, Charlie. Thanks for coming. Don't look like that," he said with a mirthless smile. "I'm resigned to it."

"What is it?" I asked, still trying to get over my shock at the deterioration in his health. The robust man I remembered seemed to have shrivelled to half his size. His clothes hung from his skeletal frame, and sunken eyes were magnified behind large glasses, which kept slipping down his nose. Tracks of a comb were visible in the pathetic wisps of thin white hair arranged across his pink scalp.

"The big C. I don't have long left and they're moving me to a hospice on Monday. I wanted to talk to you whilst I still can. Whilst I'm in my own place and can enjoy a modicum of privacy." A spasm of coughing rendered him speechless for a few moments.

I found a carafe of water on the table next to him and poured him a glass.

"Thanks."

He grasped it between both his hands. The glass shook as he raised it to his lips.

I glanced 'round the room, giving him time to compose himself. I've never been good 'round illness and wished I could be somewhere else. I felt great sympathy for him but also wondered what was so important that he'd pressured me into dropping everything and dashing down here.

There were photographs of my mother everywhere. In concert, with me at various stages of my adolescence, with Jarvis, with various conductors. With just about everyone, with one notable exception. My father wasn't in a single shot.

"She was my life."

I turned to face Jarvis. I hadn't realized he'd been watching me. "And mine," I said quietly, "and mine."

"You never knew, did you?"

"Knew what?"

"About her and me."

Alarm bells rang in my head. I had a feeling that whatever he was going to tell me, I'd definitely prefer not to hear it.

"We were—"

"Jarvis, I don't think—"

"No, Charlie, let me talk. I've kept quiet all these years out of respect for her memory, watching you chasing your tail, trying to find answers." His heavy sigh produced another bout of coughing. "Well," he said once he'd recovered, "the time has come for you to know the truth. Perhaps then you might finally find closure."

"All right." I perched one buttock on the chair opposite his, trying to look relaxed but poised for flight, just in case it all got too much. "I'm listening."

Jarvis fastened rheumy eyes upon me and after a protracted silence he finally started talking. "You don't need me to tell you how profoundly your mother affected the lives of all the people she was close to."

He paused, seeming to expect me to say something. I was too choked up to oblige and made do with a curt nod. "She was sensitive, intuitive, lovely and well… just unique. She and your father appeared to be soul mates. One of those rare couples who were completely in tune with one another and didn't need anyone else to make their lives complete."

"Yeah, that's how it seemed to me, as well."

"And that's how they were at first. Everyone was touched by their togetherness."

"But something happened?" I suggested when his words stalled and he seemed to forget I was there.

"Sorry, Charlie." He pushed himself upright in his chair. "I have trouble concentrating sometimes. The drugs, you understand."

"Of course. Don't tire yourself. I can always come back."

"What does it matter if I tire myself? I've got all day to sleep if I want to."

If he expected me to argue he was in for a disappointment. I just nodded, impatient to hear what he had to say next. Not wanting to know.

"Anyway, where was I?"

"You were explaining why my parents drifted apart."

"Yes, right, well, your father was no businessman, and that's what caused the first cracks to appear in their relationship. Then you came along and your arrival was the excuse Julia needed to find a new manager. Any number of people would have jumped at the chance of taking responsibility for her career, and so I felt extremely privileged when she asked me to look after her interests." He was afflicted by another spasm of coughing and I got up to refill his glass of water. "Thanks."

He grimaced and took an unnecessary amount of time sipping the water.

I glanced at my watch and somehow managed not to tap my foot.

"God," he said, shaking his head, spittle flying from the corners of his mouth, "this is proving harder than I thought it would. For all sorts of reasons."

"You were telling me about becoming Mum's manager." I was uncomfortable having a dying man bare his soul to me. That and my growing concern at Kara's continuing silence made me sound more acerbic than perhaps I should have.

"Ah yes, that." He sighed deeply. "Your father had always felt threatened by your mother's talent. She showed him up to be the third-rate musician that he was, you see. Not intentionally, of course. She'd never be that spiteful, and it didn't matter to her that as her reputation grew, she became the main breadwinner. But your father had been sacked by the orchestra he played in and then failed as Julia's manager. He felt like a failure and took his resentment out on her."

"I didn't know that." I stared at him, wondering at first if he might be lying. But I was unable to come up with any logical reason why he would.

"How could you? You were just a baby at the time. I took over your mother's career and helped it to flourish. That necessitated spending a lot of time with her, in out-of-the-way towns, in hotels—"

"I think I know where you're going with this and I'm equally sure that I don't want to hear it. Make your peace with your Maker, or go to confession if you feel you must, but don't burden me with your guilty conscience." I turned to leave.

"No, don't go!"

Reluctantly I halted in the doorway, my back still to him.

"If I'd just had a sordid affair with your mother, of course I wouldn't feel the need to tell you. But it was a lot more than that." He paused and I could hear the breath rattling in his throat. "We were in love, Charlie, and had been for years."

I did turn towards him now. "But your wife, she was—"

"A cripple. Yes, I know that all too well and, trust me, she knew how to use her immobility as a weapon against me. I suspect she knew about Julia and me from the first but she didn't think it would ever be more than an affair. She understood that I still had physical needs, you see. She was unable to satisfy them so what did it matter to her where I turned to for relief? She felt perfectly secure. After all, what sort of a bastard walks out on a crippled wife?"

He paused, whether because he was short of breath or for effect I was unable to tell. "Well, you're looking at him. I finally persuaded your mother that we were entitled to a little bit of happiness. What sort of life would it be if we had to carry on looking over our shoulders all the time, making sure no one even suspected? But your mother's first concern was for you, and she was adamant that we shouldn't do anything about it until you were old enough to understand. Your father had all but taken you over, supervising your piano and making you *his* son in an effort to overcome his disappointments. Julia wanted to explain to you herself what had happened, how much she loved you…" His voice broke and he paused to noisily blow his nose.

"She'd finally agreed that after the concert in Croydon that fateful evening we'd talk to you together."

"So that's what was different about her that night," I said slowly. "I sensed something but I couldn't think—"

"Yes, I'd told Marianne a few weeks before that I was leaving her. There was ample money from her compensation claim for round-the-clock carers, and it was time for me to have a life of my own."

"How did she take it?"

"Hysterically. She used every form of emotional blackmail you can imagine and recruited her family to support her cause. Every member of it berated me for being such a bastard." He half smiled. "Call me a cynic but I always thought it was because they might actually have to do something to look after Marianne themselves if I actually left her."

"Did my father know?" I asked, only now realising why he was telling me all this.

"Yes, she'd told him at the same time I told Marianne."

"I see." I walked to the window and looked out at the weed-strewn garden without actually seeing it. "But you didn't tell the police any of this after the shooting?"

"No, I didn't want to hurt you any more than you already were."

"Because you thought my father might have been behind the shooting? Might have hired someone to do the deed?"

"Or Marianne and your father in cahoots. Both of them were incandescent with rage at the thought of what Julia and I were about to do." He spread his hands over his bony knees. "Who knows what that might have led them to do?"

"So why didn't you tell the police?"

He sighed. "Because I was half out of my mind with grief. And guilt. And anyway, I knew that if a professional had been hired to do the killing, it would be next to impossible to prove it."

"It wouldn't have been, not at the time," I said, back in policeman mode. "The payment would have had to come from somewhere."

Jarvis merely grunted, probably because I wasn't telling him something he didn't already know.

"There's always a trail if you know where to start looking," I said, anger making me unnecessarily cruel to a dying man. "Hired hit men cost money. Financial records can be scoured, questions asked, alibis triple-checked." It was all too late now, of course, and next to impossible to do any of those things after all this time.

"Yes, I expect you're right."

"I am." I paced in front of him, my mind alive with possibilities. "Tell me something, Jarvis. Why are you laying this on me now?" I was unable to keep the anger out of my voice. I didn't have much of a relationship with my father, but did Jarvis really imagine I'd achieve closure for my mother's killing by turning suspicion upon Dad? "It's a little late for conscience-cleansing."

"It isn't that, Charlie. If I thought your father was behind it, I'd either have told you when you joined the police or taken my suspicions to the grave."

"So what do you—"

"You know what they say about a woman scorned."

I stared at him, dumbstruck. "You surely don't suspect Marianne acted alone. She was a cripple, for God's sake."

"A cripple with access to a phone and a family full

of righteous indignation about what I planned to do. If she shared her ideas with them, they would have encouraged her to go for it, saving them the trouble of caring for her. And, bear in mind that they didn't have to, not once your mother died because I toed the line and stayed." He lifted his eyes to my face. "If I couldn't be with Julia I was dead inside anyway so it didn't really matter where I lived, or who with." He nodded at a thick file of papers on the table. "Those are Marianne's bank statements for the time period in question."

I followed the direction of his eyes and lifted a sceptical brow. "And you've only just found them, I suppose."

"I've been clearing out, tidying up my papers for, you know… Anyway, I haven't looked at them and don't have a use for them anymore. Perhaps you'll drop them in a skip for me when you leave." He smiled and in the depths of his faded eyes I caught a brief glimpse of the vibrant man he'd once been. "You look so much like her that for a long time afterwards I couldn't bear to be with you for too long. I couldn't stand the pain or the constant reminders of what I'd almost had, or the guilt for perhaps having deprived you of your mother. That's why I didn't try as hard as I should have done to look out for you. I regret that now, and I dare say Julia will have a word or two to say to me on the subject when I see her again." His eyes drifted towards the fireplace and started to close. "You'd better go now, Charlie," he said, waving weakly in dismissal. "I doubt we'll see one another again."

He appeared to have fallen asleep. Too stunned to say anything, I did as he suggested and left the bungalow, closing the front door quietly behind me so as not to wake him.

I took a deep breath, filling my lungs with the sweet fresh air they craved after the stuffiness of the sickroom, as I thought about everything Jarvis had just told me. Then I abruptly switched my mind away from the subject and checked my phone instead. I knew if it had rung whilst I'd been with Jarvis I'd have heard it but right now any old displacement activity would do. Kara hadn't rung, of course, and so I called her for what felt like the fiftieth time that morning. Her phone was still switched off.

I stashed the papers Jarvis had given me in my top box, got on the bike and rode back to the marina, my head spinning with the implications of his revelations. The husband is always the first suspect in any investigation of this type but my father, his alibi having been checked, had been cleared. Everyone was fixated on the Iranian angle and believed my mother had died through mistaken identity. In retrospect I couldn't quite believe that this other possibility hadn't once occurred to me. I'd spent more hours than was healthy considering every angle of the situation that had changed the course of my life but had failed to pick up on the obvious. To say I felt dense would be an understatement.

Back on the boat I threw Jarvis's papers into a drawer, where they'd just have to languish until I decided whether or not I actually wanted to know. Which in itself was ridiculous. I'd spent more than twenty years trying to get at the truth, and now that it was possibly within reach I was hesitating.

It was lunchtime but I had no appetite. I was becoming increasingly concerned by Kara's silence. The time

for procrastination had passed. I *had* to do something.
A plan of sorts had filtered into my brain. I needed
to be in London, and to carry it through I needed Gil
with me. Now would have been a good time to own
a car. Travelling by train with a dog was a real pain.
My eyes fell upon an unfamiliar set of keys sitting in
the bowl on the galley surface. Kara's VW. Of course!
Monk had dropped her at her flat and her car was still
in the marina multistorey. I hastily pulled together a
few items that might come in handy if I went through
with my death-wish plan, whistled to Gil and left the
boat with him bounding along at my heels.

Driving to London was the easy part. Finding a
parking space within reach of the Cathcart Road house
was more challenging but I eventually got lucky. It
was now early evening and the first thing that struck
me was the noise. Even in July, with half the city on
holiday, my ears were assaulted by a cacophony of car
horns, music from open windows, the sound of dozens
of voices communicating in a variety of languages and
the incessant rumble of traffic on the nearby Fulham
Road. I walked past the house in question, staring up at
the myriad windows. The idea that had seemed feasible
whilst on the boat now appeared nothing short of ridiculous. But hey, I was here, no other solutions presented
themselves and so what did I have to lose by trying?

I extracted Gil's Frisbee from my back pocket and
held it aloft. Seeing it, Gil abandoned his close inspec-
tion of a lamppost and sat at my feet, eyes glued to the
blue plastic in my hand as he threw back his head and
did the excited, high-pitched howl he was famous for.
Whenever he tried that one on the boat it seemed to
reverberate around half the marina. Tessa and Mike, a

whole pontoon away, reckoned they always knew when Gil was in a playful mood. But here, amid the noise and hurly-burly of the city, his doggy excitement was barely audible.

Stupid idea, *Hunter*.

Undaunted, I tried it again. A couple walking past stopped and laughed at Gil but an old woman tutted, muttered something about dogs being a menace, and gave us a wide berth. No one else appeared to spare us a second glance. The anonymity of life in a big city had its advantages. My eyes were glued to the front of the house opposite but no wan face appeared at the windows, alerted by the noise, to give me a clue as to Kara's location. I gave up, not daring to hang around in case someone was watching me from inside.

We spent some time wandering around Brompton Cemetery, doing what we each do best. In other words, Gil sniffed and I thought.

I dwelt upon Monk, who had so cavalierly set us up. Thinking of the danger Kara now faced, thanks to him, I was hard-pressed to control my temper. Was he amusing himself now by watching me chasing my tail or should I call on him for help? He got us into this and had a damned sight more clout than I did. It was a hard one but I weighed up the pros and cons and in the end decided against speaking to him. Somehow, and I suspected it would have to be the hard way, I had to get inside that house and look for Kara. If Monk knew, he'd only throw obstacles in my path. He didn't care about anything except knowing where the hub of Kalashov's cybercrime operation was. He wouldn't do anything in his official capacity that might cause them to shut up shop and disappear off his radar.

I found a takeaway place in the Fulham Road and shared a kebab with Gil. Now that it was almost dark, we returned to Cathcart Road and tried the Frisbee thing again, more in hope than expectation. To my astonishment, during the second attempt, a curtain twitched on the top floor right. Kara's face peered down at me. She raised her hand and waved like crazy. And so did the figure that appeared beside her.

It was Jasmine.

NADIA WOKE FROM a disturbed sleep and for a moment couldn't remember where she was. Something wasn't right, though, that much she could recall. She thought she was in Cathcart Road but this wasn't the room she usually shared with Igor. She could tell from the height of the sun through a gap in the curtains that it was morning. Realisation was slow in coming. Igor had hit her, knocked her from her feet, and she'd told him she was pregnant to stop him from hurting her or the baby. And now she was sleeping in this dingy room on the top floor with two single beds.

She sat up and rubbed the sleep from her eyes. Someone else was in the room, asleep in the other bed. Red hair fanned across the pillow, the only visible sign that she was sharing the room with her sister.

"Kara, is that you?"

"Jasmine!" Kara knelt and hugged her. "What are you doing in here?"

"It's a long story. What about you?"

"I got a job here. I saw your husband take you away from Weymouth. He didn't look pleased, and I thought I might be able to help you."

Nadia dropped her head into her hands. "You

shouldn't have done that. There's nothing you can do for me. You should think about yourself."

Kara pulled a face. "Too late for that. Your stepdaughter knows who I am. God knows how she found out, but something must have made her suspicious whilst I was out with a client last night." A brief, nervous giggle escaped. "It was Charlie, but I don't think they realized that. Anyway, horrible Monika hauled me out of bed last night, confiscated my handbag and locked me in here."

Nadia pulled a face. "Monika seems to know everything that goes on in this place."

"Why aren't you with Igor, Jas? What…what happened to your face?" Kara looked appalled. "He hit you, didn't he?" Nadia said nothing and turned away. "The bastard!"

"It probably seems that way but it's more complicated than that. He's a passionate man, easily roused to jealousy." Tears flowed down Nadia's face. "I couldn't risk telling him I was in that hotel meeting you, so he thinks I was there with Anton."

Kara gasped. "What have I done? Charlie told me I'd only make matters worse and he was right."

Nadia cuddled her sister. "Igor will come 'round. Now you're here there's nothing to stop me from telling him the truth, and he'll have to believe me."

"What will happen to me, Jas? To us both?"

There was a tremble in Kara's voice that pulled at Nadia's heartstrings. "He won't harm you," she said with fierce determination. "I won't permit it."

"But look what happened to Brett."

"That wasn't Igor's doing. It was his men overstepping the mark, and Igor knows how devastated I was about it. As long as I can convince him that I've not been unfaithful, he'll eventually do what I ask of him."

"How can you be so sure?"

"I'm sure." Nadia stood and leaned against the windowsill. "His business in London will soon be completed and then we can go to Spain. He'll have nothing to fear from anyone after that and no reason to harm you. Anyway, there's nothing you can tell the authorities that will hurt him, is there?"

"No, we know nothing except what you told us."

Nadia felt relief flood through her. "Well, there you are then."

"How can you live such a life, Jas?"

Nadia's couldn't meet her sister's eye. "It's not always like this."

"No, but—"

"It's better not to think too deeply about these things. My only concern is for my children. For me they must always come first."

"Of course. But, Jas, it's not as hopeless as you think. Charlie knows I'm here." Kara's voice took on a fresh vibrancy. "He'll find a way to rescue us both, and your children. You needn't rely on the mercurial moods of a man who hits you."

"I wish it were that simple." She shook her head. "What a mess I've made of everything." She flashed a smile designed to reassure but it had little discernible effect upon her distraught sister. "But never mind that. Tell me what your Charlie's found out, sweetheart. There must be more."

"Well, a few things, I suppose."

Kara spoke for some time. There was nothing else for them to do. They spent the day in the stuffy room, sharing the same bed, talking until their jaws ached. Food was delivered but they barely touched it. Kara constantly wandered to the window, convinced Charlie Hunter would come looking for her because she hadn't been able to phone him.

Nadia didn't have the heart to disillusion her. Even if by some miracle he could work out where in the house they were being held, the place was a veritable minefield of alarms. He wouldn't reach the first floor before being discovered.

Kara's cry jolted Nadia out of her reverie. She climbed out of bed and joined Kara at the window, which was locked shut.

"Look!" Kara was waving like mad at a man with a large dog on the opposite side of the road. "It's Charlie and Gil." She turned a shining face towards Nadia. "I told you they'd come."

EIGHTEEN

GIL CHASED AFTER the Frisbee I threw down the street and I walked rapidly away from the house, feeling conspicuous. It came as no surprise that Kara had been rumbled but I *was* taken aback to discover the two girls had been put in the same room. Why would they do that? Because it was easier to keep an eye on them if they were locked up together, or were more sinister forces at play? It didn't make sense and I couldn't rid myself of the feeling that I was missing something obvious.

I whistled to Gil, waited for a green light and crossed the street, deep in thought. If Kalashov had forgiven his wife, he'd never allow her to consort with her sister, just in case she let something vital slip about his activities. Which meant she was either there acting as his spy, or he intended to finish them both off and didn't care if they exchanged information.

Such unwelcome thoughts helped me to focus, and I turned my mind to the thorny question of rescuing the girls. Any fanciful ideas I'd entertained of their being constrained somewhere other than on the top floor had now been kicked into touch, so I needed to rethink my plans. Getting to them from the inside was obviously a nonstarter, which left me with just one alternative. Even allowing for the apathy and self-absorption of the average Londoner, I was well aware from my days on the force that there were always one or two vigilante-types with nothing better to do than watch the street and report every little anomaly they observed. But there was nothing I could do about that. My main worry now was whether a man in his early forties could realistically be expected to climb up four stories on the outside of a London house without attracting the attention of those within the house. And, more importantly from my perspective, without breaking his bloody neck.

I was too deep in thought to realize at first that Gil and I had wandered in an aimless circle and were now back where we started from, opposite the house. The front door opened at that moment and I ducked out of view behind a hedge, ordering Gil to lie down beside me. When I deemed it safe I poked my head up and observed Viktor and Nikolay getting into a car that had just pulled up. I was grateful that I hadn't started upon my rescue mission yet. They wouldn't have been able to avoid falling over me if I had. I watched the car drive away, wondering where they were off to. Probably out for the night. Or perhaps they didn't sleep at the house. One could but hope. Anyway, Jasmine would probably know. If I ever got to talk to her again, that was.

The coast was now as clear as it was ever going to be, and so I went back to Kara's car and loaded Gil into the backseat. He'd had an active day and, not being too fussy about his sleeping arrangements, turned in a couple of tight circles, got comfortable and promptly dozed off. I unloaded the things I'd brought with me from the boot, cranked a window open to give the snoring Gil some air, locked the car and returned the way I'd just come.

I'd studied the façade of the building thoroughly

earlier in the day and committed its main features to memory. I stared up at it again now, hoping I might have missed something obvious that would make my life easier.

I hadn't.

There was a conservatory jutting out from the ground floor, and it appeared to have a solid roof. I made a note of the likely locations for movement detectors and automatic lights in the front garden. As long as there weren't any other surprises lying in wait, and no cameras except the one I'd noticed the previous evening, I'd probably make it at least that high. But after that there was the more daunting prospect of shinning three floors up a drainpipe. I preferred not to think about the consequences if the pipe couldn't take my weight. My only consolation was that there were solid window ledges at each level where I'd be able to catch my breath.

Provided, of course, that none of the rooms behind those ledges were occupied.

I knew that as plans went, this one was full of pitfalls. The possibilities for failure were spectacular but I wouldn't be able to live with myself if I didn't at least give it a try. I donned the webbing harness I'd brought with me from the boat. Yachtsmen use harnesses like this one to clip themselves onto the decks in big seas to prevent being swept overboard, or when they have to climb the masts and do running repairs. I found mine useful when up on the roof of the *No Comment* checking the aerials and such. I flung the binoculars I'd also brought along 'round my neck, coiled two lengths of webbing line over them and stuffed a torch into my pocket. Then I crept into the garden, crouched double, feeling like an inept cat-burglar and wondering why they always made this sort of thing look so easy in films.

I stealthily slid 'round the side of the conservatory and used the binoculars to take a close-up look at the task ahead of me. Jasmine being with Kara had its advantages. She would know where the internal alarms were so that, if I did manage to get to the girls, we'd have an outside chance of slipping out of the house unobserved. It was the thought of alarms that had dissuaded me from trying to gain access to the house from a window lower down but was an option I might need to reexamine if the climb became too perilous.

I hauled myself onto the roof of the conservatory, rather inelegantly but without too much trouble. My every move sounded unnaturally loud to my ears, even though traffic noise drowned out just about everything. Already out of breath when the hard bit hadn't even started, I decided I was definitely too old for this. I blended into the wall as best I could whilst I caught my breath, pleased I'd had the foresight to wear black clothing.

As I stood rigid against the wall, panting from my exertions, I realized that I already had a problem I hadn't anticipated. It was now dark and I couldn't see a bloody thing above my head. I had my torch but needed both hands to climb so how was I supposed to shine it? Damn, I hadn't thought about that. In the end I settled for flashing it briefly above so I could locate the precise position of the drainpipe, and stashed the torch in a pocket with a zip to avoid it falling out and giving me away. Then I pulled on my sailing gloves to ensure a better grip, filled my lungs with air and swung onto the pipe.

I managed to get halfway up to the next floor without mishap. Then my booted foot loosened a piece of masonry, which clattered onto the conservatory roof, bounced twice and fell to the ground, activating an automatic light. I clung to the drainpipe like the lifeline it was, not daring to move, my heart pounding at an unnaturally fast rate. My muscles, unaccustomed to such intense activity, were screaming in protest, but I tried to ignore the discomfort, more intent upon evading discovery.

The front door opened in response to the triggered light, and a burly individual with a strong torch examined the garden. Fuck it, it was too much to hope that all the hired muscle had scarpered for the night. Finding nothing, the man flashed the beam onto the roof of the conservatory, and I willed him not to shine it any higher. If he did, I'd be caught in the shaft and there was bugger all I could do about it.

Muttering something about fucking cats, the man eventually went back inside, and I expelled a long breath. I waited a minute or two more, just to make sure he didn't come back with reinforcements, before inching my way upwards.

The wide window ledge above me seemed more inviting than a virgin's bed, but I somehow resisted the urge to haul myself onto it when I finally drew level. There was a light coming from the room, indicating that it was probably occupied. Painstakingly I rested my feet gingerly on the very edge of the ledge, where it overlapped the window at the side, and peered into the room. Igor Kalashov was seated on a settee, a glass of what was probably vodka in his hand, in intense conversation with a woman. I reckoned she was probably the ubiquitous Monika since I could see a marked resemblance in their features.

What to do now? I was precariously balanced, my feet taking my weight, my back leaning against the drainpipe, which, mercifully, so far at least, had proved to be sturdy. Every moment I lingered heightened the possibility of detection, and it was this thought that finally galvanised me into action. Still breathing heavily, I attached one end of a webbing line to my harness. At the other end I'd attached a small but heavy fishing weight. I took careful aim and threw it over a bracket higher above me.

At least that was what I intended to do. Thanks to the conservatory roof, I'd got to the first floor level easily enough, but the climb to the second floor took it out of me. My arms were weakening, and I needed something to break my fall if the worse came to the worst. I consoled myself with the thought that there was only one more floor to go but, glancing up, it now seemed like an impossible distance to cover.

Attempting to remain positive, I returned my attention to the line I was trying to attach. My aim was off and the rope fell back down with a sickening crash, coming to rest on the window ledge. I held my breath, convinced Kalashov or his daughter must have heard it. But when the window wasn't thrown open and no one came running out the front door to find out what was going on, I figured my anxiety must be exaggerating the noise inside my head. Feeling more confident, I threw the line again, and this time found my mark. I silently offered up thanks for all the occasions when I'd had to berth a boat alone. Lassoing the bollards from on board in order to make the lines fast had improved my aim. I grabbed the loose end as it swung down towards me and attached it to my harness. It was, at best, a flimsy fail-safe but it made me feel a hell of a lot better about my chances for survival.

With a dangerous rush of adrenalin, I headed for the next floor up, heaving with my arms, feet scrabbling against the smooth wall. Panting, I eventually pulled myself onto the window ledge where the girls were being kept. The curtains were open but the room was in total darkness. For a brief, discouraging moment I thought they were no longer inside, but when I risked flashing on my torch it illuminated two single beds, both occupied.

Great! I was risking life and limb to rescue them and they were dead to the world.

I balanced on the wide ledge, still attached by webbing line to the drainpipe. Only when I felt as secure as I was ever going to did I tap quietly on the window. Immediately I heard movement inside the room and the next second Kara's astonished face appeared on the other side of the glass.

"Open up," I mouthed, accompanying the words with hand gestures to make sure she got the message.

"I can't," she mouthed back. "It's locked."

"Shit!"

What was I supposed to do now? I examined the window. Thank heavens it wasn't double glazed. I had a knife in my pocket and could if necessary loosen the putty and remove the pane of glass. But what were the chances of managing that without dropping the bloody lot? The alternative was to break it, getting the girls to muffle the sound on the other side with bedclothes. But it would still make some noise, probably quite a lot, almost certain to attract unwanted attention.

Unable to think of any alternative, I was about to indicate what Kara needed to do when my attention was caught by the window on the other side of the drainpipe. It was wide open. Now that looked like a much easier solution, except that it was presumably open because someone was sleeping in the room. Still, since I was here I might as well take a look. Using hand signals I told an anxious-looking Kara what I intended to do. She'd been joined by Jasmine, wide-eyed with shock at the sight of me there, as well she might be. Again using hand signals, I asked her if she knew who was sleeping next door but she shook her head.

Sighing at the prospect of inflicting further punishment on my protesting muscles, I swung back onto the drainpipe and, very gently, transferred myself to the opposite window ledge. I couldn't believe my luck when I peered 'round the frame. The curtains were open, as was the door to the hall, and the light from there illuminated the room. It was empty, both single beds neatly made. Not one to look a gift horse in the mouth, I lost no time in unhooking the line that was keeping me attached to the drainpipe and swung my legs over the sill. I bent my knees, which were also aching like hell, to absorb the shock and dropped to the inside. Thanks to the thick carpet I made no noise as I landed.

Only then did I pause to consider my next move, concerned that the light was on in the hallway. Did that mean the girls' room was being guarded or had someone simply forgotten to turn it off? I was about to go and investigate when a familiar handbag caught my eye. It was Kara's. I opened the wardrobe and saw the dress she'd worn the night before hanging there, along with some other clothes of hers. This was obviously the room she'd occupied before being transferred to join her sister next door. I searched her bag and found her mobile phone in it, switched off. There was a purse with money in it but no credit cards or driving licence to reveal her true identity. Presumably she hadn't been stupid enough to bring any with her. There was, however, something obvious missing from the bag, which came as no big surprise.

There was no sign of the external hard drive.

I put the purse under my arm. Knowing how women can be about their bags, I figured she'd be glad to have it back. Only then did I peer 'round the door into the corridor. There wasn't a soul about. Unsure when that situation might change, I headed straight for the girls' room. The door was locked, of course, but someone had obligingly left the key in it. I unlocked it, put the key in my pocket and went in to join the ladies.

"Charlie!" Kara hurled herself into my arms. "I didn't know you could climb drainpipes."

"Life with me is one big surprise." I winced as I closed my arms about her and my muscles protested. I'd be stiff as a board tomorrow. "Are you both all right?" I handed Kara her bag but glanced at Jasmine, who had yet to speak a word. I didn't like the look of her cut lip and I was pretty sure she had the beginnings of a black eye.

"Yes, we're fine." It was Kara who spoke. "But we're very glad to see you. Come on, let's get out of here."

"Hang on a sec. I doubt it will be that easy. Do you know where the alarm sensors are, Jasmine?"

She was busy belting a dressing gown 'round her waist and didn't seem to realize I was talking to her, even though I'd addressed her by name. It seemed as though she was deep in thought and not particularly overjoyed at the prospect of being rescued. Thinking about her children, I supposed.

"You might do better to take some of Kara's clothes from next door," I suggested. "If we do manage to make it outside, you'll be less conspicuous in street clothes."

Still without opening her mouth, Jasmine disappeared, returning a short time later in a pair of jeans and a top I recognised as Kara's. Kara was already dressed in a similar fashion.

"The alarm sensors, Jasmine," I reminded her.

"Yes, just give me a moment to think. I've never taken much notice of things like that." She tilted her head and didn't speak again for what seemed like an eternity. "I don't think there are any up here," she eventually said. "There's definitely one on the landing below, but it will only be on if everyone's in bed. What time is it?"

"Eleven-thirty."

"Then I doubt if Igor has gone to bed yet. He never goes before midnight."

"What about the ground floor? Will the alarm be on there?"

"If everyone is in, then it will be."

"Blast!" I was thinking fast. We'd come this far. There had to be a way out of this. "Where are the computers? The ones your husband's using for his scam."

"On the floor below us, the second door on the left."

"Laptops or desktops?"

"Oh, laptops, I think."

Good. That made life a fraction easier. "Will they be manned at this time of night?"

"Probably not, but there's a separate alarm that's always on in that room if no one's in there. You won't be able to get to them."

"Oh, I don't know." I flashed one of my infrequent grins at Kara, buoyed up by my success in gaining access to the house and probably getting ideas above my abilities. "A little diversion might give us a chance to nick one and to get out of the house."

"What are you thinking, Charlie?" Kara asked.

"Later." I touched a finger to her lips. "I saw Viktor and Nikolay leaving earlier," I said to Jasmine. "Will they be back tonight?"

"No, they don't sleep here."

"Good, any other security on the premises?"

"Just one man. He has a small office at the back of the ground floor from which he monitors the alarms."

"Okay, we'll worry about him when the time comes. Lead the way, Jasmine."

I locked the door again from the outside and pocketed the key. If push came to shove it might gain us a valuable moment or two. Jasmine went ahead of us and had reached the top of the stairs before Kara's voice stopped her.

"Jas, what about Anton? We can't leave him here."

"Oh yes." She seemed so annoyed to be reminded about him that the unspecified doubts lurking at the back of my mind gained momentum.

"Where do you think he is?" I asked her. "Presumably you've been worried about him."

"Well, of course she has!" Kara looked indignant

on her sister's behalf. "Would he be up here, out of the way like us, Jas?"

"Probably in that room over there." Jasmine pointed to a door with what seemed like patent reluctance.

The door was locked. I retrieved the key to the room the girls had been in from my pocket and tried it in the lock. In most houses one key opens all the internal doors and this one proved to be no exception. It turned soundlessly and released the lock with a soft click. We discovered Anton fast asleep, fully clothed, across one of the beds. His face was a mess of bloody bruises. He sat up with obvious difficulty and I guessed there must be a hell of a lot more bruising on his body, as well. His expression was wary, as though he was expecting more punishment. He blinked when his eyes fell upon Jasmine and winced at the pain it caused him simply to do that. Jasmine went to him and softly caressed his battered face.

"I'm so sorry, Anton," she said. "Are you all right?"

Stupid question. "There's no time to waste," I said. "We're going to try and get out of here. Do you think you can make it, Anton?"

"Yes." He didn't express any surprise at seeing me or ask any questions about how I came to be there. Too physically and emotionally drained to get his brain into gear, I guessed. Instead he concentrated all his efforts on easing himself off the bed. Cautiously he swung his legs to the floor, managing to stand at the second attempt. "I think so."

I gave him a minute to focus and then told Jasmine to lead the way. She did so, with me at her shoulder, leaving Anton to keep up as best he could with Kara's help. We reached the lower landing without anyone challenging us, which in itself was a major miracle. I heard voices coming from the room I'd passed on my way up that bloody drainpipe. Igor and Monika still putting the world to rights, presumably. I indicated to the others by putting a finger to my lips that we ought to be especially quiet and received nods of understanding from all three of them. Jasmine pointed to a door and I guessed she was showing me the computer room.

"What now?" Kara whispered in my ear.

"Now we think about a distraction."

I looked about. There was a tall table to one side with a bowl of potpourri on it. And almost immediately above it was a smoke alarm. Perfect! I dragged the table away from the wall and positioned it below the alarm.

"Anyone got a match?" I asked.

Kara rummaged in her bag and produced a plastic lighter. The things women carry in their bags never ceased to amaze me. I held the flame to the bowl and the potpourri took light immediately. I reckoned I had about a minute before it activated the smoke alarm. This was our one chance and it was important to time it dead right. I motioned for the others to conceal themselves behind a large chest at the top of the stairs leading to the first floor.

Once they were out of the way, I didn't hesitate. Diving for the computer room, I prayed the door would be unlocked. I was in luck and it swung inwards without making a sound. Surprisingly empty, it hardly seemed possible that high-scale crime could be activated from such ordinary desks containing two standard-looking laptops and very little else. But now wasn't the time to get all introspective so I pulled the leads from the back of one of the computers, dragged it from the desk and tucked it under my arm. I'd barely done so before the high-pitched squeal of the smoke alarm cut in.

Rushing back to the others, I dove behind the chest just as Igor and Monika came out of their room to see what the fuss was about. Their eyes were focused on the burning potpourri and, as I'd hoped would be the case, they didn't look in our direction. I could hear the heavy footsteps of the guard pounding up the stairs. He too headed straight for the fire. Igor was shouting at him to get a fire extinguisher from the computer room.

I could hardly believe it but, against all the odds, it looked as though this little ploy was going to work and we might actually get out of here.

We would have done too, if Jasmine hadn't stood up, walked calmly across to her husband and pointed in our direction.

"Darling," she said, sliding her arm into Igor's, "we have visitors."

NINETEEN

"JAS, WHAT ARE you doing?"

With an expression of total incomprehension on her face, Kara took an involuntary step towards her sister. I held on to her arm, well able to understand her bewilderment. Things had just started to come together in my own brain, and everything that hadn't quite rung true now began to make perfect sense. I made excuses for my stupidity by placing the blame on Kara. If she hadn't distracted me with her feminine wiles, I might have been thinking with said brain and seen the bigger picture a lot sooner.

I shot her a sympathetic glance. Her disappointment was about to intensify and there was sod all I could do about it. The big sister she'd always admired had never had any intention of leaving her husband, and I'd forced her hand, upset the balance, by breaking in and trying to rescue her. Had I left well alone, I suspect Kara would have come through this unscathed. Jasmine and Igor would then have disappeared into the sunset with their ill-gotten gains, with no one except the banks any worse off.

I transferred blame to Monk for playing upon my arrogant assumption that I could right half the world's wrongs. Still, if nothing else, at least I'd finally learned something about myself. If I came out of this in one piece, I vowed that in the future I'd stop meddling in things that didn't concern me and mind my own bloody business.

The goon from downstairs had extinguished my little fire and was now looking towards his boss for further orders.

"Jas?" Kara addressed her sister in a bewildered tone.

"I'm sorry, Kara, but I love Igor and can't let you ruin what he's trying to do."

"But I don't understand. I thought—"

"I'll take that." Kalashov reached for the laptop I was cradling against my chest.

"Catch."

I winked and made to throw the machine towards him. He lunged at me to prevent it hitting the ground but needn't have bothered because I didn't actually let it go. Right now it was the only thing keeping us alive, and I quite wanted to extend that state of affairs. I assessed the odds of getting out of here as we played our little game of machismo. It was two against two. Anton and me against Igor and the thug. Igor was older than both of us but Anton was in a bad way. From the agonised groans he couldn't quite suppress every time he put one foot in front of the other, I suspected that, at the very least, he had several cracked ribs. That gave the bad guys the edge but I figured we had nothing to lose by making a bit of a stand.

"It doesn't matter, Igor." Jasmine smiled at the man who'd knocked the crap out of her just the day before, a wealth of tenderness in the gesture. "Let him play his silly games if it makes him feel better about himself." Igor returned his wife's smile. "Everything's backed up."

"What's going on, Jas?" Kara asked, more forcefully this time.

"Isn't that obvious," I said, aware of Anton standing at my shoulder, almost hyperventilating with shock as he stared at Jasmine. "As soon as your darling sister found out about this operation, it changed everything."

"No!" Kara was naturally reluctant to believe it.

"I'm afraid it's true, Kara. Igor is doing all of this for my sake," Jasmine said, pride in her voice. "I never should have doubted him. Igor has always been able to remain one step ahead of the masses by using his brains and not being afraid to take risks."

"I wouldn't overestimate his cerebral qualities, if I were you." I said. "Any fool can steal."

She glared at me. "You think you're so clever but you don't have a clue what's really going on. We've been watching you and laughing ourselves silly."

"What about Kara? Have you been laughing at her too?"

She scowled. "If you hadn't interfered, Kara would never have known."

"Because she'd have finished up the same way as your brother?"

"No, that was an accident." A flash of genuine-seeming pain crossed her face. "But I was determined Kara wouldn't suffer a similar fate."

"How did you know I was here at the agency?" Kara asked, ice in her tone.

"I saw the picture Monika took of you when you came here for a job." She redirected her scowl towards Igor's daughter. "I can't believe her stupidity in taking on another girl at such a sensitive time. When I heard she'd done it I was immediately suspicious and asked to see the girl's picture. Monika didn't recognise you, of course, but I—"

I raised my eyes at Kara. "You let them take your picture?"

"I couldn't avoid it, Charlie. They needed one for their records but I thought that by the time it was printed I'd be out of here."

"In this age of digital photos?" I didn't need to press the point. She knew she'd been stupid.

"There was always a possibility that I'd be found out." Kara was speaking to me but her eyes, narrowed with bitter contempt, were trained upon her sister. "But I didn't think it would be Jasmine who gave me away."

"You ought to be grateful that it was me—"

"And so you persuaded your husband to put you in the same room as Kara," I said with quiet mordancy. "Once there you played the part of the wronged wife, just to find out how much she knew about your operation."

She shrugged. "It pays to be cautious. Igor and I had a long heart-to-heart once we arrived here. As soon as I understood that he was distancing himself from his previous activities for my sake, I was able to tell him what I was really doing in that hotel. I told him about you, Kara, and when I realized you were here at the agency, I said I'd find out what you knew as long as Igor promised no one would be hurt this time. You would have stayed here for a few days and then we'd have been gone and you wouldn't have been able to tell anyone anything."

"Why?" Kara asked, pangs of bitter disillusionment in her tone. "Why are you doing this?"

"Why?" Jasmine stared at her sister as though it was the craziest question she'd ever heard.

"Yes, why? You seem to have everything in your life you could possibly want. Money, a loving family, power—"

"Power?" She made a scoffing sound at the back of her throat as she paced the narrow hallway in front of her husband and his daughter. "Power was precisely what we didn't have. When I first met Igor, the Soviet Union was an economic disaster, which enabled criminal organisations to flourish. But there was no honour amongst thieves, and contract killings were at an all-time high. I never knew from one day to the next if I would see him again. Can you imagine how that felt?"

I shrugged. "Like an occupational hazard, I should imagine."

"And the threats against him were also directed against me," she said, as though I hadn't interrupted her. "I never felt safe, no matter where I was in the world, and if we hadn't changed direction there's every possibility we'd both be dead today."

"By why marry such a man at all?" Kara shook her head. "I just don't understand."

"Don't you?" Jasmine paused in front of Kara and looked into her eyes. "Have you never craved excitement, Kara? Have you never wanted to live on the edge and grab life by the throat?" Kara shook her head mutely. "I hated the way Father dominated the entire family, including Mother. Especially Mother. I couldn't understand why she put up with it. It was like she had no spirit, no mind of her own. And when I found out what he'd done to Brett, I couldn't accept that she didn't actually know."

"Just a minute, what did he do to Brett?" Kara stared at Jasmine.

"Ask him." Jasmine pointed at me. "He knows."

"Do you, Charlie?" She looked bewildered. "You know but kept it from me?"

"Your mother told me but didn't want you to know. She wanted to protect you from that."

"Yes," Jasmine said spitefully, "everyone wants to protect little Kara, but I suppose it doesn't make any difference if you know now." She tossed her mane of blond hair, not looking at Kara as she spoke. "Our dear father was sodomising our brother."

Kara gasped. I reached out to touch her shoulder but she didn't seem to notice.

"And when I found out, Mother pretended to be shocked." Jasmine frowned. "But how could she not have known? What sort of mother does that make her? If anyone laid so much as a finger on Sergei, I would know at once."

"A mother's intuition," I suggested mockingly.

"I…I think I need to…"

Kara rested her hands on her knees and dropped her head between them. I thought she was going to be sick but after a moment or two she straightened up again, beads of perspiration peppering her brow. There were tears coursing down her deathly pale face but she seemed a little more composed.

"Did you really imagine I'd let myself be treated like that by a husband?" Jasmine threw her head back and blew air through her lips. "Ramsay was the same. He wanted me to marry him so that he could control me and dictate the course of my life. Well, I wasn't having it, and when Igor offered me a job on his boat I jumped at the chance. His life was exciting, vibrant, and he made me feel alive like no one else has ever been able to. But most important of all, he didn't ask more of me than I was prepared to give." She turned towards her husband and brushed her hand gently along the side of his face in an intimately possessive manner that, irrationally, made me feel like an intruder. Igor grabbed that hand and kissed the back of it, almost violently.

"But you don't mind if he hits you?" I said.

"He's never done that before. And it was for your sake that I let it happened this time, Kara. He thought I was in that hotel with Anton, and if there's one thing Igor can't stand it's the thought of me with another man. I didn't tell him why I was really there in order to protect you, little sister." She pushed the hair out of her eyes and stared at Kara, as though expecting some display of gratitude. "So don't tell me I don't care about my family, about Brett, because I do. Perhaps too much. Igor wanted me to detach myself from you altogether." She sighed. "I should have listened to him, but when Brett recognised me I just couldn't help myself. I had to spend a few hours with him and make sure he was all right. And look where that got me."

"And you made up that story about your husband giving you tranquillisers just to get our sympathy," Kara said coldly.

"Oh no, that was true," Kalashov said. "She was beside herself when she found out about her brother's accidental killing, and I was afraid she'd do something stupid. I needed her to be calm until this thing is over and I can give her more of my attention. So I gave her things to make her sleep. Besides, I didn't want our children to see their mother so upset."

"How touching," I said derisively.

"I had a bit of a breakdown," Jasmine said, "and actually started believing that Igor was my enemy. I think it must have been a side effect of the pills he gave me." Her laugh was brittle. "I was actually planning to get Anton to help me escape from him." She moved to stand beside her husband and gazed up at him with open adoration. "Thank goodness he understands that I wasn't thinking straight and has forgiven me."

"I would forgive you anything." He took her hand, turned it over and applied his lips gently to the soft skin on the inside of her wrist.

"You see," Jasmine said, a triumphant note in her voice. "No one will ever come between us and nothing will stop us getting what we want."

"That must make you very proud," I said.

"What are we going to do with them?" Jasmine asked.

"Lock them back in that room," Kalashov said. "It will only be a couple more days, and then we'll be finished here for good. Once we're gone, I'll get someone to let them out, even though it would be better to have no loose ends."

"No, Igor! No more killing. Kara's my sister."

"Yes, but they know—"

"What they think they know and what they can prove are two very different things. They have nothing on us, and even if they did, by the time they present their evidence, we'll be long gone."

"It doesn't do to be sentimental," Monika said, speaking for the first time.

"Like you're not sentimental about your saintly

mother?" Jasmine said caustically. "Just stay out of this."

"Since you're soon going to leave these shores, you might as well satisfy my curiosity and tell me how you got into cybercrime," I said, suspecting vanity would make Jasmine want to spell it all out. She didn't disappoint.

"I told you how it was in Russia. With all his KGB connections Igor was able to make a lot of money very quickly. For the entrepreneur unafraid to take risks there were fortunes to be made, but the downside was that we never felt safe anywhere."

"Nadia, my love, I don't think it's necessary to—"

"It's all right, Igor. I'll never see my sister again so let me try and explain." She smiled at her husband and turned back to us. "In the early days I helped bring in some of the girls that worked here at the agency. I didn't know what they were being brought in for. Igor wanted to protect me from that and at first I thought they really were destined for jobs as waitresses and barmaids." Jasmine shook her head and smiled, presumably struck by her own naïveté. "One day I was stuck on the boat for a few days with two girls, waiting out a storm. We got talking and I realized just how intelligent they actually were. One of them was a computer expert and I couldn't believe all that talent would be going to waste just because she wanted to live in the west. I told Igor about her, unintentionally planting the idea of cybercrime into his head, although I didn't realize it at the time."

"And you subsequently stole nearly fifty million from a High Street chain."

"That wasn't us, unfortunately, but it spurred him

into recruiting the best Eastern European feminine minds in the computer world. He took advantage of the fact that women, especially beautiful ones, are usually dismissed as brainless bimbos. Men see exactly what they want to see and so we simply played on their chauvinism. Igor brought the girls over to pose as escorts and set them to work on the computers. It's taken time and patience but he's finally on the verge of eclipsing our rivals' achievements and making history in the annals of cybercrime." Her noxious smile was full of pride, like they'd done something truly noteworthy. "Everything's in place and nothing and no one can stop us now."

"Jasmine." Kara was shaking her head slowly back and forth. "What's happened to you?"

"Oh, don't worry, it's entirely safe for us," Jasmine assured her. I didn't think Kara was concerned for her sister's safety but didn't bother to set her straight. "Igor has got rid of all his other business concerns in Russia, for my sake. The criminal elements are getting themselves organized now and cooperating with one another. He's sold everything off to them, which means he's no longer a threat to anyone and is off everyone's hit lists."

"But you're stealing vast amounts that don't belong to you."

Jasmine smiled, naked avarice rather than humour reflected in the gesture. "Bah, the banks, they steal from us every day but are never called to account for it. We're merely redressing the balance. They will most likely be too embarrassed to even report the loss, so we can't be guilty of a crime that hasn't taken place."

I couldn't argue with the twisted logic behind that one.

"Pass me that laptop," Kalashov said, quiet menace in his tone.

I shook my head. "Come and get it."

"Mr. Hunter, you're being very foolish. My wife might dislike violence but personally I find it therapeutic."

"I don't doubt it. Bullies invariably do."

"I've promised Nadia that no harm will come to her sister but made no such promises in respect of you. Although I dislike doing anything that upsets my wife, ultimately I make my own decisions and she will do as I tell her."

Jasmine smiled sweetly at me and nodded. "It's true, you know. It's only Kara I care about."

"You have a funny way of showing it."

"We're wasting time here," Kalashov said. "The laptop. I won't ask you again."

I slowly shook my head. "I've grown rather attached to it." I assumed it was only concern for the machine that was preventing him from setting his goon on me. That I'd miscalculated became apparent as soon as he opened his mouth again.

"Shoot him," he said casually, snapping his fingers at his underling.

I'd been so taken up with Jasmine's pathetic attempts to justify her husband's actions that I hadn't noticed the gun in the thug's hand. But it now loomed larger than a football in my sphere of vision as he levelled it at me, his arm rock steady, eyes cold and focused. I could smell gun oil and see his finger tightening on the trigger as clearly as I could see the anticipatory half smile forming on his lips. There could no longer be any doubt that he'd kill me without a second thought.

Time felt as though it were standing still as I tamped down panic. It was deathly quiet in that hallway. Everyone appeared to be frozen in a bizarre tableau. I only had seconds to live, unless I did something. Fast. With no time to think about the consequences, I threw the laptop at the thug, hoping to buy precious seconds by putting him off his shot. Then I hit the floor hard, grabbing Kara's arm and dragging her down with me. Kalashov instinctively dived to catch the computer, just as I'd figured he would, and the bullet intended for me went straight through his heart.

Jasmine and Monika screamed simultaneously and dropped to their knees beside Kalashov. Jasmine cradled his head in her lap, manically shaking it as she yelled at him to wake up. Monika rocked to and fro, head thrown back as she kept up a bloodcurdling wail.

The thug who'd just killed his boss dropped the gun, an appalled expression on his face. Self-preservation kicked in and his head darted from side to side as he looked for a means of escape. He lunged towards the stairs but the last thing I needed was him summoning reinforcements. I stuck out a leg and he tumbled down the stairs, landing with a scream at the bottom, his limbs at unnatural angles. He didn't move and I thought, with clinical detachment, that he was probably dead.

The sudden silence as Monika abruptly stopped keening was eerier than when she'd been creating all that racket. I lunged for the gun but Monika got there before me. With a mask of unmitigated hate on her face, she fired it from almost point-blank range at Jasmine's head.

"I never did like her," she said flatly, watching with detachment as Jasmine's body crumpled on top of that of her dead husband.

Then she levelled the gun at Kara and me.

TWENTY

JESUS, WOULD THIS never end? I'd had just about enough
of people pointing guns at me today. Especially spiteful, unbalanced individuals who'd just demonstrated
that they'd kill without a second thought for the consequences.

Not surprisingly, Kara was in a catatonic state.
Deeply shocked, she stood beside me, trembling, her
mouth gaping open as she stared at her sister's body.
She appeared oblivious to the gun being pointed at the
pair of us. Not that she would have cared too much, I
was willing to bet, even if she'd known. Jasmine, for
whose sake she'd risked so much, about whom she'd
wondered for all these years, lay dead at her feet and
she didn't seem to be able to take in anything else. It
would have been better if she'd died before showing
her true colours. That way, at least Kara would have
had positive memories to hold on to. If we ever got out
of this, of course.

Where the fuck was Monk? All through this fiasco
I'd been consoling myself with the thought that he *had*
to have the house under surveillance and would ride to
our rescue in the nick of time. Yeah, like that was gonna
happen. He'd know nothing about what was going on
in here. Even if his people had seen me scaling that
drainpipe, they'd never risk intervening. Unless they'd
heard the shots. And the screaming. But it wasn't likely.

The gun had a silencer, this was a big house and I had good reason to know that the walls were constructed of thick, solid brick.

We were on our own and I had to do something to stop this crazy woman using us for target practise. Desperate times, and all that. I plumped for telling the truth.

"Give it up, Monika," I said quietly. "You don't really want to shoot us."

"Shut up!"

"Or what?"

She moved a step closer. And trained the gun squarely on Kara's chest. "Or you get to see her die, as well. It was her family, her bloody sister, who caused all these problems."

Ignore the gun and keep her talking. All the time she's talking she won't be thinking about shooting. Well, that was the theory. "How do you make that one out?"

"Her sister turned my father's head. He was sane and sensible until she came into his life. Then he was reduced to chasing after her like a trained puppy. It was sickening to watch."

"Sane and sensible?" I quirked a brow, risking antagonising her. That was the best description of the Russian Mafia I'd ever heard but decided not to say so. "Never been in love yourself, Monika?"

She glared at me. "Love's overrated. It ruins everything."

Ah, so she'd had her heart broken somewhere along the way then. "Interpol know all about your operation here," I said quietly. "They're outside. Don't make it worse by hurting us."

"What have I got to lose?" She shrugged. "It's all over now. My father's gone." Her voice caught and she paused, the hand holding the gun less than steady. Was that a good thing? It was impossible to know. "So is she." She glowered at Jasmine's body leaking blood all over the blond wood floor. "And at least I had the satisfaction of doing it myself. Doesn't matter if I kill you, as well. They can only put me in prison once."

"Or deport you back to Russia," I pointed out mildly. "The prisons aren't quite as comfortable there, I'm told."

She snapped her head in my direction. "The crime was committed here."

"What crime?" I shrugged. "You didn't shoot your father. We'll say that Jasmine was caught in the cross-fire. No one need ever know."

She curled her lips into an ugly sneer. "Do you take me for a complete idiot? You'll say anything to save your miserable neck, but the moment the authorities arrive you'll tell them everything."

"I'm a policeman, Monika," I said, hoping she didn't know I'd retired. "They might not have the death penalty in this country anymore, but do you have any idea what some of my colleagues will do to cop killers?"

"You think I care about myself."

A sudden crash distracted us all, even rousing Kara from her state of shock. Anton fell to the floor, groaning. Monika glanced only briefly in his direction but it was the chance I'd been waiting for. With one bound I covered the distance between us, grabbed her wrist to prevent her pointing the gun at me, and wrestled for control of it. I was stronger than her and it was over in seconds. The gun discharged, shattering a beautiful opaque window on the landing, sending glass showering into the night. I twisted her arm up her back until she howled with pain and stopped struggling. Only then did I turn to Anton and nod.

"Thanks," I said.

"No problem," he said, picking himself up. "It looked like you could use a distraction."

The front door burst open and several men wearing helmets and Kevlar vests and shouldering automatic weapons charged through it. Monk and Levine brought up the rear.

"What kept you?" I asked, leaning over the banisters as they stepped over the goon I'd tripped earlier.

"We weren't too sure what was happening," Monk said, ascending the stairs. "You ought to have called me before this went down."

"I had a few other things on my mind."

I passed Monika over to one of the police officers, who handcuffed her and read her her rights. Then I drew the traumatised Kara away from the bodies, into the room Igor and Monika had vacated a short time before. Monk issued a few curt orders and followed us in there.

"That was quite a climb you did up that drainpipe, Charlie," he said.

"I aim to please."

"We weren't too sure what to make of the long delay. We were just discussing whether or not to intervene when that window made the decision for us."

"Glad you could make it," I said sarcastically.

"What happened?"

Succinctly I brought him up to date. He asked a few questions along the way but made no notes. That didn't surprise me. He had total recall and nothing would be forgotten. He smoothly took control of everything after that, simply telling me to get Kara out of it.

I didn't need telling twice. I found a bottle of brandy in the cocktail cabinet and made her down a healthy slug. Then I rubbed her hands between mine, saying nothing, just trying to infuse some warmth into her. When the trembling became less severe and a little colour returned to her face, I got one of Monk's men to drop us back at her car and drove us back to Brighton. I didn't ask if she wanted to go home. She wasn't in any state to be alone so I took her back to the boat with me.

When we arrived, I helped her to undress. Then we crawled under the covers and I held her close. She lay passively in my arms, appearing to take some comfort from my presence and the fact that I wasn't plaguing her with questions. It took about an hour before the tears came, and when they finally did I thought they'd never stop. What did put an end to them, unfeeling as it might seem, was her urgent desire to remind herself she was still very much alive by making love.

Well, the lady was in shock so whatever she wanted…

AFTERWARDS WE TALKED for hours, trying to make sense of it all.

"I don't understand what made Jasmine turn out the way she did."

"Finding out what your father was doing to your brother would have been enough to turn anyone's head. Especially someone as young as she was at the time."

"Yes, but to then ally herself with criminals…"

"Well, she reckoned she was rebelling against your

father by linking up with Kalashov, but all she actually did was replace one controlling man with another. She got swept along with his glamorous existence, convinced herself it was what she wanted. Anyway, there was no way out for her by then. She'd got that bit right."

Kara leaned her head against my shoulder. "She did really seem to care for him."

"Yes, she did, which is why she wanted him to get out of his activities in Russia and do something less risky."

"I suppose." She sighed. "It's a good job Anton spilled the beans about the cybercrime. Jas obviously didn't know anything about it."

"No, he was Kalashov's one straight employee. It also explains your sister's startled reaction when he blurted out what he knew. She got the truth out of Igor when he took her to London. Then she played the part of the victim in order to find out how much we actually knew."

"I doubt we'd have been able to stop them if Anton hadn't accidentally pointed us in the right direction. Neither of us had a clue what they were really up to."

"Oh, if Anton hadn't said anything, then Monk would have. He was hoping that he wouldn't have to, and that by the time we stumbled over the truth we'd be in too deep to turn back. And that's precisely what happened." I grimaced, reluctant to put into words the admiration I felt for my old gaffer. "Wily old sod, is Monk."

We went to see her mother together the next morning and broke the news of Jasmine's death as gently as we could. Then, back at the boat, we tackled the problem that was uppermost in Kara's mind.

Jasmine's two children.

"What will happen to them now, Charlie?"

"Not sure. But Social Services are bound to become involved."

She looked at me, fresh determination in her eyes. "Do you think they'd grant me custody?"

EPILOGUE

IT WAS A crisp autumnal Saturday afternoon, almost three months after the business with Kalashov. Kara and I sat drinking fresh coffee in the kitchen of a bungalow in Saltdean. Jarvis Goldsmith's bungalow. He'd been right to suggest we wouldn't meet again. He died less than a month after moving into the hospice and, remembering how he'd looked that last time I saw him, I couldn't be sorry about that. I don't actually believe in an afterlife, but if there is such a thing I hope he's been reunited with my mother.

This time I didn't duck my obligations and went to the funeral. It was sparsely attended by some of his ageing cronies from the world of music and a few members of his dead wife's family whose pseudo-grief really got to me. They were obviously only there because they had expectations from his estate. But they were destined for disappointment. Jarvis's solicitor collared me at the end of the funeral and asked me to go and see him. When I got 'round to doing so, I discovered, to my astonishment, that I was Jarvis's sole beneficiary. This house and a reasonable sum of money were all mine. The relations made noises about contesting the will, but nothing had come of that and I, the man who desperately wanted to shake off the shackles of respectability, felt as though I was being pulled back towards normality at every turn of the cards. Emily was delighted. She seemed to think I could be happy now that I had a *proper* place to call home.

She still just didn't get it.

I was on the point of putting the house on the market and pocketing the proceeds when I thought of Kara's urgent need for somewhere to live. It took a lot of string-pulling on Monk's part, but Kara got what she wanted and was granted temporary custody of her nephew and niece. It was what Jasmine wanted too, apparently, because her solicitor produced a legal document naming Kara as guardian of her children in the event that anything happened to her and Igor. There was also a considerable sum of money set aside for their education and upbringing. That was a bit of a sticking point with Kara. She didn't know where it had come from and didn't want anything to do with illegal funds. I persuaded her to see reason. If the funds were the result of Igor's nefarious activities in Russia, then finding their true owner would be next to impossible. She reluctantly accepted that point of view and took investment advice from someone I recommended to her.

I glanced out the kitchen window at the garden. In spite of the fact that it was autumn, it was a lot neater than it had been the last time I'd been here. Two redheaded children plus Harry and Gil were helping Kara's mum rake up leaves and put them on a bonfire. It seems the lovely garden at Kara's parents' house was her mother's own work after all. Her one abiding passion. She's putting the same amount of passion into the garden here but has another outlet for it now, as well. Her grandchildren.

And her one remaining child.

She and Kara had long heart-to-hearts in the aftermath of Jasmine's death, clearing the air between them, letting their feelings out. Kara now knows all about the way she was conceived and can understand the subsequent difficulties her mother had in warming to her. The children, the innocent victims in all of this, are helping to break down the barriers between them. I offered Kara this house to live in until she decides where she wants to settle, and her mother's a regular visitor. She often picks the children up from the local school they're enrolled in if Kara's working, and needs no excuse to stay over to act as babysitter. Inexplicably she still lives in that barn of a house with her louse of a husband. Kara now refuses to have anything to do with him and won't risk having him near the children either.

"How's it going?" I asked her, nodding towards her mother, who looked ten years younger than the last time I saw her.

"We're still taking it cautiously, Charlie. One day at a time and all that but I don't feel estranged from her anymore." She smiled at me and brushed my lips with her forefinger. "It's a good feeling too."

"I'm glad."

We fell silent, smiling as we watched Saskia trying to climb on Gil's back and ride him like a pony. The stupid mutt was wagging like crazy and didn't seem to mind in the least. I marvelled at the adaptability of children. They'd been removed from everything that was familiar and placed in the care of a virtual stranger. Their opulent surroundings and exclusive schools had been replaced with the mundane, but they seemed to be thriving. They had made friends locally—something they'd never been permitted to do in Weymouth—and were behaving like normal children. They'd been told that their parents had gone on a journey.

Kara stood up to join me at the window and I slipped an arm 'round her waist. "When are you going to break the news to them?" I asked, nodding towards the kids.

She grimaced. "Soon. They have to be told. They're happy enough." She frowned. "At least I hope they are. It's difficult for me to tell. I'm still learning to be a substitute mum. Even so, it's best that they know their mum and dad won't be coming back. Social Services have been giving me some help on how to break it to them without causing too much stress."

"You're doing great. They love you." I squeezed her hand and drained the last of my coffee. "Well, I guess I'd better get Harry back to the boat. We've got a busy day tomorrow. Stamford Bridge," I reminded her.

"Ah yes, he must be looking forward to that." She smiled, not making it entirely clear which *he* she was referring to.

"He is."

I kissed her, opened the door and called to Harry and Gil. Kara and I are still an item but I never stay over when I have Harry with me. The last thing I need is Emily getting on my case about strange women influencing our son. Besides, I'm still wary of the commitment thing.

Kara isn't the only one to have made changes in her life, I reflected as I put Harry to bed that night, wondering if smudges from bonfires counted as dirt that needed to be removed. I decided not.

I responded to Brendan's plea to help with the kid who played jazz piano so exceptionally in that grimy hut. He's getting a hard time from his mates for not conforming and is threatening to stop playing. Brendan's suicidal at the prospect of losing yet another protégée, so I've taken pity on him and am doing what I can to help. Not just because he's such a talent but because the only other option for the kid is, realistically, a life of petty crime. It would be such a waste.

I poured myself a beer and sat at my desk in the wheelhouse, Duke Pearson's "Jeannine" playing softly on the stereo, staring at the file of papers Jarvis gave me just before he went into the hospice. Coward that I am, I still haven't looked at them, worried about what I might find when I eventually do.

Perhaps tomorrow, after the football...

* * * * *